BATHING BEAUTY

A gentleman did not walk in on a lady's bath. A wet cloth covered her face. She hadn't noticed him yet. He should walk out before it was too late. Except that his boots seemed to be nailed to the floor.

"Miranda?" she asked. "You here to scrub my back?"

"I'd be happy to oblige—" *Dammit, shut your mouth, Buchanan.*

Mercy sat up, trying to fit her legs into the tub, which forced her bosom out of the water. Thad had a view the memory of which he would happily take to his grave. Perhaps today, since the lady would be within her rights to shoot him. Too late, he lifted his hat to cover his eyes. He heard the cloth splash into the water. Maybe he could convince her he hadn't seen much.

"Out!" She yelled with a voice he had no doubt could carry over a herd of cattle. "Get out!"

BOOK YOUR PLACE ON OUR WEBSITE AND MAKE THE READING CONNECTION!

We've created a customized website just for our very special readers, where you can get the inside scoop on everything that's going on with Zebra, Pinnacle and Kensington books.

When you come online, you'll have the exciting opportunity to:

- View covers of upcoming books
- Read sample chapters
- Learn about our future publishing schedule (listed by publication month *and author*)
- Find out when your favorite authors will be visiting a city near you
- Search for and order backlist books from our online catalog
- Check out author bios and background information
- Send e-mail to your favorite authors
- Meet the Kensington staff online
- Join us in weekly chats with authors, readers and other guests
- Get writing guidelines
- AND MUCH MORE!

**Visit our website at
http://www.kensingtonbooks.com**

LOVING MERCY

Teresa Bodwell

ZEBRA BOOKS
KENSINGTON PUBLISHING CORP.
http://www.kensingtonbooks.com

ZEBRA BOOKS are published by

Kensington Publishing Corp.
119 West 40th Street
New York, NY 10018

All Kensington titles, imprints, and distributed lines are available at special quantity discounts for bulk purchases for sales
promotion, premiums, fund-raising, educational, or institu-
tional use.

Special book excerpts or customized printings can also be
created to fit specific needs. For details, write or phone the
office of the Kensington Special Sales Manager: Attn.: Special Sales Department. Kensington Publishing Corp., 119 West
40th Street, New York, NY 10018. Phone: 1-800-221-2647.

Zebra and the Z logo Reg. U.S. Pat. & TM Off.

ISBN-13: 978-1-4201-3087-4
ISBN-10: 1-4201-3087-0

First Printing: January 2005

10 9 8 7 6 5 4 3

Printed in the United States of America

For three strong women. Mom—I wish you could have been here to see my first book. Karen and Susan—who started me writing and believing, against all common sense, that this story just might find its way into print one day. Thank you all.

Chapter 1

Abilene, Kansas
September 1867

"Ya!" Mercy Clarke's yell carried over the rumble of hooves pounding earth. She snapped her whip at a dawdling steer. The creature bolted into the herd.

A small city bumped above the horizon. Abilene. A surge of pride rose in Mercy's chest as she watched her cattle lumber across the prairie toward their destination. She loved their warm, earthy fragrance—that powerful combination of sun-warmed hides and fresh cow dung that had once made her nose twitch. Now it seemed as inviting as coffee brewing in the kitchen.

"Move along." Luther prodded the cattle from the near side.

The lanky hired hand worked in concert with his shorter friend, Jed, herding a hundred head of cattle. It was a complicated dance—one confused steer could trample a man to death—but the cowboys made it look easy.

"Luther, you take over here," Mercy shouted, bringing her buckskin quarter horse around. "I'm going ahead. See if I can find that big packinghouse man we heard about." Time to learn whether all the risks they'd taken to get here would pay.

"Yes'm," Luther yelled without looking her way.

Jed threw a smirk in Luther's direction, not trying to hide his contempt for a woman giving orders. They'd done their job, Mercy reminded herself, but she'd be glad to shed these two when they got back to Fort Victory.

Mercy pushed her broad-brimmed hat further down on her head, but before she could pull away, her sister's voice floated to her.

"You don't need me, do you, Luther?" the girl asked from atop her small chestnut mare.

Mercy sighed. "Come along, Miranda." She waved at her younger sister before urging Annabelle into a gallop.

They sprinted for Abilene in a cloud of dust that would render their earlier scrubbing in murky river water less than useless. Miranda rode her horse with abandon, just as she did everything. Mercy had been nineteen once, but not nearly as wild as Miranda, even then.

As they entered town, they slowed the horses to a walk. Miranda's eyes grew wide and her head swiveled from side to side as she took in all the activity. "We'll have a real bed to sleep in tonight."

Mercy chuckled. After five hundred miles on the back of a horse, she too was ready for a night in a feather bed.

"Don't you laugh at me. I was so tired last night, I should have fell asleep the minute I lied down—"

"Miranda Chase!" Mercy cut in. "Lied down, indeed.

Folks'll think you're the sister who didn't have the chance for proper schooling."

"Humph! It just so happens that some of us weren't born with our nose in a book."

Mercy clamped her jaw shut, regretting her criticism. She knew Miranda loved to goad her by speaking like a rough cowhand. Correcting the girl's grammar would assure that Miranda would continue to hide her education.

Mercy was fond of her sister, but they were about as different as buckskin and lace. It wasn't just that Mercy's dark hair contrasted with Miranda's blonde. Her sister was as petite and delicate as Mercy was tall and shapely. After weeks riding herd under the same hot sun, Mercy's golden skin had darkened a shade, while Miranda's porcelain complexion had sprouted freckles, giving her a little girl look that made Mercy feel even more protective than usual.

"Anyhow, it ain't like you can't understand my point," Miranda said.

Mercy bit her tongue. She'd sacrificed for years to keep Miranda in school. Maybe one day her sister would appreciate that education.

"I see the Pearsons' store." Miranda pointed across the dusty street. The Pearsons were old friends from back when the sisters had lived in Kansas.

"Go on then. I'm sure Lydia's been waitin' for us with the patience of a heifer at calving time."

Miranda started to ride away.

"Take Annabelle," Mercy ordered as she dismounted. "She deserves a rest and some good feed." She rubbed her horse's nose. "And meet me back here at eleven o'-clock. Sharp."

"Okay," Miranda called over her shoulder as she urged the horses forward, nearly colliding with a mule pulling a farm cart.

"Dang!" Mercy muttered. "That girl is never going to learn to look before she leaps."

Mercy glanced at the new hotel and averted her eyes from the sign advertising hot baths for four bits. Time for bathing after she'd sold her cattle. She stomped and brushed at her clothing, but her efforts only stirred up more dust.

Willing her stomach to stop flipping, she marched up to the door. She'd best find Robinson and sell him on her new breed, before he spent all the packinghouse money on the usual longhorns. Mercy slipped inside the hotel lobby, looking for him. All the other buyers would follow his lead. She must persuade Robinson to bid high in order to get top price.

Mercy needed at least seventeen dollars a head to pay Lansing—the neighbor who had loaned her the money for her cattle venture. This auction was her last chance to keep her ranch and the independent life she cherished.

Perhaps she should have brought more cattle to the sale, but she didn't dare risk her whole herd on the trail. It was the first cattle sale in Abilene since the railroad had arrived. And the first time she'd sold her new breed outside of Colorado Territory.

The drive had been risky and Mercy hated gambling. In this case, she'd had no choice. Selling her cattle near home provided a living, but the prices there were too low to get her out of debt.

She lifted the brim of her hat and peered deeper into the shadows of the hotel lobby. She drew a deep breath, and released it. A woman alone couldn't afford to show any sign of emotion. Not if she intended to succeed in a man's world.

Once her eyes had adjusted, Mercy stepped onto the thick oriental carpet. All around, men sat reading newspapers and drinking coffee. Real coffee, not the muck she'd been drinking on the trail. The aroma made her mouth water.

On the other side of the lobby, a group of men surrounded a broad-shouldered fellow with a thick bronze mustache and golden hair that hung over the collar of his dark suit. They were a mixed group—two men in suits and three men with leather chaps strapped over their wool trousers—all intent on the man who towered over them.

She stepped toward the group. "Mr. Robinson?"

He stopped talking and focused on her. *Damn,* he was big. She took another step toward him, tilting her head up to hold his gaze as he studied her face.

"I'm afraid you just missed him, sir."

She spun toward the voice, a pudgy cowboy perched on a brocaded settee with spindle legs that seemed too fragile to hold him.

"Er . . . um." His eyes paused on her face before taking the long journey down to her boots and up again. She clenched her teeth, forcing herself to maintain a pleasant smile. It wasn't the first time she'd been mistaken for a man. "Er, that is, ma'am?"

"Do you mean he's already left?"

"Er . . ." The man lifted his china cup with his right hand, held it up for a moment and replaced it delicately on the saucer he held in his left hand.

His manners seemed better suited for afternoon tea with the Queen and Mercy cleared her throat to cover a laugh. "I have business with him." She took a step closer to the settee, trying to encourage a quicker response.

The fellow blinked. "Surely you aren't the . . . Oh, dear." The man squinted up at her. "You ain't the whore . . . er, the professional woman that's been arranged for . . ." He stood up, but still had to crane his neck to look her in the eye. "Hell, Mr. Robinson's a city man. He's used to women who are a good deal cleaner. And dressed . . . well, dressed—"

Several men sniggered and Mercy's cheeks warmed as she felt the entire room focus on her. "I'm here to see Robinson about the cattle sale," she said, through clenched teeth.

"Well, uh—"

"I reckon that explains the cowboy getup," said a toothless fellow seated in the corner.

This remark drew appreciative guffaws from the assembly.

"I believe you owe the lady an apology." A bass voice rumbled behind her and Mercy turned to see the blond man she'd noticed before striding forward, apparently bent on sticking his nose into her business. She pivoted back to the corner where Mr. Toothless sank into his chair, perhaps hoping the upholstery would swallow him.

Now that the blond man stood beside her, making her feel short for the first time in her life, she realized he could not be a prosperous cattle buyer. His dark jacket, worn and faded gray, fit snugly over a shirt that had probably been white at one time. The broad shoulders, which endangered the seams of his jacket, tapered into a sinewy neck and handsome face that no doubt attracted female attention wherever he went.

She judged the man to be one of the mavericks who wandered the West making their living by gambling and other questionable activities. The intensity of his azure eyes would have been frightening enough if he'd been of average stature, but he stood at least six foot four. His brawny build gave him an authority that no one in the room challenged.

Mercy's throat constricted as the stranger turned

and locked eyes with her. The fearsome glare had vanished, replaced by a look she couldn't read. Curiosity,
most likely. His thick mustache twitched as he formed a
smile. No doubt, he expected some display of feminine
helplessness. She'd as soon wrestle a porcupine as swoon
over this man.

She turned back to the other men who were examining the rug beneath their feet. The room was now utterly silent.

"No apologies necessary, gentlemen." Mercy mus-
tered a lighthearted tone and even managed to wave a
hand, as though to dismiss all of the insults the men had
hurled at her. Truth be told, she'd rather be compared
to a shameless sporting woman, than have these fellows
think she couldn't stand up for herself. "Appreciate the
fashion advice." She winked at the fellow in the corner,
then gave the maverick her most withering glare. "A gal
never knows when she may need a new trade."

She exited, accompanied by a roar of laughter, her
stomach twisting from the humiliation. She raised her
chin a notch higher—it wasn't humiliation when you
poked fun at yourself.

Mercy couldn't wait to mount her horse and return
to her ranch in Colorado. Home. Mountains, cattle and
a few cowboys who knew better than to gawk at her six-
foot-tall frame. In town, she felt like a giraffe in a mena-
gerie. She didn't belong.

A few doors down the street, she opened the watch
that hung from her belt. If she hurried, she could still
catch Robinson before the auction started.

Thad realized he was staring, but he couldn't take
his eyes off the tall beauty striding away from him. Her
grace belied her size and rough attire. Holding her

head high, she walked away from the hotel with her dignity intact, in spite of the laughter from the crowd of louts surrounding him.

Most unusual. In many ways.

He'd never known a woman tall enough to look him in the eye. The idea appealed to him. He'd nearly introduced himself when her eyes met his, but he forced his mind to think ahead to the Rocky Mountains. He couldn't dally in Abilene, even for a brief flirtation. Besides, given his usual luck with women, this one would turn out to be married. Or bad-tempered, he thought, remembering that glare.

"Don't that beat all?" The plump cowboy standing next to Thad was also watching the woman. "Can't say whether it's a man or a woman in that getup." The man favored Thad with a tobacco-stained grin.

Thad regarded the fellow. Her clothing couldn't conceal her feminine curves. In fact, a fashionable dress would have hidden those long, graceful legs. That would be a real shame.

Thad shook his head. "You, sir, are clearly in need of some powerful spectacles."

Tipping his hat to the cowboy, Thad sauntered down the street to Pearson's Mercantile, enjoying the memory of those long legs and abundant curves. At least his visit to the hotel hadn't been completely wasted. He let out an exasperated breath. Another morning gone by and all he'd met were more cowboys from Texas. *Dammit!* He needed someone who could get him to Colorado.

He pulled his hat off and combed his hair back with his fingers before pulling open the door to the mercantile. A sprite of a girl with corn silk hair disappeared into the back room just as he entered.

"Mr. Buchanan," the Pearson boy greeted him, leaning his broom into a corner and walking to the front of the store.

"Hello, Harold," Thad drawled, stepping further into the store and looking around. Like most of Abilene, the store was new, the odor of fresh paint masking the pleasant aroma of coffee brewing in the back. Lord, it had been forever since he'd had decent coffee. The boarding house proprietor was a passable cook, but if that muck she made was coffee, then Sherman's march through Georgia was a social call. He'd offered to make it himself, but she'd laughed at him and shooed him out of the kitchen. And he couldn't bring himself to pay the price of hotel coffee.

"Any news?" he asked the boy.

"Well, you just might be in luck." Harold grinned. "We've an old family friend just pulled into town for the cattle sale. Be headin' back for Colorado soon, I reckon."

"I'd be mighty grateful for an introduction."

"I ain't had a chance to talk to Pop about your situation. He'll be the one to introduce you."

"Oh." Thad took a step toward Harold. "Well, I'll be pleased to speak with your father . . . and I'll pay a finder's fee, of course."

Harold poked his spectacles up on the bridge of his nose. "He's out back now." He tilted his head toward the coffee smell. "I'll get him."

As the young man disappeared, Thad felt optimistic for the first time since he'd arrived in Abilene. He'd been stuck in this dusty cow town for two full weeks, unable to find anyone interested in guiding him across the long stretch of wilderness that separated him from his sister.

He shifted his hat from one hand to the other. Since he'd arrived in Abilene, several people had warned him that only the most experienced began the journey west this late in the year. Thad was no coward, but he was no fool either. He knew better than to gamble with the odds stacked against him. He'd wait for a guide, rather than risk his neck alone on the dangerous westward trail with winter imminent. It would be little consolation to Clarisse to learn that her last remaining brother had died trying to reach her.

An older man of average height and slim as a fiddler's bow walked up behind the counter to face him. "What can I do for you . . . Buchanan, is it?"

Harold's father, judging by the auburn hair and spectacles. The elder Pearson did not seem to like Thad one bit.

"Yes, sir." Thad reached across the counter, offering his hand. "Thaddeus Buchanan at your service."

"How can I help you?" Pearson snapped without taking the proffered hand.

"Sir, I'm in need of a guide. I understand that you've an old friend headin' for Colorado who may be able to help me."

Thad imagined the friend would be an old cowboy, perhaps even older than Pearson. The geezer might be happy to have Thad along—he was young, strong and better than a fair shot.

"Sorry." Pearson began stacking cans of tobacco on the counter. "I don't see what I can do for you."

"Mr. Pearson." Thad tried to appear patient as he gazed down at the mercantile owner. "I know I'm a stranger to you, sir. What can I do to reassure you? I'll pay any reasonable price for an escort to Colorado." Lordy, he hoped he had enough money to make good on that offer. "And I'll pay you a finder's fee if you introduce me."

Pearson's eyes, magnified by his glasses, studied him.

Thad stood, holding his hat in both hands. *Relax. Smile.* He knew his size could intimidate, but he couldn't will himself smaller. At least he was more or less clean. He didn't dare spend his money on luxuries such as a hot bath or a shave from a barber until he knew he wasn't going to be spending the winter here. He'd managed a cold dousing at the horse trough behind his rooming house, even washing some of the grime from his clothes there.

"Pop," Harold said. "Mr. Buchanan just wants to get to his sister's place near Denver and Mer—"

"That's enough!" Pearson glared at his son.

Thad trained his eyes on Pearson's. "Sir, I lost most of my kin in the war. It means everything to me to find my sister before winter sets in."

Thad ached for a reunion with Clarisse, who had moved to Colorado before the war. He longed to meet his young nephews, to be with family again. Most of all, he hoped to start a new life in the shadow of those tremendous mountains Clarisse had described in her letters. His sister had even hinted that she had a friend— a widow—who would make him a good wife. A tall woman in a buckskin jacket wandered into the corner of Thad's mind—but he shoved the image away. He wanted a wife and family, not a brief liaison with a tempting beauty.

"I'd like to help you," Pearson said. "But my friend's not a professional guide."

"I understand that, sir. But I'd be much obliged if you'd convey my offer to him."

Harold opened his mouth to speak, but Pearson silenced his son with a look.

"It's not a question of money," Pearson said. "I'm rather . . . protective of my friend. How do I know you're honorable?"

"I lost everything in the war, sir, except my good name. I figure no one can take that from me. I sure don't aim to give it away."

Pearson nodded. "I'll talk with my friend and let you know tomorrow."

"Thank you, sir. I'll be here first thing in the mornin'."

Thad gave Pearson what he hoped was a reassuring smile. He still didn't have a guide, but at least he had hope.

With a final look at the array of goods displayed in the store, he turned to the door. It had been a long while since he'd been in a well-stocked store with money in his pocket. He took another longing whiff of coffee, replaced his hat and stepped out into the sun. Best keep his money for now. The poker table was lucrative these days with all the cowboys in town for the cattle sale. If he were stuck in Abilene for the winter, his income might drop dramatically. He'd wait to make his purchases when he knew for certain he had a guide.

A wagon rumbled through the rutted street. Thad waved his hat in a vain attempt to clear the dust. Reaching into his pocket for his handkerchief, he felt the familiar weight of Papa's pipe. What would his father think if he knew his son was making his living at a card table? His practical father would likely be glad he hadn't wasted the money he'd spent sending his son to college. Thad had learned a useful skill, even if it had been outside the classroom.

He ran his thumb over the rough surface of the pipe's bowl. The pipe and the suit he was wearing were his father's last remaining worldly possessions. Sometimes Thad felt like the prodigal son for squandering his inheritance. He clenched a fist and forced it open again. Or an ass for letting the Yankees steal it.

He shoved the pipe back into his coat pocket and headed down the street. Wishing he could change the outcome of the past few years was about as useful as trying to turn bread back into flour and just as likely to succeed. He'd best forget the past. Once again, an image of a buckskin-clad beauty came into his mind and this time he allowed her to linger there. He'd wager last night's winnings that the lady could keep his mind from wandering to past misdeeds, if she were willing. He grinned. Hell, with his arms wrapped around those bountiful curves, his mind could rest entirely.

Chapter 2

With the description the auction house manager had given her, Mercy had no problem identifying Robinson. She found him studying her cattle.

"Fine looking steers," Robinson shouted at Luther who squinted back as though he didn't understand the language.

Mercy chuckled. The cowboy swallowed, half-turning to acknowledge Robinson while keeping one eye on the lumbering cattle. Luther was more comfortable talking to the herd than to a man in a suit. She stepped forward to relieve her cowhand and set Robinson straight.

"You just get the cattle into the pen, Luther. I can help this gentleman." Mercy tried to make eye contact, but Robinson seemed to focus a good bit lower.

Judging by his smirk, it wasn't the trail dust on her shirt that held the cretin's interest. Mercy felt a twinge of sympathy for the sporting woman who would visit Robinson later. His fashionable suit, slicked hair and waxed mustache testified to his efforts to make himself attractive, but he was about the ugliest varmint she'd ever clapped eyes on.

"I see you know your beef, sir," she said. No sense spoiling the sale by telling this little man what she thought of his wandering eyes. "You're looking at the future of cattle," she added, although Robinson still focused on her breasts.

He glanced up.

Mercy took a step toward him. "We'd best move out of the way or we're going to find ourselves in the pen with the steers."

Robinson stepped back into a pile of manure, releasing the pungent aroma and making a mess of his boots. Mercy bit back a laugh as he gingerly set his fouled boot down on a patch of dry earth, rubbing back and forth to dislodge the muck. Apparently, Robinson hadn't been in the cattle business long.

"You're Mr. Robinson, aren't you?" She removed a leather glove, offering him a more or less clean hand. "I'm Mrs. Clarke. Be glad to answer any questions."

"These cattle yours?"

"Yes, sir. Raised on my ranch in the shadow of the Rocky Mountains." She allowed herself a look at the herd. "You'll notice these steers are a good bit meatier than pure longhorns. That's the Hereford blood."

The man looked around. "Your husband nearby?"

She scowled. "I can speak for myself."

"I'd like to speak to the legal owner."

With his meager height, it wasn't easy for him to look down his nose at her and it irritated her that he managed it. She ground her teeth.

"As I said, I speak for myself." She cut Robinson off before he could protest. "I'm a widow."

She rubbed her thumb along the wedding band she still wore, schooling her features to hide the pain she felt when she thought of Nate.

"Well." His smile returned. "That's different."

Why it was different, she couldn't imagine. Nate had

never understood a blamed thing about the cattle business.

"You won't find more flavorful beef anywhere," she said. "And the meat's as tender as butter." Judging by his rotten teeth, he'd appreciate a tender cut of meat.

They both turned at the sound of the gate closing on the last of the steers. The auctioneer announced Mercy's ranch, the Bar Double C.

"The animals you see before you, gentlemen, are a Longhorn-Hereford mix." The auctioneer shouted the information she'd provided him, preparing the crowd for bidding on her cattle. "Rugged, sturdy animals. And plenty of fat to give the beef flavor and tenderness."

"Looks as though the auction is about to begin." Mr. Robinson tipped his hat. "Good day, ma'am."

Mercy flashed a smile that she hoped covered her fury over his patronizing attitude. Heck, she didn't need a man to run her cattle business any more than she needed a certain broad-shouldered gambler trying to protect her. She traced her thumb over her wedding band again. No, she definitely didn't need another man in her life.

Mercy sidled up to the sale pen. Luther and Jed worked the restless cattle crowded around the pen, allowing the bidders to get a good look at the lot. The auctioneer called for bids of twenty-five dollars a head to start. She scraped her boots on the fence railing, removing the accumulated manure. Too bad it wasn't as easy to scrape away the slime that Robinson's eyes seemed to deposit on her body.

She turned toward the auctioneer, leaning her back against the fence. Danged if she'd let that pipsqueak's poor manners spoil this day for her. She'd worked too hard to get here. They'd driven the cattle across five hundred

miles of wilderness—surviving cattle rustlers, bears, bob-
cats, rattlers and capricious weather. Though proud of her
accomplishment, she felt as skittish as a cat in a bullpen.
Those cows represented her future. If the buyers didn't
pay a premium for the Hereford blood, everything was
lost.

"Ah, bidder, bidder, bidder." The auctioneer's musical chant boomed over the crowd.

"Hey!" One of the auctioneer's assistants called attention to a bidder in the crowd.

"Fifteen!" The auctioneer pointed to the bidder.
"Who'll give me fifteen and a quarter?"

The bids increased to fifteen fifty, then fifteen seventy-
five. Most of the cattle sold earlier in the day had gone
for around sixteen dollars. Mercy held her breath as a
man from one of the smaller packinghouses pushed the
price up.

Robinson waited for seventeen dollars before he
jumped in with seventeen fifty.

"Seventeen seventy-five!"

"Eighteen," Robinson countered.

All eyes turned to the other packing plant man, who
walked away, spitting a great sluice of tobacco juice near
Robinson's feet.

"Eighteen once, going twice, sold to number eighty-
three for eighteen dollars a head."

Mercy rolled her eyes upward to calculate. After the
auction house took its cut, she'd have nearly sixteen
hundred dollars. She felt the knot in her stomach relax
a little. That would be enough to pay off her mortgage
and even get a little ahead.

*Don't you go counting your chickens while the fox sits out-
side the henhouse.*

She didn't know yet what her expenses would be for
the trip home. Anything unexpected, from a lame horse

to bad weather, could eat into her profit. And that was assuming they didn't fall prey to outright thievery.

While the hired hands moved the cattle to the holding pen where they would await the next train to Chicago, Mercy sauntered over to collect her money. The railroad was making western cattle ranching more lucrative and creating boomtowns like Abilene along the way.

With the arrival of the railroad, the empty prairie had given birth to a bustling city—cowboys and farmers mingling with people who dressed the part of gentlemen and ladies. Mercy shuddered, thinking of the "gentlemen" she'd met earlier this morning. Civilization? They could have it.

The auction house bookkeeper and Mercy each counted the money twice. Even though it was mostly greenbacks, the bag was bulky and heavy. Once the railroad came through to Denver things would be easier. But that was a year or two away. For now, she'd have to rely on her wits to get the money safely over the dangerous trail to Fort Victory.

She dreaded the ride home with Jed and Luther grumbling about taking orders from a woman. Their complaining was likely to be worse without the cattle to distract them. She hefted the moneybag. A generous bonus now just might help their attitude. Mercy checked her watch as she stepped into the sunlight. Just time enough to pay Luther and Jed before she met Miranda at the hotel.

She found her hired hands near the tracks, walking away from the penned herd. Both men dropped their gaze to the ground when they saw her coming. She tried to keep the irritation out of her voice as she greeted them.

"I know you're anxious to get to a saloon and start drinking your wages, but I'd—"

"Ma'am." Luther cleared his throat. "We've been thinkin' maybe you'd give us all of our pay now."

"All?"

"I know we agreed to half, but there ain't much to spend money on in Fort Victory," Jed said. "We'd just like to have our own earnings to keep safe on the trail home."

Mercy shoved her hat back on her head. "You boys aren't thinking of headin' off on your own, now are you?"

Both men focused on the toes of their boots.

"Your wages are for herding the cattle here and helping with the journey home." She could handle the dangers of the trail without them, but more eyes and more guns meant an added measure of safety.

"Our pay's mostly for gettin' the cows here." Jed raised his chin to challenge her.

"The agreement was for *both* ways."

"We're tired of chasin' cows. Been thinkin' of headin' to Kansas City. Maybe look for work there." Jed spit tobacco juice on the ground. "How much for herdin' the cattle here?"

"Half pay for half the trip." Mercy knew that wasn't fair, most of the work was in driving the cattle. Still she wouldn't reward them for breaking their word.

"A hundred dollars each." Luther had never sounded so confident. "Anything less wouldn't be right and you know it."

Mercy stared at him. A hundred dollars was a reasonable wage for a month of driving cattle. Except that they'd agreed to take a hundred and fifty for the entire trip.

"You'll get ninety dollars and be happy with that considering you're the ones breaking our agreement."

Luther glanced at Jed, who shrugged. "Done," Luther said.

She paid the men and watched them saunter toward Main Street where they could spend a month's wages in one night if they weren't careful. Damn them and good riddance. She didn't need their scrawny carcasses to protect her. Hell, she and Miranda could handle the trip alone just fine. She brushed the Colt revolver at her side and glanced around the busy auction yard. She was alone and ready for anything. Just the way she liked it.

Mercy opened the lid on her watch. Five minutes to eleven. She figured Miranda would be late as usual, but she hurried toward the hotel anyway. Marching along the dusty main street, Mercy smiled. She'd be soaking in a hot tub tonight and scrubbing with some of Aunt Emily's honeysuckle soap.

She checked her Colt again, gripping it, then letting it slide back into her holster. She glanced up and down the busy street. Carrying the bag full of money, she felt as though all eyes were on her, though an attack was unlikely on a busy street in broad daylight. With so many people out, she wondered whether she'd see the broad-shouldered man who had tried to interfere this morning. She chewed on her lip. He had meant well, he just didn't understand that she could take care of herself.

Men were always underestimating her. Arthur Lansing most of all. She couldn't wait to see the expression on his face when she handed him this cash. He was so damn sure she'd never manage it. Back in Fort Victory, Lansing was the biggest frog in the pond. Used to getting his own way. He wanted the Bar Double C, with its reliable source of water, but he wasn't going to get it. She squeezed the bag full of cash, feeling renewed confidence that she would keep her ranch.

Stepping onto the boarded walk in front of the hotel, she peered through the window. There was no sign of her sister in the lobby. Nor the big man in the faded black suit. Not that she was looking for him. Mercy paced in front of the door, then squinted up and down the dusty street.

"Lost, miss?" A portly man with a cigar clenched between his teeth leered at Mercy, his eyes roving from her face, lingering on her trousers before meandering back up.

Mercy didn't have to be polite to this one. Swinging her moneybag over her shoulder, she positioned it to block the man's view while she allowed her right hand to brush the Colt that hung at her hip.

"It's 'Missus' and I've no need of help."

The man's gaze shifted to the hand hovering near her gun; his Adam's apple bobbed. Whiskey fumes merged with cigar smoke as he took a step closer to her.

"I thought perhaps you'd like a wee bit of assistance keeping that cash safe." His eyes drifted to her bag then back to her face. Swaying under the influence of his liquor, he shoved the cigar back into his mouth, distorting his cocky smirk.

Mercy glared at him.

A flash of corn silk hair caught the corner of her eye.

"Sorry I'm late." Miranda favored her with a sheepish grin.

"Well, aren't you a lovely wee thing." The portly man's voice took on more of an Irish lilt.

Mercy put a protective arm around her sister, trying to steer her around the drunk.

He took another step toward them, pressing his brows together and lowering his lids until his eyes were sharp as steel knives. "Name's O'Reilly in case you change your mind." He leaned toward Mercy. "I'd hate to see anything untoward happen to this sweet young thing." He reached out and brushed a stray hair back from Miranda's face.

"Take your hands off my sister!" Mercy pulled the girl back. O'Reilly stepped closer, reaching toward Miranda.

Mercy slipped between O'Reilly and her sister.

"You ladies need—?" A huge figure strode onto the planked walk behind O'Reilly.

Mercy ignored him. She drove her left fist into O'Reilly's belly, then hurled her right toward his chin.

The force of the blow shot up her arm all the way to her shoulder. It was like hitting a rock. But she hadn't hit O'Reilly's chin. He had crumpled with her first blow. Mercy's second punch had landed squarely on a very solid chest.

Her moneybag started to slip and she hugged it tighter. "I . . . I'm s-sorry, I didn't mean to. . . ." She shut her mouth to prevent further babbling.

"Well." The tall blond man from the hotel lobby grinned at her. And she noticed that he had a dimple on one cheek. His right cheek. "You pack quite a punch, ma'am."

She gave him credit for not adding, "for a female." He glanced down to where she cradled her right hand in her left.

"Are you hurt?" His brow furrowed and that wicked dimple vanished.

"I'm fine." *Except that, I've probably broken a bone or two.* She forced a smile, wondering if she could coax that dimple out again. *Hell, now I'm thinking like Miranda, ready to start flirting with any handsome fella that happens along.* "Thank you kindly." She pulled herself up to her full height, dropping her throbbing hand to her side. "We don't need any help."

"No. I reckon it's O'Reilly who needs the help." He turned to examine the Irishman who had sunk to the walk and seemed intent on reconstructing his broken cigar.

The maverick turned back to Mercy, studying her from under his broad-brimmed gray hat. She suddenly felt as though she were wearing an overly tight bodice, which was ridiculous since she never wore such silly things.

"We should be properly introduced." He removed his hat and made a slight bow, flashing that roguish smile again. "Thaddeus Buchanan, at your service, ma'am."

"Mrs. Clarke." She pulled the "Mrs." around her like a shield and refused to take his offered hand.

"I'm Miranda." Her sister jumped forward and took Buchanan's hand. "Miranda Chase."

"Mr. Buchanan," Mercy interrupted, "I believe I made it quite clear this morning." Mercy looked over Buchanan's shoulder, unwilling to meet those eyes again, to let that smile melt her resistance. "I don't need your help." She pulled Miranda close, and stormed down the uneven boardwalk, brushing past several bewildered strangers.

O'Reilly's voice carried after them. "I'll not forget you!"

Mercy accelerated, forcing Miranda to trot along next to her.

"That tall fella seems to have caught your attention," Miranda teased. "Ain't seen you talk that rudely to a man in months. Not since Judge Jensen come calling on you—"

"Judge Jensen chases anything in skirts."

"You don't wear skirts, Mercy."

"He was most likely interested in you, then."

"Me? But, he's old." Miranda pulled back on Mercy's arm. "Slow down." Mercy shortened her stride. "Anyway, we were talkin' about that man there, with the broad shoulders and that darlin' dimple."

"Humph." She glared at Miranda before speeding up again. "Impertinent . . . *man*. I won't tolerate ogling."

"He wasn't ogling, he was perfectly nice."

Miranda was right. O'Reilly and Robinson were oglers. Buchanan had looked at her, seen her. That was worse.

Mercy flexed her aching right hand. At least it wasn't broken. She steered her sister across the street through a cloud of dust kicked up by a passing coach.

The women entered Pearson's Mercantile, where the sunlight streaming through the glass windows illuminated shelves and counters covered with goods. Mercy was surprised at the pleasant store James Pearson and his sister had created in the few months since they'd left their Kansas farm to become a part of the boom in Abilene. Tins of beans, fish, fruits and vegetables formed tall pyramids on the shelves to her right. Bolts of fabric in every color of the rainbow lined the far wall. Tools, tobacco, coffee and sugar occupied the shelves on the left. Behind the counter, she spotted a familiar face grinning at her.

"Harold Pearson!" Mercy called. "Is something growing on your upper lip? Don't tell me you've gone and grown up," she said, though the bright red fuzz on his lip wasn't exactly manly.

"Well, Miranda finally dragged you in here!" Harold moved out from behind the counter. "We were beginnin' to wonder if you were gonna visit us at all."

"Now you know I wouldn't come to Abilene and miss seeing my dearest friends." Mercy gave the skinny boy a quick hug. "Didn't you turn nineteen this past summer?"

"Yep. That's why I'm in here instead of out there." He pointed to the dust-streaked window. "You know Pop." Harold tilted his head and did his best impression of his father's deep voice. "I'm depending on you to take care of the store, son. Someday this will all be yours." Harold flung his arms wide, knocking a sack of flour off the pile. The bag dropped to the floor, sending up a white cloud.

Harold's face flushed red to match his mustache.

"Come along, ladies." He waved his arms more carefully. "Aunt Lydia's in the kitchen."

Lydia had the Pearson auburn hair, but hers was brushed with silver at the temples and pulled into a tight bun. When Mercy's eyes met hers, a smile lit Lydia's plump face.

She let out a little yelp of delight and raced to hug Mercy. "It's so good to see you. You'll stay to dinner, won't you? I made chicken and dumplings."

Mercy smiled, feeling a bit overwhelmed. "I wish we could, but we need to get to Uncle Will's place before dark." With plenty of time for a hot bath before supper too, she hoped.

"No?" Lydia pouted.

"We'll come back to town for supplies before we leave," Mercy said. "Perhaps we can visit longer then?"

Lydia beamed another bright smile. "Fine. Harold and James won't mind dumplings again. Now sit and rest for a bit and tell me your news. I'll get you some cold cider to wet your whistle."

Mercy and Miranda obeyed, taking seats at the table while Lydia bustled about.

"We thought you and Miranda would come back to Kansas to stay and bring Fenton so we could help care for him."

Mercy nodded, understanding Lydia's concern. Her father hadn't been the same since the bulls had turned on him and Nate two years before. At least Pa had survived. "Pa is getting better. He hasn't had a blackout in months."

"Wouldn't he be better off here—at home where he'd be close to friends and family?"

"We do miss you all, but Kansas isn't home any longer." Mercy drew her lower lip between her teeth while she searched for the right words. "You'd have to see our ranch to understand why we love it so." She could picture her home in her mind's eye. "The sky is wide open like Kansas. But then there are the mountains—great, rugged peaks that reach clear to heaven. It's hard to put into words."

"Sounds like paradise."

"We're not all in love with vast emptiness, Aunt Lydia," Miranda put in. "I myself am enjoying civilization."

"Well, well." James Pearson entered the kitchen with Harold tagging behind him. "Lydia, imagine mistaking Abilene for civilization. You're going to have to give this girl your talk about the wonders of Philadelphia."

"That's enough teasing, brother." Lydia turned to the pots covering the huge cast-iron stove that dominated the kitchen.

"It's good to see you, Mercy." Pearson patted Mercy's shoulder and sat beside her. "It's been ages since we've had a letter."

"I'm sorry. It gets busy running the ranch and I lose all track of time."

"And Mercy's been worried sick about repaying Mr. Lansing," Miranda burst out. She blushed, glanced at Mercy, and then set about studying the cider in her glass.

"Miranda's being a bit dramatic." Mercy turned from Miranda to Pearson. "We're getting along very well. No need to worry."

Pearson cleared his throat. "Well, we have been concerned about you. I know you've had a lot of responsibility dropped on your shoulders since you lost Nate and your Pa was hurt."

Mercy glanced at Miranda, wondering how much she'd told James about their business, but Miranda continued to gaze into her cider. "Nothing I can't handle," Mercy said. "Truly. I don't want you and Lydia fretting over us."

"But you've gone into debt." Lydia sat across from Mercy.

"This cattle sale will take care of that." Mercy glanced from Lydia to James. She wasn't going to waste her breath convincing them that she'd done the right thing investing in her breeding program. Today's auction was proof enough.

"Miranda tells us you came all this way with only two men to help."

Mercy nodded. "James, please. I came to visit, not discuss business."

"Well, you're carrying a lot of cash now. I hope these are good, trustworthy men."

"To tell you the truth they aren't going back with us." Mercy squeezed her jaw tight too late.

"What?" Pearson asked.

"You mean Luther and Jed aren't—" Miranda said.

"No!" Mercy snapped. "No. Luther and Jed aren't heading back with us. And I'm glad they aren't."

"You won't have any men with you?" Lydia sounded as though Mercy had just announced her intention to capture the throne of England.

"They were useless. We're better off without them."

"You and Miranda, alone?"

"Miranda is better with a pistol than most men I've known and you know I can handle myself." It was true. Mercy had taught her sister well. Still looking at her petite sister, Mercy's stomach twisted. There had to be a way to avoid putting Miranda at risk.

"Two women alone . . ." James ran his hand through

his thinning hair and pushed up to his feet. "I have an idea."

"What do you mean?" Mercy stood to follow him.

"You just sit here with Lydia." James placed one hand on her shoulder and with the other directed her back to her chair. "There's someone I want you to meet. I'll be back shortly."

As he left, Mercy turned to Miranda who shook her head and shrugged. Lydia bent to peek into the oven. Harold picked an apple from a bowl in the center of the table, avoiding her eyes.

"Harold?" Mercy asked.

He rolled his eyes to the ceiling while he chewed. "I wonder if he's gone to fetch that man."

"What man?"

"A real nice fella." Harold took another bite, chewing methodically. It took all of Mercy's restraint to keep from grabbing the apple and demanding the rest of the story.

"Lookin' for a guide to Colorado Territory," Harold continued at last. "He's got a sister lives outside of Denver."

"Does this man have a name?" Mercy stood, fisting both hands.

Harold nodded. "Buchanan."

"Buchanan? Your Pa thinks *that* man should look after me?" She stomped out of the kitchen muttering, "I need Thad Buchanan like a leaf needs a caterpillar."

The saloon reverberated with scraping chairs, banging glasses and male voices. The smell of whiskey mingled with the pungent aromas of men, tobacco and burning oil. The commotion wasn't enough to distract Thad from thinking about a certain lady. All of the in-

tricacies of poker—calculating the odds, studying the
players for signs that would give away their hand, watching the dealer for any dishonest tricks—promised to
keep his mind busy. He'd forget about women altogether and more important, he'd forget his worry
about finding a guide.

The dealer shuffled and distributed the cards. It had
been a slow game. O'Reilly, quite drunk, but never free
with his money, kept up a constant chatter, complaining
about women business owners.

"Even the one they're built fer—pleasuring men.
They supply the skill, but a man oughta run the business."

The two trail-weary cowboys—Luther and Jed—guf-
fawed. "It's a damn shame to see a whore wastin' her
time countin' money. But that ain't half so bad as a
woman bossin' a man," Jed said.

"Amen!" Luther punctuated his comment by down-
ing a shot of whiskey.

"There oughta be a law." O'Reilly lifted his glass and
both cowboys laughed again.

Jed and Luther seemed to believe everything the
Irishman said. *Idiots.*

"I wonder, gentlemen, whether you believe all women
lack the talent to run a business. Or could it be," Thad
focused on O'Reilly, "you've been bested by a woman
and just don't like the competition."

O'Reilly glared at Thad through a cloud of cigar
smoke, then waved for another drink. Thad did a mental calculation of the chips sitting in neat stacks before
him. He'd learned long ago to count his chips without
touching or looking at them, so as not to draw the attention of the other players. He'd more than tripled the
twenty dollars he'd started with today, while O'Reilly
had bought more chips twice, just to stay in the game.

Jed and Luther had nearly exhausted their chips and had threatened to retreat to the bar. Instead, they remained at the table, complaining about their losses.

"I never did see such a lucky streak!" Jed said.

"Makes you wonder, don't it?" Luther replied. "Maybe it ain't luck." He glared at Thad. "I heard tell men like him make their own luck."

Thad ignored them. He did make his own luck, but he wasn't cheating as the cowboys implied. He turned back to O'Reilly who was rifling through a stack of chips waiting for the deal. Rumor had it O'Reilly made his money rustling cattle. Whatever his source of income, it wasn't poker. O'Reilly tossed in another four-bit ante.

The Irishman fanned his cards, examining each one in turn. "I've got you this time, Buchanan." O'Reilly grinned, displaying a large gap between his front teeth.

Thad knew the look. O'Reilly had aces, or wanted Thad to believe he did. He fanned his own cards and glanced at them. His heart started pounding—two aces, king, four, and two. He refused to allow his lips to curl into a smile. Whether the Irishman was bluffing, or not, Thad's hand was just as good. All heads turned to O'Reilly who threw in ten dollars.

Jed and Luther folded, leaving O'Reilly alone with Thad. O'Reilly was still grinning—his crooked teeth giving him a clownish look.

Thad threw in two five-dollar chips. O'Reilly wouldn't get away with the bluff.

"Cards?" the dealer asked.

O'Reilly and Thad each requested two cards. Thad glanced at his draw, careful not to show any reaction as he observed ace, king. He glanced at O'Reilly who sneered back.

"I'll bet another twenty," O'Reilly said.

He'd asked for two cards, so it was unlikely O'Reilly

had four of a kind. He was most likely just supporting his bluff. Thad reached for his chips. "Call," he said, tossing eight more chips into the pot. "And raise another twenty."

O'Reilly roared with laughter.

"You ain't got nothin', Buchanan! I don't believe it." He lapsed into a brogue. "You're trying to bluff me. Well, I ain't fallin' fer it." He threw a handful of chips into the pot. "I'll see that raise. Now show me yer cards."

O'Reilly didn't wait for Thad to display his cards. Showing three aces, he reached for the pot.

"I don't know where your aces came from, O'Reilly. Mine were dealt me." Thad laid his full house face up on the table.

The dealer looked from O'Reilly to Thad, his Adam's apple bobbing.

"What?" O'Reilly roared. "You dirty cheat. You've been stealing me money all afternoon."

O'Reilly leaped to his feet, drew back his fist, and threw a roundhouse punch. He tumbled to the floor as Thad stepped away. The saloon grew silent—all eyes on the poker table.

Thad reached down to help O'Reilly to his feet. "Now, Mr. O'Reilly, you know—"

A chair crashed across his back and Thad turned to face Luther as the crowd roared its pleasure. Whether the crowd was pleased to have Thad take a blow, or simply pleased for the entertainment of a fight, he couldn't be sure.

"I can't abide a cheat," Luther growled through clenched teeth as his right fist connected with Thad's chin.

Surprised by the punch, Thad staggered back. Glimpsing a movement, he threw his right arm up in time to shield his face from the bottle O'Reilly wielded. Glass shattered against Thad's elbow, soaking his sleeve with whiskey. Thad drove his left fist into O'Reilly's gut and the portly fellow doubled over, gasping and sputtering as he dropped to his knees still clutching the broken bottleneck.

Thad spun back to Luther. He held up his hands. "Now listen here. I've never cheated. Check the cards, you'll see O'Reilly's the one who—"

Luther and his smaller comrade attacked Thad, fists and feet flying. Jed nearly toppled Thad with a well-placed kick behind his knee before Thad sent him sprawling.

"Jed!" Luther shouted, but Jed remained motionless where he'd landed.

Luther swung another right hook, but Thad blocked it and smashed his fist into the cowboy's face. Blood spurting from his nose, Luther came back at Thad with both arms swinging.

Thad dodged and tried again to explain, but the blood seemed to arouse the crowd and Thad couldn't even hear himself speak.

The fight went back and forth for a few moments, neither man landing a serious blow. Then Thad saw his opportunity to end it. He faked a jab with his left fist. When Luther dodged, Thad slammed a right to the cowboy's chin. Luther fell backward and lay still.

Several men came forward to congratulate Thad, but most returned to their drinking. Thad surveyed the saloon. O'Reilly was gone. The mess was limited to the broken bottle and chair his attackers had used. The poker table had been overturned. Three chips remained on the floor. Thad guessed the crowd had collected the rest. He retrieved the chips.

"I checked O'Reilly's cards," the dealer said. "You were right. Two of his aces don't match the deck."

Thad nodded, weighing the small disks in his hand.

"For your trouble," he said, handing the chips to the dealer.

Thad bent to collect his hat from the floor then turned to the door in time to observe a familiar figure exiting.

"Mr. Pearson!" Thad chased the shopkeeper outside. This was turning out to be one hell of a day.

Chapter 3

"Mr. Pearson, please," Thad called again. "One moment, sir."

Pearson turned, taking in Thad's appearance. "I had you figured for a gentleman, Buchanan." Pearson shook his head. "My mistake."

"Sir, I can explain."

Pearson raised his hand. "No explanation necessary. You live your life as you see fit. But I am not sending my friend on the trail with a drunken gambler."

"James." The shopkeeper turned. Mrs. Clarke was approaching behind him.

"Harold told me . . ." She broke off, looking up at Thad.

When she wasn't lecturing, her contralto voice was as smooth as warm honey over cornbread. His lips started to stretch into a smile, the pain reminding him of the punch he'd received earlier. His hand went to his face and he felt his mustache damp, most likely with blood from his lip. He snatched his hand down, placing it behind his back.

"Ma'am." He nodded, removing his hat. "I'm—"

"A no-account gambler?" Mercy raised her eyebrows. She took a step closer and sniffed. "And a drunk?"

"It's not what it appears. I don't drink."

"Use whiskey for cologne, do you?"

Thad opened his mouth to explain, but thought better of it.

"Mercy," Pearson said. "I had thought Buchanan here—"

Mercy spun to face Mr. Pearson.

"I've made my decision, James. I'm no child and I won't be treated like one." She took a step toward Pearson and placed a hand on his shoulder. "I appreciate your concern." She looked back at Thad and shook her head. "I'm sorry, Mr. Buchanan. The trail can be dangerous. I won't put my sister and myself at risk by bringing along someone who isn't . . ." Her eyes met his. "Completely reliable."

She turned and walked away.

Thad put his kerchief up to his lip as he watched Mrs. Clarke stride away with her thick brown braid swinging against her buckskin jacket. Why did he seem forever to be staring at that woman's backside?

He turned to Pearson. "That's your *old* friend?"

Pearson glared at him, then turned to follow Mrs. Clarke. Thad closed his eyes. *Hellfire.* He'd just lost his best chance of reaching Colorado.

Riding across the silent prairie beside her sister, Mercy's mind wandered again to the maverick with the blue eyes that could see deep inside her. And a smile that could melt her heart. Hell, never mind her heart, that face and those shoulders sent liquid heat right through her. She gritted her teeth and shoved that thought clear out of her mind. She had other worries.

She must get home and keep her sister safe. James

was right when he said she and Miranda would be foolish to make the journey alone. True, they weren't likely
to have any trouble from Indians. The government had
moved them all out of Colorado Territory. That left
only the minor difficulties of wild animals, storms and
thieves.

They needed—not a man—just more people. Enough
that they could trade watches at night and have plenty
of eyes alert for danger all day. It didn't have to be a man,
and it certainly didn't have to be Thaddeus Buchanan.

She smiled. His sheer size would scare off the wolves
and coyotes. But he was a gambler. Even assuming he
was as strong as he looked, he wouldn't be good for anything practical. He might not even ride well enough to
keep up with Miranda. And Lord help them all if he
brought whiskey with him.

"Mercy?" The breathless voice reminded her that
Miranda was riding beside her. "Is that Uncle Will's
barn?" Miranda pointed.

Mercy looked and nodded. "That's the place."

Miranda clucked her tongue, urging Princess to a
gallop. Mercy held Annabelle back while her sister
raced ahead toward their uncle's farm. She was anxious
to see her relatives, especially Emily. This reunion
wouldn't be easy though.

She leaned forward and let Annabelle run, gathering strength from the powerful beast under her. She arrived in time to see Aunt Emily throw her arms around
Miranda. Little cousin Jake held Princess's reins while
he looked around, perhaps trying to avoid a hug from
his cousins.

"Come here, Jake." Mercy wrapped her arms around
the boy, eliminating any possibility of escape.

Her heart leaped to her throat as she saw her youngest cousin peering out from behind her mother's skirts.

The little girl's tawny hair and big brown eyes were so like Nate's it was hard for Mercy to look at her without imagining the children she'd not been able to give her husband. The girl even had his name.

"Don't be shy, Natalie," Emily coaxed. "Mercy and Miranda want to see you." Emily pulled the girl around to stand in front of her, keeping a protective hand on her shoulder.

"We brought you something," Miranda said.

The girl gave her a tentative smile.

"Did you bring me something too?" Jake asked.

"Jacob!" Emily scolded.

"Of course we did, Jake," Mercy said. "We brought something for all of you."

Miranda handed Natalie a bundle and the little girl looked up as if waiting for an explanation. "It's for your baby doll," Miranda said.

"Ellie?"

"Is that her name?" Miranda stooped so that she was at the child's eye level.

Natalie nodded.

Mercy's throat tightened as she watched the exchange. It had been a mistake to come here. Everything about this place reminded her of Nate.

"Mercy knitted the blanket and I made the dress," Miranda said.

"What did you bring me?" Jacob tugged on Mercy's arm.

"A rattle," Mercy said.

Jacob scowled. "A baby rattle?"

"Nope. From a rattlesnake."

Jacob's eyes opened wide as Mercy unwrapped the rattle and handed it to him. Little Natalie pushed over to get a closer look as well.

"Did you kill it with your bare hands?" Jake asked.

She laughed, squatting down beside him. "No, I'm afraid not." Mercy touched the delicate rattle cradled in Jake's palm. "I came upon this fellow already dead."

Jake kept his eyes on the prize he held. "I bet you wouldn't be scared of no live rattler neither."

"It's just plain good sense to be scared of a rattler," Mercy said.

"Why, Mercy Clarke—what happened to the fearless fifteen-year-old girl I met so long ago?"

She smiled at her aunt, knowing she was teasing. All the same, Mercy couldn't help wishing she could be fifteen and fearless again.

Three hours later, Mercy stepped into hot water and bent to scrub her legs. The steam tickled her nose. She splashed water on her legs to rinse the soap from them and then sat, draping her legs over the side so that her long body would fit into the tub. Days in the saddle and nights on cold, hard ground had left her aching everywhere. The muscles in her back relaxed as the warmth soaked into them.

Ahh. She'd waited all day for this, enjoying the anticipation as she allowed Miranda to bathe first. She surprised Aunt Emily by not arguing against throwing out Miranda's bath water. This was no time to economize. She wanted her bath clean and she wanted it hot. *Lovely.*

She rubbed the bar of honeysuckle-scented soap into the cloth and made lazy circles from her shoulder, down her left arm. Her hair, already washed and pinned to the top of her head, dripped cool water on her neck.

She tried to empty her mind of all thought outside of this tub. To truly relax for the first time in weeks. Months? She cupped a hand to bring water up to her shoulder and watched as the warm suds dripped back into the tub.

How many days would it take to get home? A week to
Fort Kearny. Miranda would want to stay overnight.

Bloody hell! She had to stop thinking at least for a few
hours. She shut her eyes tight and started humming the
first tune that came into her mind.

A minute later, she was singing full out, as she scrubbed.
"Oh, Susannah! Oh, don't you cry for me. . . ."

She glanced at the door, hoping Miranda would come
in to scrub her back. The girl was probably distracted,
playing with their cousins or gossiping with Aunt Emily.
Mercy pulled the warm, wet cloth over her face to soak
out weeks of trail dust.

Thad and Harold tied their horses to a post in the
quiet yard in front of the house that belonged to Mercy
Clarke's uncle. Harold had told him Mrs. Clarke's given
name. Mercy. He hoped her name described her char-
acter—he could use some compassion. If she'd allow
him to tell his story, he was certain he could persuade
Mercy to take him to Colorado territory. His fight at the
bar had made the wrong impression on her, but he
could overcome that.

"Where do you suppose everyone is?" Harold looked
around.

There was smoke and voices around the far side of
the house and they headed in that direction when a
honey-sweet contralto singing "Oh, Susannah!" caught
Thad's attention.

"I'm gonna check the house." He tilted his head toward the front door and Harold nodded.

Thad knocked on the front door as Harold continued around the house. Thad was certain that voice belonged to Mercy. She continued singing. Likely, she
didn't hear the knock. He removed his hat and let him-

self in. There was no one in the front parlor. He hesitated a moment before following the voice down the hall.

The song stopped. She was humming now, soft and low, and—*oh, Lordy*. She sat in a tub in the middle of the kitchen naked as the day she was born. Only this was no fragile newborn. Those long, shapely legs—bare, wet and gleaming in the sunlight that filtered through the kitchen curtains—drew his eyes to the tub. He ached as he watched a soap bubble slide over her collarbone and disappear between the two full breasts that floated just beneath the surface of the water.

He took a step toward her and froze. *What's wrong with you, Buchanan?* A gentleman did not walk in on a lady's bath. A wet cloth covered her face. She hadn't noticed him yet. He should walk out before it was too late. Except that his boots seemed to be nailed to the floor. He just kept staring at those legs.

"Miranda?" she asked. "You here to scrub my back?"

"I'd be happy to oblige—" *Dammit, shut your mouth, Buchanan.*

Mercy sat up. Pulling her legs into the tub forced her bosom out of the water and he had a view the memory of which he would happily take to his grave. Perhaps today, since the lady would be within her rights to shoot him. Too late, he lifted his hat to cover his eyes. He heard the cloth splash into the water. Maybe he could convince her he hadn't seen much.

"Out!" she yelled with a voice he had no doubt could carry over a herd of cattle. "Get out!"

Chapter 4

"Don't go in there!" Thad heard a girl shout and he let go of the doorknob as though it were a hot coal.

From where he stood on the front porch, he saw Harold approaching with Miranda on his arm. Thad understood now why the boy had been so eager to guide Thad to this farm. Harold had attached himself to Miranda like a billy goat to a hillside.

"My sister's bathing." Miranda giggled. "She'd have you skinned alive if you walked in there."

He relaxed a little. They thought he was going in, not coming out.

Skinned alive? His shoulders went taut again. He stepped away from the door. Maybe he could still escape.

"You've met Mr. Buchanan, Miranda?" Harold smiled at her as though she were the only person present.

"Sure have. He nearly got hisself beat to a pulp trying to rescue us from a drunk." Miranda laughed.

Thad remembered Mercy's fist in his chest. He scowled. Was the girl laughing at him for trying to be a gentleman?

"Come meet my relatives, Mr. Buchanan." Miranda waved for him to follow her.

They moved away from the door, but Thad wished they'd move faster. He wanted to be miles away before Mercy Clarke emerged from the house. The embarrassing bathtub incident had surely cost him his chance to persuade Mercy that he should join her trip to Colorado. How could he convince Harold to depart before she appeared and suggested skinning, or perhaps hot tar?

Damn. He'd been determined to convince the woman to take him along with her. He could be useful—provide a bit of protection for two vulnerable young ladies. Mercy would never believe that now.

Around the side of the house, Miranda's relatives were preparing for supper near a makeshift summer kitchen. Miranda introduced Thad to her Aunt Emily, a woman who seemed far too young to have adult nieces. Uncle Will was a bit older, but young enough to laugh with his children as they recited their day's adventures. Thad couldn't help smiling as Uncle Will patiently instructed his young daughter to put a spoon at each place rather than all the spoons at one place. The little girl, Thad reckoned, was teasing her papa and he knew it.

Before Thad could protest, one of the older boys had added a place for Thad and Harold as well.

"Harold tells me you have a sister near Denver?" Aunt Emily asked.

"Yes, ma'am." Thad turned to face Aunt Emily who was struggling to remove a Dutch oven from the coals. He grabbed a towel and lifted the heavy iron pot. "She runs a mercantile about sixty miles from Denver." Thad kept a wary eye on the house as he set the Dutch oven down and took the seat Aunt Emily indicated.

What would he say when Mrs. Clarke accused him

of . . . immorality? It wasn't as though he'd intended to spy on her. He'd only wanted to talk to her.

He couldn't have known she'd be naked. Good Lord. He still might have escaped if she hadn't invited him to scrub her back. Not that she was inviting *him*. She'd thought he was her sister. For all her unpolished appearance, he knew Mercy was a lady, not the type of woman who allowed strange men to . . . He should have kept his mouth shut.

It was hard enough trying to think what to do with those legs in plain view. When her breasts appeared above the water and . . . He swallowed. Whatever the punishment was for accidental sins, that view might just have been worth it. Remembering the scene was causing Thad the same discomfort he'd experienced inside when he was so near those legs and . . . all. Thank goodness, the table offered him more cover than his tight-fitting pants.

He'd covered his eyes the moment he'd regained his senses. Perhaps she hadn't seen him looking. He glanced back at the house.

"Mr. Buchanan?" Miranda's voice penetrated his worried thoughts.

She had asked something. He turned to her. "Hmm?"

"Sixty miles north or south of Denver?"

"North. Fort—"

"Not Fort Victory?" Miranda almost squeaked.

Thad nodded. His sister was in Fort Victory and he was never going to get there.

"Your sister runs the mercantile in Fort Victory?" Miranda laughed.

Thad checked over his shoulder again. Mercy was coming around the corner wearing a yellow gingham dress that swirled about her legs as she marched directly for him with . . . was that a bullwhip? She released the end of the loop and allowed the whip to hang down

to its full length. Her eyes fixed on his. He was dead—
she'd definitely seen him looking.

"Clarisse Wyatt is your sister?" Miranda asked.

Mercy froze a few feet from him. Her head swiveled
from Thad to Miranda, then back to Thad.

He ripped his eyes from Mercy, turning to face Miranda.
"You know Clarisse?" It didn't seem possible.

"She's Mercy's best friend in the world. Isn't she,
Mercy?" Miranda put her hands on her hips. "What are
you doin' with that whip?"

Thad whirled back to Mercy. Her knuckles were
white where she gripped the whip's handle. She relaxed
her hand and turned from Miranda to him, studying his
face with clear green eyes. Her damp hair was pinned
loosely up on her head, revealing a graceful neck that
he hadn't noticed before. Little wonder.

He'd been wrong earlier about putting her in a
dress. It might be a shame to hide those legs, but the
dress hugged curves that her jacket and loose-fitting
men's shirt had nearly hidden.

He pushed up from his seat. His mother would be
appalled that he'd failed to stand to acknowledge the
approach of a lady, but damn, this woman was distracting. How was a man supposed to think when she kept
dazzling him with her figure and those captivating
green eyes?

"You're a friend of my sister?" Thad looked deep into
her eyes, willing her to hear his thoughts. *They don't
know I saw you bathing. We can keep this secret between us.*

Mercy blinked. It was as though a shutter had closed,
hiding a part of her. She looked at her gathered family,
then back at him. Her hands worked the whip back into
a circle.

He held his breath, waiting like a soldier who knew
the enemy was hunkered down just across the field.

Mercy lifted her eyes back up to his. "You're Clarisse's baby brother?"

Thad grinned. His tiny sister loved to call him baby brother. He studied Mercy, unsure whether he'd been forgiven or not. Best to play the cards he'd been dealt. "It's a family joke. There was a time when I was a good deal smaller than Clarisse."

Mercy pulled her shoulders back and lifted her chin. He thought for a moment that she would demand an apology. Or worse. His eyes dropped to the whip, which she now held at her side. Her face revealed her battle for control, her lips pinched together so tightly he thought they'd become one.

Now, or never. "I'm very anxious to see my sister again," Thad said. "I've never even met my nephews."

She looked away for a moment, before leveling a serious gaze at him.

Thad plowed ahead before she rejected the idea. "I'd pay fifty dollars to go along with you." He could almost see her mind working, considering. "In gold coin."

"Seventy-five," she said.

Had he heard right? She was going to take him to Clarisse?

"I know how anxiously Clarisse has been waiting for you to come. Reckon I couldn't face her if I told her I'd left you behind in Abilene."

Seventy-five dollars, hell that was nearly half of what he'd managed to save. But he was going to see Clarisse again.

Mercy placed her hands on her hips. "If you're traveling with me, you'll be following my rules. First, no whiskey. The trail's dangerous enough with everyone awake and alert. We can't have a drunk to look after."

"No, ma'am. I don't drink." Not to excess, he didn't.

She raised one eyebrow, clearly not believing him and proceeded with her list. "No gambling."

"I'm no gambler either."

"Mr. Buchanan, I saw you at the saloon."

"Poker, Miz Clarke, is a game of skill."

"Humph!" Mercy crossed her arms in front of her chest, but her eyes told him she was ready to laugh. "I'll do my best to get you to Fort Victory, but the first sign of trouble and I'm leaving you behind. Is that clear?"

"Yes, ma'am." Thad extended a hand. Mercy hesitated before taking it. Her grip was as firm and confident as any man's, but her skin was womanly soft. Except that, unlike any woman he'd met, her lean fingers fit around his broad hand. "I appreciate you letting me join your party."

The humor left her eyes, and he had another glimpse inside her. She nodded, slipping her hand out of his grip. The invisible shutter closed again, locking him out.

"You're welcome." Her eyes wouldn't meet his. "For Clarisse's sake."

The bells on the back of the door chimed as Thad entered Pearson's Mercantile. He spied Harold leaning on a broom while reading a book. Lydia Pearson greeted Thad from behind the counter.

"Mornin', ma'am," Thad said, removing his hat and stepping up to the counter.

"May I help you?"

"Yes, ma'am." Thad scanned the shelves behind the counter. "I wonder if you could grind some coffee for me?"

Lydia started toward the back shelf.

"With a little chicory?" he added.

"Why, that's the way I like it too," Lydia said as she scooped some beans into the hopper.

Thad leaned over the counter toward her. "And a bit of cinnamon?" he whispered.

Lydia grinned. "Cinnamon?"

"Yes, ma'am. Just a pinch."

"Hmm." Lydia raised an eyebrow, then turned to the shelf full of spices. "Sounds good—I'll have to try that myself." She found the cinnamon and turned back to the grinder. "Are you goin' to need anything else?"

"I will be wantin' a few things."

"Harold, will you help Mr. Buchanan, while I grind his coffee?"

"Yes'm." Harold shoved the broom into a corner and set his book on the counter. He grinned at Thad. "You'll be one of my last customers before I hit the trail tomorrow."

Thad found the cabinet that displayed soaps, shaving equipment and colognes. He smiled when he saw the bay rum. He looked around the store recalling the mental list he'd made earlier. "A needle and some white thread, to start."

Harold bent behind the counter. "Seems like an odd thing for a man to be buyin'."

"It's what I need."

Harold inserted the needle into a scrap of paper, then went to fetch the thread.

"You've been friends with Miz Clarke for a long while?" Thad asked.

Harold grinned. "Since I was knee high to a grasshopper."

"I take it she's a widow?"

"Yup." Harold's grin widened. "But you might be in for a disappointment—ain't no man gonna distract her from that ranch of hers."

Thad suspected he could distract her and it might make the journey a more pleasant one for both of them. Or it just might get him whipped.

Harold set the thread on the counter. "What else can I get for you?" Harold caught a look at himself in the mirror behind the counter and reached up to flatten the hair at his crown.

Thad bit his lip to keep from laughing at Harold's primping. "I notice you carry bay rum." Thad nodded in the direction of the toiletries, remembering his father giving him his first bottle of bay rum and his first razor when he was sixteen.

"Yes, sir." Harold walked over to the display. "Just got that in. Haven't had a chance to try it yet myself, but I understand it drives the ladies mad." He looked up at Thad. "I hope you're not plannin' on, um, socializing with Mercy."

"The cologne can be very soothing after a day in the sun." He lifted one of the glass bottles and studied the label. "Broke a bottle on my way to Abilene. I wonder if . . ." He looked around the store. "Yes." He walked across the room and pointed into another glass display case. "How much for one of those?"

Harold walked around behind the counter and pulled the shiny flask out of the display. "This is genuine brass."

Thad waited.

"It'll cost you five dollars."

Thad released a long breath. Five dollars was a small fortune, but it could save him money in the long run. He held the bottle of cologne next to the flask. "I'll take the bottle and the flask."

Harold piled Thad's purchases on the counter, keeping a running tally as he went. Soap, a new jackknife, and three extra handkerchiefs. "That'll be thirty-two dollars and forty-seven cents, Mister Buchanan."

Thad looked around the store again. "I don't suppose you'd have a white shirt in my size?" He walked over to the shelf piled high with men's shirts.

"I reckon we have just about any size you could want." Harold reached down to the bottom of the stack, pulled out a large shirt and held it up in front of Thad.

"That'll do. I'd like to greet my sister wearing a clean shirt." Running his hand over the stiff fabric, he suddenly felt his long awaited reunion with Clarisse was really going to happen.

"Here's your coffee, Mr. Buchanan." Lydia placed the sack next to the pile her nephew had started. "I've got to check on the supper, Harold."

"I'll mind the store, Aunt Lydia," Harold whined. "For one more day," he mumbled, then winked at Thad.

The bell on the door chimed as more customers entered.

"Be with you in a minute," Harold called. "You wear two guns, Mr. Buchanan," Harold said. "That's good. You'll be wantin' to buy some ammunition, I reckon."

"I have plenty."

"You sure? Might be good to stock up, seein's how we'll have two ladies to protect." Harold grinned. "Though I must tell you, Mercy's a better shot than any two men I've ever met."

Thad looked the lad in the eye, trying hard not to stare at the wispy moustache he was trying to grow. "Don't know if that should comfort me, or not."

"Well, it ought to comfort you, I guess. Unless you get her riled."

"Reckon I'll do my best to avoid that."

"You men aren't plannin' on riding with Mercy Clarke, are you?"

Thad recognized Luther's voice from the poker game. He turned to see Luther and Jed approach the counter.

"What of it?" Harold asked.

"S'pose we should warn 'em, Luther?"

"Don't rightly care what happens to the cheat here."

Luther pulled a face that suggested he was smelling skunk. "I suppose it'd only be fair to warn the boy, though."

"Warn me of what?" Harold asked.

"That woman is trouble," Luther said.

"What—"

Jed interrupted. "The bitch has a mouth like—"

"Just a minute there," Thad growled. "You're talkin' about a lady."

"Hell no, we ain't." Jed thrust his chest toward Thad.

"We don't aim to start a fight." Luther pulled his friend back. "Point is—if she hired you boys for protection—"

"She didn't hire no one!" Harold stepped up to Luther. "She's a friend of mine. And Buchanan here paid her to guide him."

"You paid?" Jed asked. "Hear that, Luther? I think Buchanan here just might be another girl who likes to wear men's—"

Thad grabbed Jed's shoulders. "I would hate to see this fine mercantile suffer any damage over the likes of you. But I will gladly take you outside and remind you what my fist can do to your jaw."

"Gonna punch someone, cheat?" Luther said. "Start with me."

Thad let Jed go. "Not inside the store."

"Leave your guns with the boy here and we'll meet you outside," Luther said.

"You remove your guns first," Thad said.

Jed pulled on Luther's arm. "Come on, Luther."

"We ain't got nothin' to prove to you, Buchanan," Luther said. "Just remember what I said, boy. You ride with that woman—you're headin' for trouble. She's carryin' over a thousand dollars cash and plenty of folks know it."

* * *

Mercy sat in front of the dressing table with her eyes closed as Emily ran a brush through the hair that hung over Mercy's shoulder and down her back like a woolen shawl. She thought she'd outgrown her impulsiveness years ago, but the past few days she'd been rushing decisions without thinking. If she'd stopped to deliberate, she never would have agreed to let Harold Pearson come along. Buchanan, Miranda and Harold. She sighed. Now she'd have three people to look after on the trail. And if Buchanan didn't submit to the rules she'd set for him, there could be trouble.

"I miss this," Emily said.

Mercy opened her eyes to look at her aunt's reflection in the mirror. "Brushing my hair?"

"And talking." Emily chuckled. "Natalie's the only female companionship I have these days. And she usually wants to talk about insects."

"Now that sounds mighty interesting."

"At least she's stopped hunting snakes." Emily shuddered. "I was always afraid I'd find one under my pillow, or in my yarn basket."

"If I'd known about her interest in snakes, I'd have given her a rattle too."

"Now don't you go encouraging her." Emily affected a stern look. "I'd as soon have my daughter playing with dolls."

Mercy smiled at her aunt's reflection.

Emily returned the smile, then resumed brushing. "I wish I had your thick, elegant hair."

"Elegant?" Mercy wrinkled her nose. "More like a nuisance. I've considered cutting it all off."

"You wouldn't!" Emily stopped brushing and bent to look directly at Mercy.

"No, I wouldn't." Mercy sighed. "But I have considered it."

"Pshaw!" Emily shook her head as she worked a knot out of Mercy's hair with her fingers. "That's a silly notion. You know you're an attractive woman and your hair is one of your best features."

"Which might matter if I had any intention of attracting someone, which I do not!"

"You don't mean that."

"I most certainly do. I'm content with my life."

Emily sat on the cedar chest next to the dressing table and Mercy took up the brush. If she kept moving maybe she could avoid Emily's scrutiny. "For two days you've avoided my questions. Now, I want to know how you are doing. And I don't mean how many cows calved this year, or how well Jake's Creek is running through another dry summer. I mean you—in your heart—how are you?"

Mercy turned back to her own reflection. Her gaze settled on the gold band gleaming in the lamplight and she felt the familiar tightness in her throat.

"It's been two years, Em." She set the brush down on the table. "I've done my grieving. I have a new life and I enjoy running the ranch—truly." She turned to look at Emily and saw the unspoken question. "Of course I miss Nate. I miss him the way I'd miss my right arm if it were cut off."

Emily placed her hands over Mercy's and squeezed hard.

"I expect a part of you will always miss Nate, but . . . Miranda tells me you've had some suitors and you—"

"Suitors?" Mercy laughed.

"A traveling judge."

"Judge Jenson is nobody's suitor. Leastwise not the kind who wants marriage."

"Well, what about your neighbor?"

"Lansing?" Mercy shook her head. "Did Miranda call him a suitor?"

"She said he proposed marriage." Emily squeezed Mercy's hands again. "Miranda also said he has a young boy."

Mercy sighed. "Miranda has it completely wrong." She took up the brush and pulled it through her hair. "Yes. He asked me to marry him, to be a mother to his boy." She scowled at the memory. "I'm not the romantic I was at twenty-one, but even so . . . Em, he said it would be good for business. We'd put our two ranches together and I'd take care of Jonathan—his son. I've known that little boy since the day he was born and I . . . care for him. But I won't enter a marriage for the sake of a child and a ranch. I like my independence too well." Mercy smiled at her. "Yes, losing Nate was hard. Oh, Em—I've gained something too." She set the brush on the dressing table. "When there's a man around, everyone naturally looks to him for decisions. Now they look to me. Marrying Lansing, I'd lose so much. At least Nate consulted me on most things. Lansing wants to dress me in finery and keep me in the house. I'd never make another decision beyond what to have for dinner."

"Well, I hope the man plans on hiring a cook," Emily teased.

"It'd serve him right," Mercy laughed. "Having to eat my cooking."

Emily shook her head. "Your lack of skill in the kitchen is my greatest failure in life."

Mercy smiled. "It's not your fault I never wanted to spend much time in the kitchen."

"Nate's letters were filled with admiration for how you ran the ranch. He said you knew the business better than anyone, even your pa."

"Really?" Mercy's throat tightened. "I didn't think he noticed. He never seemed interested in the business."

Mercy stood and walked to the window, half-listening to Emily's recollections of Nate's letters. Stretching her thumb across her palm, she touched the smooth gold band on her finger. By the light of the moon, she could see the apple trees, the garden, and the prairie extending beyond. It was her fault Nate had felt a failure. She never understood why her success as a rancher made him feel like less of a man, but somehow it had. And perhaps that was part of the reason he'd stopped thinking of her as a woman.

The prairie disappeared into shadow as a cloud passed in front of the moon. She brushed at her temple as her head started to throb. Emily stepped close to her. Mercy continued to gaze out the window, inhaling the cool evening air. The clouds moved, revealing the endless prairie again.

She felt a comforting hand rest on her shoulder. "Mercy, your heart has been torn and battered these past six years. It's natural to want to protect it."

"I don't know what you mean."

"I think you do."

Mercy kept her mouth clamped shut. Her aunt had been like an older sister to her since her marriage to Uncle Will some twelve years ago. Em had the best intentions, she just didn't understand.

"Let me plait your hair like I used to do." Emily tilted her head toward the dressing table and Mercy sat on the three-legged stool again so that her petite aunt could reach her hair.

Mercy relaxed while Emily ran the brush over her head. "I loved him. But he's gone and I've come to accept that."

"As you accept that you are alone?"

Damn. She should have bit her tongue. "Yes. No. I'm not alone. I have Pa and Miranda."

Emily set the brush down and wove Mercy's hair between her fingers. "Don't you mean they have you?"

Her aunt spoke quietly. "Good ol' reliable Mercy, never thinkin' of herself."

Emily regarded Mercy in the mirror.

"I told you, I'm content with my life."

"Maybe we don't understand content the same way. You figure content means making dang sure nothin' dangerous or frightenin' comes along."

"Are you calling me a coward?"

"Not likely. Not the woman who takes charge of running a ranch and bossing her own cattle drive." Emily pulled the plait tight and continued weaving. "You're brave about most things and avoid some others."

"Avoid?"

"I understand," Emily said. "You're reluctant to hand your heart over to a man who has the power to break it."

"Nate never . . ."

"I'm not blaming Nate."

"You shouldn't. It was my—"

"Now don't you go blaming yourself, either." Emily pulled a ribbon around the plait. "I know it was hard on both of you . . . when you didn't have a child."

Mercy kept her eyes on the dressing table. "Turns out it was for the best."

"Why?"

"How could I run the ranch now if I had small children to look after?"

Emily squeezed her shoulder, but didn't say anything.

"It is possible for a single woman to be happy."

"Of course it is," Emily said. "I'm glad you've found some joy in your work. I—"

Mercy lifted her chin. "I know you want what's best for me, Em, but I honestly don't need a man."

"I never said you needed a man. On the other hand, if a man should happen along . . . Take Mr. Buchanan."

"You take him," Mercy teased. The idea of leaving him with Emily appealed to her. Keeping a good distance from that man seemed a whole lot safer than spending long days and nights with him on the isolated trail.

"Maybe I will." Emily very nearly giggled. "I like a man with broad shoulders and," she leaned close to Mercy's ear, "a nice round seat."

"Em! What would Uncle Will say about you looking at a man's bottom?"

"Don't you suppose Will knows just exactly which male parts I most enjoy?" This time Emily did giggle. "Of course, he is rather possessive." She grinned, her eyes shining in a way that made Mercy feel hollow for some reason. "He might not like it if I flirted with Thad Buchanan. But the way that fella was lookin' at you I don't reckon I'd have a chance with him anyway." She winked at Mercy.

"I'm not interested in that . . . hulk of a man."

"No?" Her aunt studied her face. "Seems to me the two of you would fit together pretty well. It's nice to have a man who's bigger and taller so he can wrap his arms clean around you and keep you warm on long winter nights. And he is somethin' to look at, don't you think?"

Mercy felt heat rising to her cheeks and she was grateful for the dim light. "No." She shook her head. "Not especially. Just another handsome face." *Mercy, you are such a liar!*

"Well, let's just say you did set your cap for him. It wouldn't be so wrong, would it? To consider yourself for once. Maybe be a little selfish."

"What? Abandon my ranch and my family? Take up poker and whiskey?"

"Take a chance on love. Maybe tear down that fence

you've been building 'round your heart to keep folks out."

"I haven't built any fences, I'm just . . . busy, is all."

"Taking care of your pa and Miranda."

"Yes, that's right, Em. I have a lot of responsibilities."

"You have a lot of excuses to hide behind."

"I'm not hiding."

"Hmm." Emily sounded skeptical, but she didn't press the point. She walked over to the window and leaned out. "It is lovely out tonight. I think we may get some rain. That'd be a blessin'." She turned back to Mercy and placed an affectionate hand on her shoulder. "G'night."

Mercy pulled her aunt into a tight embrace. "Good night, Em."

Mercy watched the door close. The room was warm, but she was shivering. She put out the lamp and crawled under the blankets, knowing she'd never sleep. Staring up at the ceiling, she tried not to think about her aunt's words.

Your heart has been torn and battered these past six years.

Not the two years since Nate had died. Aunt Emily knew her secret. Everyone had worried about her when Nate died, but Aunt Emily knew the truth. Her grief had begun long before he died. She would not go through that kind of pain again, ever.

Throwing the blankets off, she fumbled in the darkness, pulling her jacket on over her nightgown and slipping out the window into the night.

Walking slowly, Mercy breathed in the farm smells around her—ripening apples, drying hay, cows in the barn. The moist prairie air had cooled, but the earth beneath her feet still held some of the sun's warmth.

Breathing the fresh cool air eased the throbbing pain in her head. Now if she could just find a curative that would keep her mind from straying to painful memories. A certain man's wicked grin flashed in her mind's eye. *No!* She refused to think about Thad Buchanan.

She lifted her shoulders and pulled in another deep breath. Tomorrow they'd begin the long journey home. She'd be too busy keeping everyone safe to think about broad shoulders and strong, inviting arms.

Chapter 5

Before dawn the next morning, Mercy cinched up the pack on Clover's back, working more by feel than by sight in the dim light of a single lantern. Her horse, Annabelle, and Miranda's Princess stood nearby, ready to go. Moving around the mare's head to check the bridle, she rubbed the white markings on Clover's golden brown forehead. The animal nuzzled Mercy as she crossed in front to check the pack on the other side.

She had purchased the mare from Uncle Will to carry the supplies they'd bought in Abilene, not to mention Emily's honeysuckle soap, and the supper she'd packed them.

"Emily's fried chicken and biscuits will be a blessing. Tomorrow's soon enough to start eating beans." She was going to miss Emily.

Mercy rubbed the horse's neck before double-checking the packs for balance and assuring that all the straps were tight. They could move faster if they carried only enough supplies to last three or four days at a time. It would be easy to purchase food along the way, so long as Miranda didn't spend too much time socializing at every stop. It had taken over a month to drive the cattle here, but they could make it home in three weeks depending on weather and luck.

Preparation was even more important than good fortune. She'd done everything she could think of to make their journey safer. Mercy hated the idea of carrying so much cash on the trail, but Lansing had insisted she make a lump sum payment in cash. One thousand dollars. She shook her head. She'd had no choice but to deal with Lansing when the banks in Denver had refused to finance the importing of the Hereford bulls. She'd accepted his terms and that meant paying in cash. She grinned, remembering the bankers who had laughed at her plan. This auction had proven her right and those men wrong.

"Damned shortsighted." Mercy brushed a hand over her hair, though it was perfectly smooth, as Miranda had secured it in a tight braid less than an hour ago.

She checked the last strap for a third time. She was working methodically because it was important to get it right, not because she was trying to postpone the meeting with Thad.

"Don't want to have these straps rubbing on you, do we girl?"

Clover nickered, nudging Mercy's shoulder with her nose. Mercy gazed into the horse's patient eyes for a moment and sighed. If only people were as easy to understand.

Her face heated when she remembered the way Buchanan had looked at her after the bathtub episode. His thoughts were easy enough to read then. She'd make him forget that incident as soon as possible. She rubbed her wedding ring. By the end of the day, Buchanan would understand she was strictly business.

Miranda burst into the barn. "What a beautiful sunrise! It's gonna be fair weather today. That's a good omen, don't you think?"

She went straight to Princess, allowing the horse to nibble a treat out of her hand. Mercy hoped it was a carrot and not something that was going to ruin the animal's teeth.

Miranda grinned. "It's an apple core. Did you think I would take Aunt Emily's sugar?"

Mercy knew her sister would help herself to sugar and so did Emily. No doubt their aunt had made a point of giving the girl the apple core.

Miranda glanced at the bundles on Clover's back. "Did you get everything packed?"

Mercy smiled at her sister. "Yes." She patted the leather pouch that had been full of cash after the auction. "I found space for your curtains in the moneybag."

She smoothed her hand over her jacket, feeling the extra bulk created by the greenbacks Aunt Emily had sewn into the lining. She'd done an excellent job of distributing the bills so that there were no visible lumps. Thieves would have to kill Mercy to get the money.

She thought of O'Reilly's threats in Abilene. That drunk didn't scare her. Still, he could have spread the word that she was carrying the sale money. After paying Jed and Luther and purchasing supplies, she had nearly twelve hundred dollars left. She glanced at her Sharps rifle, cleaned and ready in its holster on Annabelle's back. Her old Remington revolver would be easy to reach from where it sat in a bag on top of her change of clothes. She brushed her right hand over the modified Colt Army she carried in a holster on her belt. Mercy would be prepared for any trouble.

She remembered Miranda standing nearby and smiled to hide her worry. "We could have used the space to carry something more useful."

"Oh, but that fabric will brighten our cabin. You'll see—come winter you'll be glad for a little color."

"If we tire of our flour sack curtains, we could always buy something nice at the Wyatts' store in Fort Victory."

"But not the same lovely shade of yellow. It's perfect and Aunt Emily weren't gonna use it and it's just the right amount to make curtains..." Miranda stopped and Mercy realized her grin had given her away. "You're teasin' me now. You like the fabric as much as I do."

Mercy responded with a shrug. Truth was she enjoyed making Miranda happy. She knew living on the lonely ranch was hard on her sister.

Miranda patted the horse's shoulder. "Clover, I'm glad you're coming along." She rubbed her face against the horse's neck. "Every time I look at you I'll think of Uncle Will and Aunt Emily, too. I miss them both already."

Mercy glanced at Miranda and sighed. "I'll miss them too." Mercy cleared her throat. "Princess is ready. Let's get on outside."

Miranda led Princess out the wide barn door and Mercy followed with Annabelle and Clover.

"We'll be stoppin' at Fort Kearny, won't we?" Miranda asked, then continued before Mercy could answer. "It is about halfway and we'll need fresh supplies. I think Harold would like to meet Captain Jamison. Harold's very interested in military things and the captain loves to talk about his war exploits."

Mercy opened her mouth to respond, but Miranda stopped her with a gasp. "There he is waitin' for us." Miranda pulled Princess to a stop. "Mr. Buchanan's about the biggest man I ever did see. Do you reckon he's as strong as he looks?"

Mercy pulled up next to her sister. The last thing she expected was for Thad to arrive on time. Perhaps he wasn't as unreliable as she feared. More likely, he just didn't want to be left behind.

Miranda's voice took on a teasing singsong quality. "I don't suppose there's any point in me admiring the man. He only has eyes for you."

"Miranda!" Mercy growled. "Do you want him to hear you?"

Mercy studied Buchanan, who stood in front of Emily and Will's house checking the packs on his horse. As he reached across the animal's back, his jacket lifted enough for Mercy to get a clear view of his backside. Aunt Emily was right—it was nice and round. Mercy remembered his solid chest against her fist and wondered how that rump would feel against her palm.

Dangit! She'd spent the night chasing thoughts of Thad Buchanan clean from her mind and now they were back again. She chewed on her lip for a moment. Hell, her mind wasn't really the problem. It was those female parts she hadn't thought about in years suddenly wanting to have their say. She wasn't going to pay any attention to those feelings.

Men, on the other hand, didn't have any discipline. She couldn't expect Thad to keep his distance. Since he'd stumbled upon her bath and seen far too much of her, he probably thought he wanted her. She was going to make certain that he didn't cling to any hope of getting another view of her naked body. Her trail clothes would help discourage him. She'd make it clear that she was the boss on this journey—that would help too.

Like most men, Thad would no doubt prefer a sweet, demure female in gingham and lace. She'd show him the opposite in every way.

"This is a business arrangement. I won't have you embarrassing Mr. Buchanan with your foolish teasing," Mercy said.

Miranda drew herself up, mustering all of her dignity. "Very well. I ain't sayin' nothin' to embarrass *Mr. Buchanan.*" She glared at Mercy. "But I don't believe it's really his feelin's you're considerin'." Miranda stomped up to Buchanan, greeting him with her usual enthusiasm.

"Mornin', Miss Chase." Thad tipped his hat to her.

"Please call me Miranda." The girl grinned back at Mercy. "And my sister prefers Mercy. Mrs. Clarke reminds her of her dear deceased husband," she whispered loudly enough for Mercy to hear.

Mercy bit her lip. She'd have liked to keep things more formal. No doubt, her sister knew that.

"I'm sorry." Thad looked from Miranda to Mercy. "Well, you ladies please call me Thad." He tipped his hat to both of them.

Mercy glared at Miranda who tied her horse and sauntered up to where Harold Pearson had just emerged from the house. Names didn't mean a thing. Mercy was not about to let Thad Buchanan get close to her. Not in any way that mattered.

She took a deep breath and placed a welcoming smile on her lips. "Good morning, Thad."

"Mornin', Mercy." He tipped his hat again. "We have fair skies to start our journey."

"Yes. Should be able to make good progress today." Mercy tethered the animals to a rail, shoving her leather gloves into her pockets as she approached Thad. He looked as though he'd had a shave and a bath since their last meeting. His mustache had been trimmed considerably.

"You have . . ." Her mouth went dry. She'd almost said he had lips. She swallowed, searching for something more sensible to say. "A good hat. A broad-brimmed hat is essential for the trail."

His eyebrows came together as though he were trying to solve a puzzle. She averted her gaze and found herself focusing on his shoulders, then his chest. Her eyes dropped. Heavens, his pants were so tight she could see the muscles bulging on his thighs. "Impressive . . . um . . . hat." She cleared her throat, realized she was staring in a most inappropriate manner and looked up. "The weather. A good omen. The fair skies is . . . are a good omen for us." Embarrassed by her babbling, she turned her focus on his horse, a much safer view.

"Magnificent beast, isn't he?" Thad moved to her side. "I'll wager you won't find a stronger horse on either side of the Miss'ippi River."

Mercy couldn't resist running her hand along the horse's thick black mane. He turned to look at her, then relaxed as she rubbed his neck with practiced hands. "He'll need a strong back to carry you." She glanced at Thad, turning quickly back to the horse. It wasn't like her to dwell on a man's build. She blamed Miranda for putting it in her mind.

The horse was the largest Mercy had ever seen, standing substantially taller than her own long-legged quarter horse.

"He looks up to the task, I must say."

"Better'n sixteen hands." Thad gave the beast a possessive pat on the rump. "And definitely as strong as he looks."

She looked up at him. *Had he heard Miranda's comment?* There was a hint of humor in his eyes, but he couldn't have heard from across the yard. He smiled, then turned to give his horse another affectionate pat.

He took a step closer to her. "I call him Zeus."

She wasn't sure whether he was trying to tease her, but she'd teach him that she could give as well as take. "I'm glad to see, or should I say—smell—that you have decided to use different cologne." She regretted the comment the instant it left her tongue.

Thad's dimple appeared. "Bay rum." He tilted his hat back on his head to reveal his full face. "Glad you approve, ma'am."

He thought she was flirting with him. As if she'd be interested in a whiskey-drinking, gambling . . . As her cheeks warmed yet again, she turned to greet Harold. She had to get back in control.

"You just about ready?"

Harold patted a shiny new gun at his waist. "Yes, ma'am."

She made a mental note to supervise some target practice for the boy to make sure he knew how to handle that weapon. Mercy turned back to Thad and his azure eyes locked with hers. She curled the fingers of her left hand, rubbing her thumb along her ring. It wasn't only a reminder of Nate, it was a shield that helped her keep men at a distance. She would use every tool she had to keep this particular man in his place. She turned at the sound of Miranda giggling with Harold.

"I believe we're nearly ready to go, Thad."

He grinned. "That suits me, ma'am."

His smile nearly made her forget the final thing they needed to resolve.

"There's just the matter of payment to be settled first. I believe you owe me seventy-five dollars."

"No, ma'am." Thad raised his hand as Mercy opened her mouth to protest. "I will owe you seventy-five when you get me to Fort Victory. I don't owe you yet."

"That's ridiculous." Mercy took a step closer, tilting her head to look Thad in the eye. "How do I know you even have seventy-five dollars?"

Thad pulled a bag out of his jacket pocket and poured several gold coins into one of his wide palms. "There's more'n enough here, I assure you."

"How do I know you won't gamble it away at the first settlement we reach?"

Thad dropped the coins back into the bag. "I never gamble."

Mercy chortled. He almost seemed offended. "I saw you playing poker just three days ago."

"Poker is not gambling."

"I know—it's a game of skill."

"I'd be happy to demonstrate."

Mercy shifted her weight from one foot to the other. She was keenly aware that Harold and Miranda had stopped their conversation and were now listening to hers. And now Aunt Emily and her family were gathering to say their farewells.

"I won't argue the point with you." She glared at him. "I require payment in advance."

"I'll pay twenty-five now. The balance when we arrive in Fort Victory."

She thought of Clarisse waiting for her only remaining brother. Her friend had lost so many of her kin in the war. Mercy allowed herself a thorough look at Thad's face.

His eyes, so like Clarisse's, probed hers again, but this time there was no hint of flirtation, only sadness. She knew that look too well. "Forty dollars now. Thirty-five when we get to Fort Victory."

"Yes, ma'am." He smiled again, though the pain didn't leave his eyes. "That's acceptable." Thad captured her hand in his.

She wished she hadn't removed her gloves as his grip sent a rush of warmth into her arm and on to the pit of her stomach. He let her hand go and fished four gold eagles out of his bag. She pocketed the money without taking her eyes from his face. She'd known he was handsome that first day, but now that he was washed and clipped, she could see the finely sculpted lines of his cheek bones, his chin angled, but not pointed, softened by the thick bronze mustache trimmed to reveal his full lips. And that one dimple.

An artist might say it ruined the symmetry, but to her mind, it enhanced the charm of his whole face. She could imagine women swooning over this man. Seeing the twinkle return to his eye she wondered if he expected swooning from her. If he did, he'd be disappointed.

Mercy glimpsed Miranda and Emily exchanging a look and a whispered confidence. She expected her sister and aunt had decided Thad would make a fine Prince Charming who could sweep her away to happily ever after. With her sister conjuring such fairy tales, this was going to be a long trip.

She marched over to collect hugs from all the relatives, saving Emily for last.

"I'm going to miss you," Emily spoke the words that lingered in Mercy's heart.

Not trusting her voice, Mercy pulled Emily into another embrace.

"You take care of yourself, Mercy," her aunt whispered.

"I will," Mercy said as she stepped back.

Emily reached up to touch her niece's cheek. "I mean it. You take care of yourself, not just everyone else."

Mercy nodded. She blinked back a tear as she stepped over to Annabelle. Taking her hat from Annabelle's saddle, she pushed it down on her head, as she assumed the familiar role of cattle boss.

"Mount up everyone," she shouted. "We're headin' home."

The sun was well on the decline and they were still riding. Thad shifted in his saddle, trying in vain to find a more comfortable position. He was anxious to get to Colorado, but this madwoman acted as though it were possible to cover all five hundred miles in one day. If she kept this up, the horses wouldn't last the distance.

Riding in the lead, Mercy appeared at ease in her saddle, her back straight, her head moving back and forth, as she surveyed the prairie. Thad watched her chestnut braid, the swishing motion hypnotizing him.

The day had started with promise. He wiped his sweaty palm against his thigh, remembering the warmth of her hand in his—that hand, tough from work, yet womanly soft. In spite of their battle over the money, it seemed like a friendly beginning. And he liked the way she seemed flustered by his appearance. When she'd dropped her guard and smiled, he glimpsed a light in her eyes that she kept concealed most of the time.

Whatever she was hiding, the barrier seemed impenetrable. He'd tried to strike up a conversation as they rode, but her responses were limited to nods and grunts. The only break in the prairie silence was the pounding of the horses' hooves and the constant chatter from Miranda and Harold riding to the rear.

He shook his head. Too many hours in the hot sun, the gentle rhythm of the horse under him and sheer exhaustion were making him drowsy. They hadn't taken a dinner break. Instead, they'd made a few brief stops to water the horses and nibble on jerky and dried fruit. He touched his sunburned cheek. He hadn't even had time to dig out his bay rum. The cologne cooled a sunburn, but only if it was applied regularly.

Mercy lifted her hand, signaling them to stop. At last, General Sherman would let the troops rest. He bit his tongue. He wouldn't be discourteous to a lady, even if she were behaving more like an uncivilized Yankee.

Thad suppressed a groan as he swung down from Zeus's back. His legs felt like jelly. He led his horse to the watering hole, then bent to splash water on his face. He was an experienced rider, but he had never covered so many miles at one time. When he pushed upright,

Mercy was next to him. He smiled, trying not to let on how miserable he felt.

She didn't return his smile. "How are you doing, Thad?" she asked, her tone making it clear that his response was of no consequence to her.

"I'm fine, ma'am." From her raised eyebrow, he figured his answer sounded like the lie it was.

"I understand from your sister that you served in the Rebel Army."

Thad cringed at the use of the word "rebel." "I wore the uniform briefly."

"Not cavalry, I don't suppose." She let her eyes wander down to his legs and back up. He shifted, trying to appear relaxed, though his muscles were screaming for rest.

"Not cavalry. I grew up riding, though."

"Hmm." Mercy gave him a challenging look. "I thought maybe you were tiring. It has been a long day."

He stood taller. "I'm fine." He crossed his arms across his chest. "I was hoping we could put on a few more miles today."

"Good." She flashed him the look of someone who'd drawn four aces. "We have plenty of daylight and no need to cook supper. I think we can go another two hours."

Two hours?

When they finally stopped to make camp, Thad could barely move. He lifted the saddle off Zeus's back, feeling his muscles contract as he turned to set it on the ground. The ache spreading up his legs and back would make him miserable tomorrow, but he wouldn't utter a complaint to his guide.

He reached into his bag and pulled out the flask he'd purchased. Opening it, he poured some of the cologne into his palm and splashed it onto his face and neck. The liquid felt cool on his sunburned skin. He breathed in the spicy fragrance, feeling invigorated. Glancing up, he noticed Mercy watching him, though she turned back to the packhorse as soon as their eyes met.

Harold gathered fuel, while Miranda laid out the cold supper.

"Can I do somethin' to help, Miss Miranda?" Thad asked.

She favored him with a bright smile. "Could you get the fire lit?" She pointed her chin in the direction of a small pile of dried dung. "We don't need to cook supper, but Mercy will be wantin' her coffee."

"Coffee?" Thad grinned. That was something he understood.

He lit the fire before walking the short distance to the creek to fill the coffeepot. Moving and working helped ease his aches. He set the pot at the creek's edge and looked over his shoulder to be sure the others didn't see him. Holding his right arm straight, he lifted it out to the side nearly to shoulder height. He did the same thing to the front, using his left arm. He pulled his right higher, until the pain forced him to stop. The long day in the saddle had made his arm stiffer than usual. He kneaded his shoulder with his left hand for a moment, working the pain back to a dull ache.

He shrugged both shoulders a few times. His right arm was nearly as strong as his left now and it moved well enough. He'd been lucky. The pain reminded him that he'd survived the war. He'd learned to feel grateful for that. Thad bent to fill the pot with water.

As he returned to camp, he watched Mercy still working with the horses. She seemed full of energy as she sorted the packs and checked each animal. She seemed to be talking to the horses, probably conspiring to leave

Thad in the wilderness tomorrow. The further they got from Abilene, the more Mercy seemed to regret having him along.

Get some sense, Buchanan. Did you expect her to throw herself into your arms? She has other concerns and so do you.

He started the coffee cooking and returned to check Zeus again. The gelding seemed content to munch on a thick clump of grass. Thad had been fortunate to find a saddle horse of this quality for sale in Abilene, and doubly lucky that his owner was not much of a poker player. He patted the beast's rump.

Mercy caught his eye again as she checked her side arm and rifle by the failing light. He remembered the warning from the two cowboys in Abilene. She leaned her rifle against her saddle and joined her sister near the fire. He checked the pair of Remington revolvers he wore on his gun belt before ambling over to join the ladies.

Mercy poked at the fire and leaned toward the pot hanging over it. "Coffee nearly ready?"

"It should be," Miranda said.

"I noticed you checkin' your weapons," Thad said. "Hope you're not expectin' trouble."

"I always expect trouble." Mercy turned to the fire, keeping her back to him. "Your comment surprises me. A man with your military experience should understand the value of vigilance."

The woman could irritate a mosquito. She seemed pleasant enough except when she was speaking to him. "I'd just like to be kept informed if there is a particular danger."

She snapped her head to glare at him. "I'll keep you safe, if you follow my instructions."

"I never asked for your protection, Mercy." Thad spoke through clenched teeth. "Nor do I need it."

She jumped up. If she'd been a man, he'd have

taken the move as a threat. As it was, he found himself clenching his fists.

"You hired me to guide you," she snarled. "That means I'm in charge of this group." She leaned toward him. "Do I make myself clear?"

He met her glare. "I'm paying you to guide me, not to boss me." He relaxed his fists.

Mercy blinked and turned away. She pushed a stray lock of hair back from her face and took a deep breath. "I know the trail and I know the dangers." Her voice now seemed composed. "I can't have you questioning me." She glanced at the fire, then back at him. "But I won't treat you as a hired hand, if that's what worries you."

It wasn't what he meant at all, but he knew better than to expect any understanding from this woman. "I think you'll find you can count on me in a fight."

"Let's just hope that won't be necessary."

"Amen."

She turned away from him. Apparently, their discussion was over.

"Where's Harold?" Mercy asked.

Miranda pointed to a snoring lump on the other side of the fire. Mercy strode over to where the young man was curled up on the ground. "Harold," she growled, giving his bottom a nudge with her boot.

"Ow! Please! I've been bouncing on that all day."

"Come get your dinner," Mercy said. "Emily's chicken and biscuits will be the last real food you eat for a while."

"I'm too tired to eat," Harold whined, placing his arm over his ear and curling deeper into his blanket.

"Suit yourself," she said. "I'll wake you when it's time to start washing the dishes."

"I'll do it tomorrow."

"No, you won't. We'll need them for breakfast at dawn. You'll take care of the dishes tonight before you sleep." Her voice was firm but kind. Nothing like the way she spoke to Thad. "You're dishwasher on this crew. That was our bargain, Harold."

"All right, all right," Harold muttered as he finally stirred.

Thad brought two plates and, sitting next to Harold, handed him one. "You'd better eat to keep your strength up."

"Thanks." Harold yawned and took a nibble from a chicken leg.

Thad smiled as he watched the food revive the lad. He looked up to see Mercy sitting with her hands wrapped around her tin cup. She inhaled the aroma appreciatively before taking a sip.

"This is good coffee, Miranda. Did you do something different?"

"No." Miranda looked across the fire at Thad. "I mean, not exactly. Thad made it."

Mercy looked into her cup then across at Thad. He half expected a word of thanks, but she took another sip then turned back to her plate.

Thad was determined to get a civil word from the woman.

"If you like it, I'd be happy to take charge of the coffee makin' for the entire journey."

With nothing but the dim light of the fire, it was difficult to read Mercy's expression, but Thad thought he saw surprise. Perhaps he'd found a chink in her armor.

"Fine." Mercy took another bite of her biscuit, chewed and swallowed it. "Don't see any harm in you makin' coffee," she said before taking another bite.

Lord, he'd never please that woman. Nor did he have any reason to do so. He bit into one of Aunt Emily's biscuits. Even a day old, it held the flavor of home. A younger version of Aunt Emily would be the sort of woman for him—pleasant, cheerful, and maternal. The opposite of Mercy Clarke in every way.

All he had to do was survive a few weeks under Mercy's command, then he'd reach his new home. He'd meet the nice widow that Clarisse had in mind for him and settle down to farming and raising a family. There would be an end to loneliness and a real chance to make something of his life.

His eyes strayed across the fire to where Mercy Clarke sat sipping coffee.

"I reckon we made fifty miles today." Miranda broke the silence.

"Maybe," Mercy said. She leaned back to look up at the sky.

Her long silhouette against the night sky—legs stretched in front of her and back arched—created a dangerous temptation for Thad. In his younger days, he'd have put good sense aside and pursued that desire. No longer. Thad had learned to control his impulses.

"We'll make good progress as long as the weather holds." Mercy straightened and met Thad's eyes across the fire. "I don't think we all have the endurance to keep up this pace, though."

"I was hopin' we could go further tomorrow." Thad prayed she wouldn't accept that challenge, but he wasn't about to let her accuse him of slowing the group down. "No need to stop so often."

"Dang, but you're plum loco," Harold said. "I can barely move my legs tonight."

"There ain't no need to hurry so much, is there, Mercy?" Miranda asked. "Even if we're willin' to spend all night standin' while our seats—"

"Miranda! Watch your tongue."

"Well, it ain't easy to sit after a day in the saddle, is

it?" Miranda glared at her sister. "And you know it ain't good for the animals to go all day with no rest."

Mercy held Thad's gaze. "I suppose, for the sake of the horses, we can slow down a bit." She turned to Miranda. "Don't forget, Pa needs us home."

"You know Buck'll look out for him," Miranda said.

Mercy nodded. She stood and set her tin plate next to Harold. "Get on with the washing up. You'll have time to sleep before your watch."

"My watch?"

"Don't worry," Mercy said. "If a shake doesn't wake you, I'll kick you where you sit down."

"Hell . . . aw, heck!" Harold pushed off the ground with all the grace of an old man.

Thad stood and took a step toward Mercy. "When's my watch?"

She turned to him. "Why don't you rest tonight?"

Mercy stepped away, but Thad set a hand on her arm to stop her. "I'll take my watch. Seems to me Harold's the one who needs his rest."

Mercy looked up at him, her face inches from his. He imagined touching her smooth, warm cheek. Her eyes dropped to his hand, still resting on her arm and she stepped away, turning to where Miranda worked near the fire. She looked back at Thad.

"I'll watch first and wake you . . . when I tire."

Mercy turned and headed for the horses, her long strides emphasizing the sway of her hips. Thad imagined kissing his way up those long legs to. . . . Hell! So much for his newfound self-control.

Chapter 6

The campsite was quiet, except for Harold's snoring. Mercy contemplated the mound that represented Buchanan's bedroll. She'd pushed him hard today. She had meant to keep a cool distance between them, not to treat him rudely and insult him. Her childish behavior had been embarrassing. This morning she couldn't take her eyes off the man's impressive shoulders and ridiculous dimple. Then all day long, she'd been impolite. She breathed a quiet laugh. Truth was she'd been downright rude.

It was no way to treat the brother of a good friend. Clarisse and Mercy had become very close in the last six years. Though their families had fought on opposite sides in the war, the two women had refused to let the issue come between them. They had consoled each other and cried together when news came of family and friends that had been killed. Uncle Jake and two of Nate's brothers had died. Clarisse had lost two brothers as well. And her pa.

She remembered now Clarisse talking about her baby brother. After learning that he'd been wounded,

Clarisse had waited for months for news of whether he would live or die. Mercy turned to look at the big man stretched on the ground trying to sleep. Clarisse had mentioned the color of his eyes, his golden curls and even his dimple. But she'd been describing a young boy.

Clarisse had not seen the man her brother had become. She couldn't describe the confident way he carried himself and those eyes that seemed to burn right down into a woman's soul.

She was glad to be bringing Clarisse's brother to her, but damn, the man flustered her. She walked over to dig her hairbrush out of her bag and detoured to check on the horses again. She'd driven them too far today. That extra two hours was unnecessary, foolhardy. Hell, if one of the horses came up lame they'd lose time. And they couldn't afford to buy another horse if it came to that.

She watched Thad roll over and pull his hat over his face. It was that face and his flirtatious grin that had her acting like a cat in heat. She'd wanted to avoid him at all costs. Not that a handsome face and muscular body tempted her. Her face warmed. Hell, there was no point lying to herself. That body was temptation itself. She could well imagine resting against his broad chest with those arms wrapped around her.

She crossed her arms over her bosom. No harm in thinking about it so long as she didn't act on it.

Mercy found her brush and released her hair from its plait. Bringing a handful of hair in front of her shoulder, she pulled the brush through it. She settled well away from the fire, to get a better view of the dark prairie that surrounded them. All day long, the open space had protected them. No one could approach them without being seen. Night, however, provided excellent cover for bandits.

She finished brushing and wove two braids. One

braid made a hard lump under her head when she
slept. Not that she would get much sleep tonight. She'd
barely dozed safe in a feather bed at Emily and Will's
place. She returned the brush to her bag, then spread
the last glowing embers of the fire to hasten its death.
The half moon provided little light, making their camp-
fire a beacon to anyone looking for prey. She moved to
the edge of camp, wrapping a blanket over her shoulders
and settling cross-legged with the Sharps rifle across her
lap.

The night quiet brought the prairie sounds close.
Harold's snoring, the movement of the stream some
yards away and a critter splashing in the water. Likely a
fox. Not big enough to be a man. Still, she watched in
that direction for several minutes to be sure whatever it
was didn't approach the camp.

Mercy stood to stretch. Keeping her rifle with her, she
circled the camp. A million stars decorated the black sky
above without a cloud anywhere in sight. They'd been
lucky with the weather today. Rain would slow them down.
A thunderstorm would stop them.

The night dragged on and Mercy fought to keep her
mind alert for danger. She ached from hours in the saddle and she was tired. No need to wake Thad yet. She
yawned. She wasn't truly worried that she'd fall asleep.
More likely, she'd be distracted by the memories that
often haunted her. She knew she couldn't change the
past and yet her mind constantly went over each of her
mistakes as though she could make things right. She
stretched and sat down again, pulling the blanket closer
around her. The fact was, she couldn't live the past
again, but she could keep from making those same mistakes in the future.

Thad stirred, then rose. He tramped over toward the
creek and back to where Mercy sat.

"You didn't wake me."

"No need. I'm not tired yet."

"You don't trust me."

"What do you mean?"

"If you trusted me . . . Is this because of the, er . . . bathtub incident?"

"What has that got to do with anything?" She had hoped to forget that ever happened.

He sat a few feet away from her. "I owe you an apology." He brushed at his knees a few times, then stretched his legs out in front of him. "Is that why you're angry with me?"

"Angry? No." She pulled the blanket tighter around her shoulders.

"Please, let me explain." Thad pulled his hat off and set it beside him. "I heard you singing. At least I thought it was your voice and I wanted to talk, to ask again if you'd bring me along. So, I followed the voice . . ."

"When you saw me . . . why didn't you just leave?"

"I couldn't," he said.

"Couldn't?" Surely, he didn't expect her to believe that.

"I was . . . mesmerized. Damn! Excuse me, ma'am. I know that sounds silly. But it is the honest truth. I was transfixed by your beautiful legs and your . . . er . . ."

"Stop!" she growled. "If you think to flatter me—"

"No. No." He cleared his throat. "I mean . . . it isn't flattery. It's honesty and I'm . . . making matters worse—"

Transfixed. The man was shameless. "A real gentleman would never have walked into that room and he certainly would not have stayed."

"I did say I wanted to apologize."

"I think it's best we don't discuss this further."

"Yes, ma'am. I . . ."

She stood and felt the power of towering above him for a change. "Wake Miranda before dawn. I'll go rest now." She stomped off. At least in the blackness he'd never know that her neck and face were on fire with embarrassment. She turned to see him standing, staring after her. *Damnation!*

She marched back to him. "Have you ever fired a Sharps?"

"A few times."

She held the rifle out to him. "Best take this . . . while you're watching."

As he reached for the gun, his fingers slid across the back of her hand, gentle as a breeze on a summer night. He gripped the gun on either side of her hands. She let go and took a step back. It seemed for a moment as though a butterfly were dancing through her belly. She sucked in a deep breath, turned and stepped away.

As the third day of their journey dawned, Thad watched Mercy fixing her hair while he set the coffee to brewing. It was almost a ritual, the way she pulled the brush through in long, steady strokes. He forced his gaze away, not allowing himself to contemplate weaving his fingers through her hair. He glanced at the coffeepot, poked at the fire and lifted his gaze back to Mercy. Sitting cross-legged caused her pants to stretch, emphasizing the curves of her hips and legs. If she was intentionally trying to hide that feminine body of hers behind her rough men's clothes, it wasn't working.

Miranda bent near to remove the cooked bacon from the large pan over the fire. "It's her one vanity," she whispered.

"Hmm?" Thad stared at Miranda.

"Mercy. Claims she's not vain. Maybe she ain't except when it comes to her hair." Miranda grinned.

Thad smiled and shrugged, hoping he didn't appear too interested in Mercy. Fortunately, Harold arrived just then to distract Miranda.

"No beans this mornin'?" Harold asked with mock outrage. "Don't know how we'll get through the day."

Miranda laughed. "We're out of canned beans. Sorry. No time to cook the dried beans this mornin'. You'll have to make do with bacon and johnnycakes." She leaned toward him and whispered, "I cut the bacon thick the way you like it."

"Keep cookin' like that and I'll be too fat for my horse to carry me."

Miranda grinned. Thad turned back to Mercy who was studying the way Harold's packs rested on his horse. Her smiles were far more subtle than Miranda's. Just a small upturn at the corners of her lips—as elusive as a trout breaking water. But he had seen the spark of light flare in her eyes, then vanish. He knew that there was something more to Mercy than stern expressions and a sharp tongue.

He left the coffeepot and turned to packing his gear. The woman was a puzzle he could never hope to solve. If he kept trying, it just might drive him mad. Once they reached Fort Victory, he'd probably never see her. He expected she seldom left her ranch to come into town. And he hoped to have his own farm as soon as he could earn the money to buy some land.

The golden johnnycake batter hissed as Miranda dropped it into the pan. She was by far the more social of the sisters. But too young for Thad, even if she weren't smitten with Harold Pearson. Thad was only twenty-three, but sometimes felt like an old man. He glanced back at Mercy, who'd managed to get all that hair into a single thick braid and was now pouring a large cup of coffee. Watching her enjoy the fragrance, he wondered whether she ever allowed herself to indulge in other sensual pleasures.

Buchanan, get that thought out of your mind right now. Lord, walking in front of firing cannons was less of a gamble than getting involved with Mercy Clarke. He pulled the rope tight around his bedroll. She'd never make a wife for him. Even if her temperament suited him, her interests did not. He wanted a woman who would have a hot meal ready for him when he returned from the fields. Mercy ran the cattle herself. She left hearth and home to Miranda.

Mercy set her cup down and fingered her wedding band. He'd seen her playing with that ring a thousand times in the few days they'd spent together. Perhaps he'd judged her unfairly. It could be that losing her husband had forced her to take on a man's role. No, she was too damn ornery to let a man make the decisions. He'd wager she was runnin' the ranch even when her husband was alive.

Thad secured the last of his things to Zeus's saddle. He had his future waiting for him in Fort Victory. If all went well, they'd reach their destination in less than three weeks. He could control his lust for that long.

Thinking of Mercy's fist slamming into his chest, he was certain he could.

Mercy sat cross-legged on the ground, her hands wrapped around her warm cup as she breathed in the rich aroma. Thad had been kind enough to offer to make the coffee and she hadn't even thanked him. He poured some coffee for himself now and took a plate heaped with pancakes from Miranda.

"What will you bet I can sit without spilling a drop of this precious elixir?" Thad asked Harold.

"Two bits says you'll drop somethin'," Harold said.

"My money is on Thad," Miranda said.

"Smart lady." Thad winked at Miranda.

Mercy clenched her jaw. The man was an outrageous flirt—just the type her innocent sister was likely to set her cap for. She'd best keep an eye on Miranda. Thad held the cup and plate out as he sat easily without losing any of his beloved coffee. Miranda demanded her payment from Harold.

Mercy took another mouthful from her own cup, beginning to feel her energy return. A night on the hard ground wasn't very restful. She was unlikely to get a good night's rest until they arrived home. Truth be told, she wouldn't sleep at home either. She hadn't had a full night's sleep since Nate died.

She shook her head against the threat of memories. No point dwelling on the past. She had a responsibility to get home safely with Miranda and Harold, which wasn't going to happen so long as she sat around sipping her coffee. She drained the cup so fast the hot fluid stung her throat.

Buchanan had saddled his horse and she still had Clover to pack. The early morning sun had already dried the ground. It would be another hot day.

"Let's get a move on, Harold," she said, handing him her plate. "The sun's been up for an hour," she muttered as she headed over to saddle Annabelle and Princess. She couldn't pack Clover until the dishes were done.

Harold stacked Mercy's plate with his own. He sighed, but said nothing.

"I'll help Harold." Miranda jumped up.

Mercy had threatened to leave Harold at the next settlement if he didn't stop complaining and she wondered if he'd asked Miranda to intervene for him.

"Harold agreed to wash the dishes if I let him come along," Mercy reminded her sister.

"But his hands are getting raw!"

Mercy cleared her throat to keep from chuckling over the way Miranda made raw hands seem a great injustice. She glanced at Harold who stared down at his plate. "You have your job, Miranda."

"I've already filled the canteens and my bag is packed."

"And Harold was still snoring when you started the fire before sunrise." Mercy looked from Miranda to Harold. "Very well, if you don't mind, I suppose it will get us on the road faster." She turned toward her horse, then back to Miranda. "Be sure to use cream on your hands when you're done. And give some to Harold too."

"I ain't using no ladies' cream!"

Mercy barely managed a straight face. "Suit yourself."

"Mercy." Thad stepped closer to her.

"Don't tell me you want to help with the dishes?"

"No, ma'am. I believe Harold's doing a fine job." The twinkle in Thad's eyes suggested he too found Miranda's protests amusing.

"What is it then?" Mercy asked.

"It's Sunday."

"Sunday or not, we need to put some miles behind us."

"I agree, ma'am," Thad said, rising to go to his bag. "But I think we can spare a few minutes on the Lord's day to read the scriptures." He pulled a thick leather-bound book from the bag.

Mercy stared at Thad. There was a time when she hadn't regarded bible-reading as a waste of time. She made sure the family was in church whenever the preacher came to town and saw to it they read from the family bible every Sunday. That was a long time ago. Now she didn't care.

"Please, favor us with a reading, while Harold and Miranda wash up." It would do no harm to let him read so long as it didn't cost them any time.

"My pleasure." Thad sat on a large rock and thumbed his way through the well-worn book until he settled on a passage. "Something from Psalms to praise God for the beautiful day, I think." His bass voice was soothing.

As the words washed over Mercy, she thought of the tiny church in Kansas that her pa had helped build when she was a little girl, and all the Sunday meetings and funerals and weddings she'd attended there. Including her own wedding to Nate. She'd worn a blue dress and sung "Amazing Grace." Nate's favorite. Her throat constricted as she remembered his words. *"Amazing Grace" is supposed to make a man think about God. All I could do was think about how beautiful you are in that blue dress.*

Thad finished reading. His lips slowly curved upward until he radiated a full smile. Who did he think he was, flashing that dimple at her?

"You amaze me, Mr. Buchanan," she snapped. "You think you can spend your week in a saloon and make up for it with a reading from the bible on Sunday morning."

Harold and Miranda stood frozen, staring at her.

Thad was the first to recover. "I reckon we'd better be on our way now," he said, pushing himself to his feet and replacing the Bible in his saddlebag. He turned and looked at Mercy. For a moment she was certain he was going to say something more, but he simply led his horse away.

She rubbed her throbbing temple. She couldn't seem to stop herself snapping at the man. *Blast!* At least she'd found a way to avoid that damn smile of his.

* * *

The group rode silently that day, Mercy in the lead as usual, until they reached a watering hole where they stopped to rest the horses. Miranda forced her sister away from the men.

"Don't you think you should apologize?" she whispered.

"What ever for?" Mercy hated it when the little pest was right.

"Well, big sister, you're the one who always taught me that we oughtn't to judge others."

Mercy shrugged.

"You were wrong and you know it," Miranda said.

Mercy turned away, splashing into the stream to fill her canteen with water once she was clear of the debris that littered the bank. Keeping Thad angry had one big advantage—he was more likely to keep his distance. When she turned, she saw Thad coming toward her. *Damn.*

"Mercy." Thad saw his chance to get her alone for a moment. "It seems we have started our relationship on the wrong foot."

"You misunderstand." Mercy sidestepped him. "I believe you are paying me to get you safely to Colorado, is that not correct?"

"Of course." Thad followed her, though he dearly wanted to hold her still and force her to listen to him.

"Good." Mercy hung her canteen on Annabelle's saddle. "Then we have no relationship to discuss."

He moved to the same side of Annabelle, inches from Mercy. "Just a minute." He raised a hand to stop her interrupting him again. "We are only a few days into a journey, which, by your own estimate, will take us at least three weeks. I, for one, would prefer the trip to be a pleasant one and I think it can be if you will stop making unfounded accusations against me."

"Back in Abilene, you came out of a saloon, reeking

of whiskey." Mercy ticked each point off on her fingers. "You'd been gambling and had been in a fight. That much I saw for myself. Later, I heard the fight was because you'd been cheating—"

"Falsely accused of cheating." Thad managed somehow to keep from raising his voice. "If we were still in Abilene, I'd introduce you to the dealer—he knows the truth." Thad shoved his hat back to get a clear view of her face. The sun touched her cheek, giving her a warm glow. Thad forced his mind back to the discussion. "I'm surprised you'd believe O'Reilly—"

"O'Reilly? That—" Mercy clamped her jaw shut.

"I could suggest a few descriptive words, but they wouldn't be suitable for a lady."

She caught his eyes and gave him one of her almost smiles.

"I heard it from Luther," she said.

Thad nodded. "It was O'Reilly who put extra aces in the deck and accused me of doing it. Luther and his friend . . ."

"Jed?"

"Yes, that was his name. Those two cowboys were happy to believe that I was cheating, rather than admit they don't know how to play poker."

"Hell, I . . ." She cleared her throat. "I should have known better than to listen to Luther." She put a hand on her right hip. "That still leaves the whiskey."

"O'Reilly broke a bottle on my elbow."

There was that smile again, only this time it stayed and lit up her eyes like a mountain creek shimmering in the sun. Her tongue swept across her lips. Lordy, he wanted to touch that mouth for himself. He leaned a bit closer.

"It seems you have an explanation for everything, Thad. Poker is a game of skill and so is talkin' your way out of trouble. I suppose you think—"

His lips covered hers just enough to taste, to feel the tender warmth. Her hands came up against his chest and she leaned into his kiss. He reached for her waist, ready to pull her closer when she pushed back hard, nearly stumbling as she stepped away from him.

She grabbed the bullwhip hanging from Annabelle's saddle. "You take a step closer and I'll use this on your pathetic hide."

"I'm—"

"Don't apologize!" she growled. She peered over the horse to where Miranda and Harold were splashing in the creek several yards away. "Lucky for you they didn't see anything. It never happened."

He had half a mind to grab that bullwhip and remind her that something sure as hell had happened. For one insane moment he'd let desire rule over reason, but he hadn't been alone—she'd kissed him back. She could deny it from here to Colorado, but they both knew the truth.

"No, ma'am." He grinned. "Nothing happened here."

"Maybe you think this is just another game." Mercy glared at him. "I assure you this is one you won't win."

Chapter 7

Three days later, they made camp at midday. After her foolishness of the first day, Mercy had been careful to set a reasonable pace, but they all needed a respite. Besides, stopping early would give Miranda time to cook a real dinner. Though dinner would be dried beans unless Mercy found game later. She'd hunt after the heat of the day had passed. Meanwhile, the women had washed themselves and were now washing clothes in the creek. Mercy wriggled her toes in a pool of clear water, warmed by the late summer sunshine.

Harold was taking the opportunity for some target practice. He was a terrible shot and Mercy was half tempted to take his gun away from him entirely. But it was better to have Harold armed, if he could learn how to use the dang pistol. Buchanan had offered to help the younger man. At least the gambler appeared to have one useful skill. She chewed on her lip. The man had a real knack for kissing too, although that wasn't a talent she wished to encourage. She flicked a handful of damp hair back over her shoulder.

Mercy scrubbed hard trying to get the grime from her extra chemise. She loved the wild outdoor life, but still liked to have clean undergarments. Besides, the scrubbing action was helping to soothe her irritation at the silent Mr. Buchanan.

"You aren't fooling me, Mercy." Miranda started in scrubbing one of Harold's shirts.

"Harold should do that himself," Mercy said.

"I offered to do it for him." Miranda gave her a challenging look. "And don't change the subject. We were talking about your attraction to Mr. Buchanan."

"Attraction?" Mercy dropped her chemise in the water and grabbed it before it floated away.

"That's why you're being so rude. Why don't you admit it?" Miranda grinned. "Better yet, why don't you do something about it?"

Mercy lifted the chemise to examine it, then returned to scrubbing. She should have apologized to Buchanan days ago, but every time she approached him, she found herself criticizing him or arguing with him. This morning it was Harold's horse. That boy was thoughtless in the way he packed. He put all the weight on one side of his saddle. A trip like this was hard enough on a horse without making him carry an unbalanced load. She had gotten into the habit of checking Harold's bags and repacking everything. Buchanan thought she should teach Harold, rather than keep doing it for him. Even knowing Buchanan was right, she'd raised her voice and argued with his suggestion. Being around that man had made her lose touch with her good sense.

At least he wasn't flashing that vile dimple at her anymore. He was far more likely to scowl at her than to smile. She glanced over at him, then back to her scrubbing. Miranda was wrong. It was not that he was attrac-

tive, though he was that. There was something about his
eyes—looking into them frightened her.

Buchanan had no problem speaking to Harold. She
glanced over at the men, who were jawing as they set
some targets. Harold could talk the ears off a corn stalk.
Satisfied her chemise was clean, she spread it over a
rock to dry before submerging her spare shirt in the
creek.

Everything about Buchanan radiated quiet strength
until she looked into his eyes. There she saw turmoil,
sadness and a loneliness that could break her heart.
Except that her heart was already dead and buried.

She never should have brought him on this journey.
No, that wasn't true. She was glad to play a part in re-
uniting Clarisse with her youngest brother. Still, Mercy
would assure they arrived in Fort Victory as soon as possible. She'd push them all for extra miles each day, so
long as the weather held and the horses weren't over-
taxed. Once they were home, she wouldn't have to en-
dure his company again. She brushed a lock of loose
hair back from her face and turned to listen to her sister.

While the women washed in the creek, Thad asked
Harold about Mercy's continued hostility. He shouldn't
have kissed her, but she'd been angry with him even before he'd made that foolish mistake.

"Was Mercy's husband killed in the war?" Thad
thought that might explain her attitude.

"Naw." Harold piled empty tins on top of a rock.
"Trampled by a bull."

"When'd that happen?"

"Two years ago—nearly." The men stepped fifteen
paces from the cans. "I reckon she ain't over it yet.

Miranda says Mercy blames herself for the accident 'cause she convinced her husband to move to Colorado."

"That hardly makes sense."

"You figure women are supposed to make sense, Mr. Buchanan?"

"Call me Thad." He looked over his shoulder at the two sisters, knee deep in the stream, scrubbing.

Mercy had bathed and was now hatless as her chestnut hair dried, the sun reflecting off the copper and gold that streaked through it. She usually wore her hair knotted in a thick braid that reached halfway down her back. Loose, it hung below her waist like a heavy curtain. Mercy reached up and pushed an errant lock back. A part of him was still sorely tempted to explore all that beautiful hair, those generous curves and sweet lips. Hell, he'd settle for a civil conversation.

Whatever the ladies were discussing, Mercy was sure excited. He suspected Mercy could get worked up about the proper way to cook a can of beans. Thad smiled, imagining a heated discussion between the women over whether up or down strokes cleaned more efficiently. He stroked his chin.

"I guess you're right. Women are a mystery."

"Mr. Buchanan . . . Thad?" Harold looked up at him. "Did you get to do much fightin' in the war?"

"Nope."

"Can't imagine they'd stick a big fella like you behind a desk. Did they?"

Thad glared at Harold. "Concentrate now. You're gonna aim for the center can." Though he'd be pleased if the lad hit anything in the pile, including the rock.

Harold raised his pistol.

"No. Two hands. Your aim will be much steadier." *And the kick isn't as likely to knock you down as it did yesterday.*

Harold aimed carefully and pulled the trigger. Twice. The cans didn't move. Thad sighed.

"Let's stand a little closer." He paced forward five steps.

"So, what did you do in the war, Thad?"

"Not much." Thad focused on the target. This should be an easy shot. "Try again."

Harold held the pistol up, his tongue slid out the corner of his mouth and his face creased in concentration. Bang! A miss. Bang! A hit.

"That's it!" Thad thumped the boy on the back. "Good."

Harold slipped the gun back into his holster, and grinned up at Thad. "So, what exactly did you do? Were you a spy?"

Thad sighed. "I'm no hero, if that's what you're wonderin'." Thad marched over to the rock with Harold following.

"I just wanted to know what it's like—bein' in a real battle."

Thad bent to stack the cans again.

"Infantry or artillery?" Harold asked.

Thad brushed the dust from his knee. Harold was not going to let the subject drop. "Infantry, same as my father and brothers."

"You saw the battles up close then?" Harold asked.

Thad paced away from the target.

"I mean," the young man continued. "Artillery is away from the real fightin', but infantry—"

Thad spun around and Harold slammed into him. He glared down at the young man. "It wasn't like a stage play where the closest seats are the best." He fought the urge to shout. "You had to be there to know . . . I did what I had to do. We all did. And when it was over I worked like hell to forget what I saw—what I did."

"Gee, I'm sorry, Thad. I only . . ." Harold's eyes dropped to the ground.

Thad blew out an exasperated breath. "No, I'm sorry to have snapped at you. The war is not something I want to talk about."

"Okay," Harold said.

Thad clapped Harold on the shoulder. "Now let's get back to work before Mercy pulls out her whip."

"Aw, she ain't as tough she pretends to be." Harold shook his head. "Heck, Mercy's soft as bread puddin' underneath that granite exterior."

"I'll just bet she is. Bread puddin' that's been settin' out in the sun bakin' for a month."

Thad prowled along the creek looking for a place to throw his line in. He scanned the horizon—nary a tree in any direction. He shook his head. The Kansas prairie was nothing like the green hills of Tennessee and, according to Miranda, it was only going to grow more desolate as they traveled west.

Mercy had been gone for an hour looking for game. He'd told her there'd be no critters out in this heat. Naturally, she wasn't going to listen to him. He'd be damned if he was going to eat beans again tonight just because Mercy was too stubborn to ask for help. He found what he was looking for—a rock casting a broad shadow over the water. He bet there'd be a whole mess of fish gathered in that shade, escaping the heat of the sun.

Thad continued downstream for another twenty yards before crossing and hiking back up to the rock. No sense in alerting the fish to his presence. He leaned over the rock and peered into the water until he spotted the telltale bubble of a fish feeding at the surface. He pulled his hook and line out of his jacket pocket and set the jacket over the rock.

Patience catches fish.

His father's words had never made sense to him. Not until hunger forced him to understand the need for deliberation. How he must have irritated his father with all his chatter, his splashing in the water and complaints when the fish weren't biting. He'd learned a good deal in the past few years about how to survive. A delicate balance of caution, tenacity and recognizing opportunity.

He slid a bit of bacon over the hook and tossed it into the water.

Mercy stole back into camp feeling as though her rifle had doubled in weight. Unless they were willing to eat prairie dogs, their dinner would be beans again. There simply wasn't any game out there. Her head ached and she was desperate to sleep.

Miranda was working over the fire and as Mercy drew closer she smelled something that definitely wasn't beans.

"Fish?"

Miranda nodded. "Mr. Buchanan caught them for us. Aren't they wonderful?"

Harold was already digging into a plateful.

"I didn't think there were any fish in that creek," Mercy said.

"They are a mite small." Thad took the plate Miranda handed him and passed it to Mercy.

"But there's two for each of us." Miranda bubbled as she cut a wedge of cornbread out of the Dutch oven to add to Mercy's plate.

Mercy glanced at the plateful of food, then at Thad. He was full of surprises. "Thank you."

He beamed. "My pleasure, ma'am."

When he offered her a cup of coffee, Mercy took

that as well. Miranda filled her own plate and sat next to
Harold, which meant that Mercy would have to sit with
the men, or sit alone.

"Come on." Miranda patted the ground next to her.
"You aren't going to eat that standin' up, are you?"

Mercy joined the group. She was too weary to argue
and it was easy enough to sit quietly while Miranda told
Harold all about Fort Victory.

"Between the miners, the soldiers and the ranchers
we have all kinds of folks," Miranda said.

"All kinds of men, sounds like," Harold mumbled
through a mouthful of fish.

Miranda scowled. "We have some interestin' women
too. Though I reckon you'll find them for yourself
soon enough." She pulled a bit of fish off the bone with
her fork. "There's Mr. Buchanan's sister—Clarisse. She
runs the store. And you'll have to meet Rita—she's
Spanish."

Miranda disclosed this last fact as though it were a
well-kept secret. Mercy shook her head. Even Harold
would notice Rita's exotic appearance and thick accent
the moment he met her.

"Is she pretty?" Harold asked through a mouthful of
cornbread.

"She's too old for you, Harold Pearson," Miranda
nearly shouted.

Thad seemed to be listening with interest.

"There's some advantages to older women, ain't there,
Thad?" Harold asked.

Buchanan stopped chewing and looked at Mercy.
She met his gaze, accepting the challenge.

"I don't know whether older or younger makes so
much difference, Harold. I reckon there are other things
a man looks for in a woman."

His eyes drifted slowly over Mercy until she felt as

naked as she had in the bathtub. She raised her coffee cup to her lips to hide the fact that she was blushing.

He turned back to Harold. "I could name any number of important things to consider when choosing a woman. Kindness, gentleness." He glanced back at Mercy. "A meek and humble woman, Harold. That's what every man wants."

Chapter 8

Thad crossed the central yard of Fort Kearny, headed for the large brick building that served as a dining hall, saloon and general meeting place. Four days of riding and he still couldn't get that kiss out of his mind. It hadn't even been a whole kiss. More like the start of a kiss. Though a very promising beginning. That was the trouble, really. He always hated it when he couldn't finish what he'd started.

From inside the dining hall Thad heard a jolly crowd singing "Oh! Susannah," accompanied by a skilled piano player. The instrument was in tune, unlike the discordant box he'd endured in Abilene.

They'd made it halfway through their trip in only eight days. At this rate, they would arrive in Fort Victory ahead of schedule. Feeling refreshed after a haircut and shave, Thad was searching for the women. Mercy and Miranda had gone to purchase supplies while the men visited the barber. If the storekeeper hadn't suggested he look in the big hall, Thad would never have thought of it. After the way she'd chastised him for frequenting the saloon in Abilene, Thad couldn't imagine

Mercy going into such a place herself, let alone allowing her sister to set foot in it.

Thad stood in the doorway, observing the jovial crowd around the piano while his eyes adjusted to the dim light. He fought an urge to stride across the room and rescue Miranda who was standing at the center of a raucous male throng. She did not appear to desire rescue. In fact, Miranda appeared comfortable as the men competed for her attention with flirtatious winks and smiles. The impromptu choir belted out the popular tune, with considerable enthusiasm, sacrificing tone quality in favor of volume.

Where was Mercy?

Once again, he scanned the room, not believing the protective older sister would allow sweet Miranda to wander into this den of iniquity alone. The song ended and the piano player launched into another tune. Then he heard it.

Mercy's strong contralto voice carried over the rumbling male chorus. Moving closer, still not believing his ears, Thad looked over the gathered men and saw her seated at the piano—her left hand setting a rhythm of broken chords while her right danced the lively tune "The Blue Tail Fly." She was enjoying herself.

The one officer in the crowd stood close to Mercy, singing at the top of his lungs. Unlike many of the others, the captain was singing in the correct key, which was about the most that could be said for his abilities. His thin voice was all throat and strained to the limit as he worked to produce more volume.

Mercy glanced up at the man and the captain threw her a wink before resting his hand on her shoulder. Thad smiled, expecting Mercy to give the man a well-placed elbow, but she simply went on with the song. When it ended, the captain bent and whispered something that caused her to chuckle before starting in on another tune.

Thad shoved a fist into his pocket. Mercy was a grown woman and could flirt in public if she wanted, but she ought to be watching out for her younger sister.

He heard Miranda giggle as one of the men next to her winked and used her own braid to tickle her under her chin.

Thad was surprised when one of the men next requested "Rock of Ages," which seemed an inappropriate choice in a place that was serving whiskey. But there was a murmur of agreement among the men and Thad realized they were amusing themselves with familiar songs, not thinking about their significance. Besides, judging from the tables, chairs and stacks of benches in the corner, the room probably also served as a church. Mercy segued into the popular hymn, her voice once again leading.

"Beautiful Dreamer," one of the men bellowed when the hymn ended.

"Ah, a romantic in the crowd," Mercy joked and the crowd of admirers all laughed while Thad could only shake his head and wonder if this was the same woman who seemed determined to make each day on the trail as miserable as possible. At least when she turned the captain's hand slid off its resting place on Mercy's shoulder.

Without further hesitation, she launched into the beautiful Stephen Foster ballad and the crowd hushed while she sang the first verse. "Now come on, you're all supposed to be singing," Mercy coaxed and the men joined in for the next verse.

Thad inched up to the group, adding his voice to the chorus. When the men parted to allow him to join the inner circle, Mercy glanced up, beaming a smile such as he hadn't seen on the entire journey.

He returned her smile, then glanced at the captain, who grabbed a songbook from the piano and began to leaf through it. Watching Mercy sing, her lithe fingers caressing the keyboard, he thought he'd never seen her so happy. Perhaps the saying about music soothing the savage breast was true after all, he mused. Or perhaps the air of Fort Kearny had magical powers. Today, for the first time, Mercy had agreed with Thad when he had objected to Miranda's request that they spend the night here, where they could have a hot bath and sleep in a real bed. As tempting as that sounded, Thad preferred to gain a few more miles. They'd agreed to stop only for a meal and fresh supplies. When Thad noticed the barber, he decided to add that errand and Harold had followed him.

While the group sang "Listen to the Mockingbird," Harold strolled up to Miranda. Making no secret of his displeasure at the men surrounding her, he edged toward her until they were shoulder to shoulder. For his efforts, he was rewarded with one of Miranda's brightest smiles. The two appeared smitten with each other. Thad smiled at the lad's slicked-down hair and freshly waxed mustache. The barber had done an excellent job taming that patch of fuzz so that it did appear more like a mustache and less like a dust ball. Thad turned back to Mercy to keep from laughing aloud and noticed her Sharps rifle at her feet, along with one of her saddlebags. She was enjoying herself, but was also on her guard.

Thad was just about to suggest they have their meal and move on when someone requested "I Dream of Jeanie with the Light Brown Hair."

"Thad, you sing it," Harold shouted.

"Be happy to," Thad said, moving closer to the piano.

Without his asking, Mercy adjusted the key and looked up, her lifted eyebrow a silent question. Thad nodded, mentally adding an excellent ear for music to the long list of Mercy's talents. Watching her fingers glide over the keys without apparent effort, he couldn't help comparing her with the dainty woman described in the song, who was "borne like a vapor on the summer air." Mercy was graceful, but he'd never compare her to a vapor. The floating Jeanie had no substance. She flitted about in her pretty way and ultimately was lost when she "strayed far from the fond hearts round her native glade." Mercy was fiercely loyal to her sister and absolutely dedicated to her ranch. She would never stray and it would take a damn strong wind to blow her away. Of course, a man might wish for her to vaporize and be gone when she unleashed that temper of hers.

Mercy joined the song on the last verse, adding a layer of harmony. When they finished, the room erupted into applause. Mercy turned on the stool, her eyes locking with Thad who grinned back at her. The room was warm, but he suspected that wasn't the only reason for the color in her cheeks. He'd seen the same pink glow after he'd kissed her—only this time she was smiling.

"Amazing Grace," the man next to Thad called out.

Mercy looked at the man. "I . . ." A look of alarm replaced her relaxed smile. "I don't know that one."

"I'll be happy to step in." The captain looked at Mercy. "If you'll permit?"

Mercy surrendered the stool to the captain, who sat and played the hymn. Out of the corner of his eye, Thad watched her back away and weave through the crowd. By the time they started the hymn, she had slipped out the door of the saloon.

Outside, the blinding sun hit her with a blast of heat, but Mercy was shivering.

Nate's voice came to her. *No one sings "Amazing*

Grace" like my Mercy. Then he would wink at her and she knew he wasn't thinking about her singing voice. She closed her eyes, trying to shut out the image.

The voices of the men carried out the open windows of the saloon. "I once was lost, but now am found, was blind but now I see."

Yes, she could see now. It was love that had blinded her—love that had left her open to the worst kind of pain and loneliness. *Never again.*

" 'Twas grace that taught my heart to fear . . ."

The song continued pulling her away. . . .

A bitter October wind had pressed against her back that day while she had gazed at the Rocky Mountains looming over her ranch, solid and formidable against the slate–gray sky. Most of the folks who lived around Fort Victory had gathered to pay their last respects and they were singing Nate's favorite hymn. "Amazing grace, how sweet the sound. . . ."

She tried to sing the song for Nate, but the lump in her throat made singing impossible. Feeling numb, almost as if she were watching herself rather than actually standing there, she tried to concentrate on everything she must do to manage the ranch and take care of her sister and father. But the anger, fear, and sorrow had drained her mind. All she could think was—it would snow soon.

"It's grace hath brought me safe thus far . . ." But grace hadn't been enough to keep Nate safe. Mercy rubbed the thumb of her left hand against her wedding band and refocused on the pine box the men were lowering into the ground. Her sister leaned against her, sobbing.

I will not cry.

There was no telling whether their father would walk again, or whether he would even survive his injuries. Mercy would be running the ranch alone. She had always been strong, and now it was more important than ever to keep her head. She tightened her arms around her sister, vowing to protect Miranda no matter what.

The sound of stone hitting wood had drawn Mercy's eyes back to the box as the men had begun to shovel dirt over it. She had thought of Nate inside that box and had known she was truly alone . . .

The cry of an angry mule called Mercy back to the bustling activity of Fort Kearny. A man fought to pull his mule away from a water trough as a gray stallion nipped at the mule's nose. Mercy walked over to where Annabelle stood tied between Thad's gelding and Clover. She ran her hand along Annabelle's smooth buckskin-colored neck.

"Mercy?" Miranda's voice startled her.

Mercy took a deep breath, mustering a smile before turning to look at her sister. "You gave me a start."

Miranda grasped her arm. "Are you all right?"

She looked back at her horse. "What do you mean? I'm fine."

"You left so suddenly."

"There was so much smoke in that room it was hard to breathe." Mercy turned to her sister, flashing her most reassuring smile. "Besides, it was high time I checked on these horses."

Miranda nodded, but still looked concerned. It wasn't possible that Miranda understood the real significance of the song—the way Nate had teased Mercy about how she looked in her blue dress, had made her feel pretty for the first time in her life. Not just a female body, but womanly and wanted.

"The men are busy." Miranda gave Mercy's arm another squeeze. "We could find a place to talk, if you'd like."

Mercy widened her smile. "We'd best get that dinner and find a place to camp before we lose our daylight.

Go find Harold and Thad. I'll join you inside in a few minutes."

Miranda drew a breath as if to speak, then nodded. She turned and walked back toward the saloon. Mercy caressed Annabelle's neck again, combing fingers through her mane.

"Oh, Annabelle, when am I going to be able to put all this behind me?" Mercy whispered.

The horse accepted Mercy's caresses with what sounded very much like a sigh, but if Annabelle had an answer, she chose not to reveal it.

As far as Thad was concerned, dinner was torture. Captain Jamison joined them. He grabbed the seat next to Mercy, and quizzed Thad about his background. When he learned Thad hailed from Tennessee, his demeanor changed from friendly to suspicious.

"Are you a Union man, Mr. Buchanan?"

"I'm an American, Captain." Thad met the officer's gaze.

Jamison gave Thad a wary look, then turned back to Mercy. "I wish you could stay a few days."

Mercy ladled chicken and dumplings onto a plate and handed it to Jamison.

"Please, Mercy?" Miranda took the next plate Mercy passed and gave it to Harold.

Mercy glared at Miranda. "We've got to get home." She turned to smile at Jamison. "As tempting as it is to stay here and enjoy your hospitality."

Thad chewed on a dumpling, swallowing hard to get it down. He might as well have been eating beans for all he tasted of his supper. Watching Jamison ogling Mercy was enough to make Thad's stomach turn. At least they'd managed to avoid discussions of the war.

"Miranda says you're a decorated hero, Cap'n," Harold said before shoveling another dumpling into his mouth.

"Tut, tut." Jamison beamed at Miranda. "You know modesty prevents me from claiming to be a hero." He glanced at Mercy, then back to Harold. "In fairness to the young lady, I will admit that I received numerous citations for valor."

The man had the humility of Lucifer.

"You saw a lot of combat then?" Harold asked hopefully.

Thad shoveled another dumpling into his mouth.

Jamison smiled. "Yes, I saw at least my share." He touched his thumb to a scar that ran along his jaw. "Had my face redecorated by a Rebel bayonet just before the bastard succumbed to a bullet from my Colt revolver."

Harold's eyes widened.

"Not that I'm asking for sympathy, mind." The captain winked at Harold. "I've had more than one lady tell me they find the scar attractive." He glanced meaningfully at Mercy who had the sense to look down at her plate.

Thad couldn't bear any more. He excused himself to go outside and smoke his pipe before they left. Before he reached the door, Thad was pleased to see that his departure prompted Mercy to check the watch that hung from her belt.

"We'll be out in a few minutes, Thad," she called after him.

Thad made a quick bow to the table and turned to smile at Jamison, hoping the man could read his thoughts. *Enjoy the next few minutes, Captain. I'll have the next week.*

Chapter 9

They took advantage of the evening sun to ride more than two hours, following the Platte River away from Fort Kearny. The land was flat and open, treeless for the first hour. They finally stopped at a place where the river split around a tree-covered island.

They made camp along a shallow side stream near the island that stood up out of the river like a lopsided slice of cake. The downstream half of the island sat about six feet above the water, while the part nearest their camp sloped down into the river.

The days had been so dry that, even after the short ride, any respite from the hot, dusty trail was welcome. The group lingered near the river's edge for a few minutes before they started working on their nightly chores.

Mercy and Thad cared for the horses while Harold and Miranda crossed the shallow stream to gather firewood on the wooded island.

Thad and Mercy worked in silence for a time.

"I want to apologize for Captain Jamison," Mercy said. "Except I'm not sure why I feel the need to apologize."

She glanced at Thad, then back to Annabelle. "Oh, dear . . ."

"He is a bit . . . much?" Thad said.

"More than a bit, I fear." She pulled Annabelle's saddle off. "He was a friend of my uncle's . . . during the war."

"You don't have to explain."

"I just wouldn't want you to think . . . He's a family friend. That's all."

Thad nodded, apparently considering this statement. She blew out a breath, having embarrassed herself in front of Thad again. She should learn to keep her mouth shut.

He looked across the creek, then turned to help her unload Clover. "I guess you trust that Pearson boy pretty well," he drawled.

"I don't know." Mercy set the supplies she had removed from the packhorse on the ground, puzzled over the sudden change of subject, but relieved just the same. "Harold's never been on the westward trail. I keep a short rein on him."

Mercy returned to inspecting Clover for any sign the pack had rubbed her sore.

"Except I notice you often allow him to be alone with your sister."

"I see what you mean." She smiled at Thad. "But there's nothing to worry about. Harold's a friend. They played together as children."

As if to confirm her words, the sound of Miranda's playful laughter floated over the water and they turned to look toward the thick stand of cottonwoods and willows that grew on the island. "He's like a brother to her."

"I know it's not my place . . ." Thad turned back to Mercy. "But in my experience a man does not look at his sister the way Harold looks at Miss Miranda."

Mercy studied Thad's intent blue eyes, glimpsing the grief that never seemed far beneath the surface. For a moment, she wondered how a man who had survived so many losses still managed to feel concern for near strangers. It was probably just Miranda. She was petite, pretty and so young. Naturally, Thad felt protective of her.

Mercy forced her eyes away from Thad's, to the trees which shielded Harold and Miranda from view. Miranda had been a girl when they left Kansas six years ago and now she was a young woman. Once again, Mercy heard Miranda's laughter, this time harmonizing with a deeper chuckle from Harold. Mercy stalked across the creek and into the woods, cursing herself for failing to recognize the signs earlier.

When Mercy approached them, Miranda was leaning back against a cottonwood tree with Harold braced against her, his lips covering hers. Seeing them so intent on each other, Mercy felt a strange weight in her chest.

"Haven't found any firewood?" she asked.

Harold and Miranda turned simultaneously, Harold nearly losing his balance as he pulled away from Miranda. Both their faces flushed the same strawberry–red color.

"Miranda." Mercy kept her voice calm. "We need to talk."

"We didn't . . . we haven't done anything," Miranda sputtered, then let out a long sigh.

"I suggest you get back to camp now, Mr. Pearson," Mercy ordered.

They watched Harold walk away, hastily gathering wood as he returned to camp. Mercy led Miranda to a large flat rock a dozen yards upstream from camp. She motioned for Miranda to sit, while she paced back and forth wondering how to begin. She glanced over at the camp and watched Harold drop the wood in a pile where they would make their fire in the morning.

"You're too young for this," Mercy started, then realized her mistake. "I know. I know. You're both nineteen . . ." Mercy trailed off, sitting down on a flat rock next to Miranda. She searched for a way to explain the danger of giving one's heart away without confessing to her own secret pain.

They sat for a moment, watching the dark water dancing over the stones of the creek bed. The bubbling, cheerful sound contrasted with Mercy's somber mood. She inhaled the moist air that lingered around the stream, then turned to watch the men in camp.

Harold seemed to be trying to imitate Thad as the two of them organized camp. Fortunately, Thad was a very patient man. He had removed his jacket and vest, which left his shirt clinging to his back so that Mercy could see the muscles working as he lifted Miranda's saddle. Mercy shook her head. She was supposed to be concentrating on Miranda's problem, not thinking about Thad Buchanan. Annoyed that she'd allowed herself to be distracted, Mercy picked up a stone, splashing it into the water. Miranda startled and turned to Mercy.

"I know you're angry," Miranda said.

"I'm not angry." Mercy placed a hand on her sister's shoulder. "Just worried about you."

"I know I should have said something to you sooner about me and Harold." Miranda kicked at the top of a stone that was buried in the dirt. "But you've been acting so odd on this trip. We used to talk about everything, but lately, I don't know . . ."

"You didn't tell me about your feelings for Harold because you thought I'd forbid it?" *I just might, too, if I thought it would keep you from falling in love.*

"No. I was afraid . . ." Miranda kicked the stone free

and watched it tumble a few inches away. She stared at it as if expecting to find the right words written on its speckled surface. "I know you miss him, Mercy, but you never want to talk about him. I was afraid if I told you that I love Harold . . . well, you'd think of Nate. I didn't want to hurt you."

At the mention of her husband's name Mercy felt the familiar pain, as though her heart were caught in a vise. She tightened her jaw and turned to face her sister.

"You can't know you love him." Mercy shook her head. "You're not ready."

Miranda's blue eyes sparked with anger, but Mercy watched her suppress it. "I'm not a little girl anymore."

"I didn't say you were, but . . . I just don't want you rushing into anything."

"You married Nate a few weeks after you met him."

"You're quite right. I did rush into my marriage."

"I only meant—you know what it means to be in love."

Mercy tried to ward off a headache by rubbing her temples. "I know you're full of joy right now." She well remembered the giddy feeling of first love. "But there may be pain down this road you've set yourself on. If only you would wait a few years." Mercy stopped, knowing her advice was too late. She couldn't spare her sister the anguish that came with loving someone and losing him.

"I also know what it's like to lose a love." The words tumbled out as Mercy's usual composure broke. "To be breathing, and eating, and walking on this earth every day and yet feel dead inside." She walked away and faced the trees, her back to Miranda. "I don't want that for you."

"Mercy," Miranda whispered, placing a hand on her older sister's shoulder. "People die. I know that. We both lost our mothers before we even had a chance to know them."

"It's not the same."

"I can't know exactly what you're feelin', but I know it'll hurt if I lose Harold. That don't mean I oughta spend my life alone, never lettin' myself feel for fear of losin' someone. I don't think you really want that for me. I can't believe you'd choose that for yourself."

Keeping her back to Miranda, Mercy wiped her eyes. "You go on and help the men set up camp. I'll collect more firewood." She splashed across the stream and tramped into the woods.

Her tears were flowing by the time Mercy was beyond sight of the camp. She sat on a fallen log and allowed the familiar ache to envelop her. She couldn't tell her sister that the loss she felt was not simply about Nate dying. What hurt most was knowing that she had let him down in so many ways and would never be able to make it up to him. She gazed at the clear sky, the moon already on the horizon. Soon the sky would be black, covered with a million stars. Once, Nate had loved to watch the night sky with her . . .

"I ordered this sky just for you," Nate had said, walking up behind her, pulling her against his chest, gripping her as if he thought she might escape. "Other men buy their wives mere diamonds. Not me. I spoke to God this morning, 'Put an extra ten thousand stars in the sky tonight, will you? It's my wife's birthday and she loves stars.'" He nuzzled the back of her neck. "So what do you think?"

"It's lovely. And they look especially nice floating over our ranch." She twisted her head, planting a kiss on his cheek. "Thank you."

He turned her and kissed her more thoroughly. They'd been married less than a year and everything was still magical.

"I got you something else. Something much smaller. Come back to the house and see."

He took her hand and led her back into the house where he pulled a blue satin bag from his pocket and handed it to her. "I was lucky the Wyatts had one in stock. I thought they might have to send to Denver. Hope you like it."

She tipped the bag into one hand and out dropped a gold chain followed by a small gold watch.

"Nate . ."

His face fell. "You don't like it?"

"It's beautiful." Mercy shook her head. "It's just too much."

"We can afford it. That's part of my surprise. I've had a letter from the lawyer for my father's estate. I guess my mother never persuaded him to disinherit me after all. The money will be deposited in a bank in Denver. In fact, it's probably already there."

"That's wonderful!" Mercy hugged him. "We can buy those Hereford bulls."

Nate shook his head. "It's only a thousand dollars."

"Oh." Mercy hid her disappointment behind a smile and squeezed her husband's hands.

"Look inside the watch," he said.

There were tiny words in fine engraving. "As each hour passes, I love you more."

The watch had kept reliable time ever since, but Nate's optimistic words had not been so accurate. To start with, they had disagreed about how to spend the inheritance.

He wanted to go to Europe and Mercy had dismissed his idea as silly. Instead, they'd used the inheritance along with money borrowed from Lansing to import Hereford bulls from England. They hoped to breed them with their longhorn cattle and improve the quality of meat they produced. It wasn't easy bringing anything from England during the war and they had waited for years.

During that time their hope of having children faded away until acquiring the bulls and making a success of the ranch became the most important thing in Mercy's life.

They finally found a way to transport the animals. A ship carried the beasts from England to Panama. They were herded across the narrow isthmus, then shipped to California. When the bulls arrived, Mercy and Nate traveled to San Francisco to collect them at the dock. By then Nate had seemed a stranger who happened to share her bed, but nothing else.

Mercy had hoped that a few days enjoying the city together would help bring her husband back to her. She'd been especially excited about their visit to the theater. She'd chattered all the way back to their hotel with little response from Nate.

"I had no idea it would be so different," she said as she lit the lamp in their room. "Seeing a play in a real theater, I mean."

The bed stood between them, its brass railing gleaming in the lamplight. They'd been in San Francisco for two days and hadn't used the bed for anything but sleep. She hoped Nate would suggest something different tonight, but if he didn't, she would. Her husband shrugged out of his coat.

"I never thought I'd hear Shakespeare's words spoken by real actors." She stepped over to him and turned so that he could help with her buttons.

She'd been disappointed that Nate hadn't mentioned anything about her wearing his favorite blue dress. Looking back on it, she realized she'd been foolish. Her dress had been far too plain to wear to a big city theater. She'd probably embarrassed him.

"It was a fine performance," he said, patting her shoulder to signal he was finished with her buttons. "If you don't mind, I'm a bit tired."

He slipped out of his remaining clothes and under the sheets as though she weren't there.

Mercy joined her husband in bed. She gave herself to him as best she could, but he had soared away without her. She was a failure as a wife and he had stopped wanting her.

Maybe if she'd been willing to move to Chicago he would have been happy. Instead, he had died before she'd found a way to break through the wall that had come between them.

"I'm sorry, Nate," she whispered to the wind.

The only response came from the leaves rustling in the trees around her. Pushing the ache back into its secret place in her heart, she covered her eyes with the kerchief she had wet at the stream.

The sharp crack of gunfire disrupted the silence of the woods. Mercy scrambled to her feet. Drawing the Colt that rested against her right hip, she raced toward the sound—through the woods toward camp.

Chapter 10

Mercy tried to tell herself the shots she heard were Harold at target practice again. But she knew the sound too well—rifle fire—and it was too rapid to be coming from one weapon. She never should have gone off alone leaving the camp unprotected. Her Colt was loaded and ready, but that only gave her six shots. If she could get to her saddle, she'd have a second revolver and her Sharps rifle, but there was no use in wishing for what she didn't have.

She slowed as she approached the edge of the trees, keeping herself hidden as she surveyed the camp. Thad crouched low behind his saddle and a pile of supplies, aiming Mercy's rifle toward the low, tree-covered ridge downstream.

She spotted Harold on the ground several yards from Thad. *Damn!* He was writhing in pain. *Where was Miranda?* Mercy's stomach knotted as she searched for some sign of her sister. Then Thad moved, revealing a bit of Miranda's corn silk hair as he used his body to shield her.

Mercy heard shots coming from the ridge and watched

Thad lean protectively over Miranda before returning fire. Mercy couldn't get a shot at the ridge from her position. She fought the instinct to run to camp. She'd have only a slim chance of hitting one of the attackers with her .44 at that range, but they would have an excellent shot at her with their rifles.

She raced back into the woods to circle behind the shooters, moving swiftly, but silently. Harold was wounded and Thad couldn't hold the men off indefinitely.

She cursed herself for failing to show Thad where she stored the extra ammunition. Perhaps Miranda would tell him. *Unless Miranda was also injured,* she thought, the knot in her stomach tightening.

"Where the bloody hell are those shots coming from?" Thad kept his voice low and squinted into the trees. *And who the hell was ambushing them?*

"Let me up!" Miranda said in a hoarse whisper. She struggled beneath him. Thad pinned her small frame down easily with his legs while he watched for the attackers to reveal themselves. "I've got a gun and I'm a damn good shot!"

Thad raised an eyebrow at the profanity. He imagined Mercy would wash Miranda's mouth out with soap if she'd heard it.

"Your revolver wouldn't do any good at this distance."

"Then at least let me go help Harold!" Miranda pushed up again, but Thad locked his legs tighter.

"No." Thad thought he saw movement to his left and raised the rifle. "We'll help Harold as soon as we can. Meanwhile, it won't do him any good for you to get yourself shot."

He felt Miranda relax a little but didn't loosen his grip. A volley of shots peppered the ground around them again. This time he saw the source and returned the fire.

"Where's Mercy?" Miranda asked.

Thad squinted toward the woods, but saw no sign of her. If they had surprised her . . . No. She could take care of herself.

"She has her Colt on her," he said. "I reckon she's got to get close enough for it to do some good."

All I have to do is keep these men occupied until she can get into position. He fired off another round in the direction of the ridge.

Mercy crept to within a few yards of two men who crouched, aiming rifles toward the camp. She leveled her Colt at the center of the larger man's back.

"Drop your guns and turn around slowly," she commanded. Her voice held much more confidence then she felt.

Both of the men froze. She stepped toward them and they lunged forward, launching themselves over the edge of the ridge. Rifle shots rang out from camp. Mercy hit the ground to avoid Thad's shots. Crawling forward, she reached the edge just in time to see the two men emerge from the woods on horseback and ride away.

As Mercy raced across the stream, Miranda and Thad sprang into action. By the time Mercy reached camp, Thad was by Harold's side and Miranda was approaching them, carrying the calico she'd intended for curtains. She ripped the fabric and handed it to Thad in strips. Mercy examined her sister. She was uninjured, thank the Lord.

Mercy knelt at Harold's head. Thad was straddling Harold's legs, trying to hold them steady as he worked on the injury. Mercy felt bile rising in her throat as she saw the extent of damage to Harold's knee. She turned her focus to the young man's face, grabbing his hands and trying to keep him still.

"Mercy . . ." Harold's voice was hoarse, his face pale and tear streaked. "God help me. My leg's on fire."

"There's no fire. You've been shot, Harold." Mercy tried to make her voice sound reassuring. "Don't worry, we're going to take care of you."

"I'm going to die." Harold squeezed his eyes shut.

"No, you're not." Thad's voice carried a weight of authority that Mercy had not heard before. "We're going to get you to the doctor at Fort Kearny. You're not dying—you hear me?"

Harold nodded, his eyes still shut tight. Thad directed Miranda to keep pressure on the wound while he went to his saddle to fetch something.

From the beginning of their journey, Mercy had been certain Thad was carrying liquor in his bags. She'd expected him to get drunk regularly and try to ply Harold with drink as well. Now she was grateful that he carried it.

"For medicinal purposes," he mumbled as he held the bottle to Harold's lips and forced him to take small sips.

Thad and Mercy left Miranda to tend to Harold while they built a travois to carry him back to Fort Kearny. "We'll use those oil cloths you're carryin'." Thad pointed at Mercy's saddle, then grabbed Harold's blankets. "We'll need blankets and rope. We can tie him on with his head below his leg—"

"He's lost a lot of blood," Mercy whispered. She watched Miranda wipe a wet rag across Harold's forehead.

"Yes." Thad's voice remained calm. "That's the point. We have to keep his leg up to slow the bleedin'."

"I'm not sure he'll make it all the way to Fort Kearny," Mercy said.

Thad glared at her. "I promised to get him to a doctor and I aim to keep that promise. Are you going to help, or not?"

She nodded. "I only—"

"Maybe you could use your influence with the Almighty. I'm sure that, like the rest of us, He's used to takin' orders from you."

Mercy clamped her jaw shut. This wasn't the time for an argument.

"Harold's going to be fine," Thad said, pulling the ropes tight as he lashed two branches together. "He's young and strong. He'll survive."

The last stars disappeared as pink dawn drove the indigo night away. The longest night of Mercy's life was slipping away quietly.

It had taken hours to get Harold to Fort Kearny, dragging him behind his horse on the crude travois that they had thrown together. Thad's plan to keep Harold's leg raised and tightly bandaged had worked to slow the bleeding. Still they stopped frequently to check Harold's bandages. They fumbled in the darkness, pouring water into him and doling out the precious brandy, which seemed to ease his pain a little. Mercy had reassured the others that they wouldn't be attacked so long as they traveled on the open plains. But she'd remained vigilant and noticed Thad was also alert for danger.

She was utterly exhausted, but too anxious to sleep. Instead, she leaned against the wall of the infirmary, watching the sky, listening to the sounds of Fort Kearny coming to life and reviewing every moment from the sound of the first shots, until she'd watched the attackers ride away. There was something familiar about the two men. If only she'd seen their faces.

"Coffee?" Thad stood beside her with two cups.

"Thanks." Mercy took a cup, wrapping both hands around it, allowing the warmth to soak into her fingers before she raised it to her lips and took a sip. "Not as good as I've grown accustomed to drinking."

"They wouldn't let me in the kitchen, I'm afraid."

Mercy smiled at Thad, then took another sip of the watery brew that really didn't compare to his. Though she doubted even Thad's strong coffee could revive her after what they'd been through this night.

"I arranged for you and Miranda to have a room in one of the married officer's houses. You should try to get some sleep."

"Miranda won't leave Harold's side."

"You both need to rest. The doctor gave Harold so much laudanum he won't know who's with him for some time."

Mercy nodded and took another sip. She stared up at the fading moon. "I can't believe I let this happen." She glanced at Thad. "I should have been there to protect Harold."

"I was there." Thad shook his head. "The gunfire seemed to come out of nowhere and Harold went down with the first shot. Perhaps if I'd seen them coming, or heard something . . . If I'd reacted a bit faster."

Mercy placed her hand on Thad's arm. "Please don't blame yourself. I'm mighty grateful for your quick actions. The way you protected my sister and held those men off with my rifle made all the difference."

"I wish I could've done more."

"It wasn't your fault, Thad." Mercy pulled her hand back when she realized it had been lingering on Thad's arm.

"If only the doctor had been able to save his leg."

"As you said, Harold is young and strong. He'll recover."

Thad nodded and looked at the infirmary wall as if he could see through it into the room where Harold was recovering from the gruesome surgery. "He's alive, that's the important thing."

Mercy took another sip of coffee, now bitter and cold. "Perhaps I will try to get some sleep." She poured the remaining coffee on the ground. "How about you? Did you get a room for yourself?"

"No need. I'll go in and see if I can convince Miranda to let me spell her. Tired as I am, I don't think I'll have any trouble sleepin' in a chair."

Mercy started to protest that she and Miranda didn't need the bed, but she knew it would offend Thad. He was too much of a gentleman to consider sleeping in a comfortable bed while ladies slept on the floor. "I may still have enough influence with Miranda to convince her."

Thad opened the door. "After you, ma'am."

Mercy paced over to the window and stared out at the bustling fort. Everyone had a job to do except for her. Days were passing and Lansing's deadline loomed closer than ever.

"Damn," she muttered. She paced back to the door. "Hell!" She lacked the vocabulary to express her frustration. What she really wanted to do was to kick something, or at least shovel some manure.

She had been volunteering in the stable yesterday when her monthly curse hit hard. She should have known it was coming—there had been drops of blood on her clothes for days. Curling up in bed was very tempting right now. She paced across the room again. Damned if she was going to let a female problem keep her in bed. Bad enough that she had to live with this monthly reminder of her failure to have children.

That's enough feeling sorry for yourself—time to think about Harold. He'd come through the worst of the fever. Now, he faced a lifetime without his leg. She wished she had that moment back when those two men were within range of her Colt. Although she knew she wouldn't have shot them in the back and even if she had, it wouldn't have done Harold any good.

She rubbed the back of her neck trying to ease the tense muscles there. There was no way in hell they'd ever get back on schedule now, but they could still get home before the payment was due. They must. Lansing would never accept a late payment. He wanted her ranch too badly. *Dammit.* They were going to have to leave Harold here.

She worried her lower lip.

It could take them as much as a week to follow the Platte River the rest of the way home. Longer if they ran into more trouble. Another day or two was all they could afford. And that would leave them with little time to spare for the remainder of the journey. Two days. She could survive another couple days of captivity.

She paced around the small room she was sharing with Miranda. There was one important job she must do. Mercy pulled a chair up to the desk near the window. She'd postponed writing to the Pearsons to tell them about Harold's injury. At least she now felt confident that he would live. The army doctor was taking good care of Harold and she trusted that he would continue to do so. She'd leave enough money to see Harold was cared for until he was strong enough to take the stage back to Abilene. She rolled her eyes to the ceiling to calculate.

She'd have barely enough left to pay Lansing. No

matter. They could sell cattle to the mining camps for living money. And next year they'd bring more cattle to the sale in Abilene.

She stared at the blank piece of paper and sighed. How to begin. Her eyes drifted closed. She'd felt exactly like this when she'd sat down to write Nate's mother of his death. No, it hadn't been exactly like this. The guilt she'd felt about Nate was different. She never should have married him. He'd have been safe working in his father's law office in Chicago. Safe and far away from her . . .

She had fled into the shadows of the barn that awful day, not wanting to face him. Nate had been persistent and he had found her hiding place.

"You're right to blame me." He had touched her shoulder, then recoiled as though he'd touched a hot stove. "It was a stupid thing to do."

She turned to face him. If he insisted on having this conversation, she wouldn't lie to him. "You're right. We've lost a good horse through your carelessness."

"I'm sorry."

"What do you want me to say? That it doesn't matter?" She hadn't meant to raise her voice, but all the frustrations of the past months seemed to pour out of their own accord. "Well, it does matter. We've been at this for four years and I swear your mind is still back in Chicago. It certainly isn't here."

"I said I was sorry." Nate kept his voice quiet, which made Mercy angrier.

"Being sorry doesn't change one thing."

"No, it doesn't." Nate reached a hand toward her, but used it instead to brush the hair back from his forehead. "Sometimes I wonder what life would be like if we could go back and change things. What if I'd stayed in Chicago? I'd have made a good lawyer, I think, instead of an incompetent rancher. And you'd have married someone like Buck."

A part of her wanted to shout, "No, I love you, Nate. Buck knows horses and cattle, but he probably thinks Shakespeare is a weapon owned by a fellow named Shake. He'd never look at the stars at night and make up stories out of the pictures he sees."

She should have kissed him and told him he would have been a great lawyer. That she'd move to Chicago and learn to live in the city. Her marriage vows required at least that much of her. All she did was glare—blaming him.

He turned and walked away from her when she grabbed a shovel to muck out the stalls. It had been the perfect work for her mood. She'd left the cattle to the men while she hid in the barn, scooping and humming, trying to control her temper.

"Mercy!" The panicked edge in Miranda's voice had made Mercy drop her shovel and run outside.

"What's the matter?"

"I've been looking everywhere for you." Miranda stopped to gulp air.

"What is it? What's happened?"

"There's been an accident." Miranda took another breath and swallowed. "Pa's hurt real bad."

If she'd taken a moment to think, she would have been better prepared. She should have hitched the wagon and ordered Miranda to fetch bandages from the house. Instead, she'd run after her sister. When they found him, Pa lay bleeding on the ground, with Buck and Nate kneeling over him.

Mercy dropped to her knees next to Nate. "What happened?"

Her father was unconscious. He'd bled through a kerchief they'd wrapped around his head. She bent low over him, finding the reassuring rhythm of his heart pulsing at his neck and hearing the sound of his breathing—slow but steady.

"A bull charged me for no reason," Nate said. "Pa stepped in to turn him away and . . ."

She examined Nate, who was pale as a sheet and shivering. He was clutching his left hand in his right.

"You're hurt," she said.

"Just some broken ribs, I think. And my wrist . . ." He winced as he tried to move it. "Not broken, I don't think."

Her father wheezed and they all turned to him, but his eyes remained shut.

"You'd best look after your pa," Nate said. "I'll be fine."

Mercy turned and ran her fingers along Nate's wrist. Though swollen, it didn't feel broken. His hands were cold and damp; his shirt filthy with mud and hoof prints. She knew Nate was hurt worse than he let on, but she thought Pa needed her more.

"Mercy, I'm sorry . . ." Nate's eyes drifted down to her father.

"Don't worry about Pa." Mercy turned to Miranda. "Get Nate back to the house. He needs to lie down."

"No, need to fuss over me—"

"It'll be best for Miranda to get away from here," Mercy interrupted. "Buck and I can take care of Pa." Nate opened his mouth to speak, but she cut him off. "We'll talk later."

She hadn't kissed him, or touched him or even smiled at him. She had simply turned her attention to Pa.

Miranda and Nate had been in the aspen grove by the creek a hundred yards from the house when he collapsed and started coughing blood. It had taken time for him to die, but Miranda was afraid to leave him alone long enough to get help.

Mercy sometimes imagined that it was she and not Miranda who was there holding Nate's hand in the end. But even in her imagination, she never seemed to have the right words to say.

Chapter 11

Thad threw his cards in, disgusted with himself. It was the music that was distracting him. Who ever heard of playing Bach in a card room? He glanced over at the piano. No, it wasn't the music. It was the musician. Mercy had been playing for the past hour and in that time he'd lost nearly twenty dollars. He'd been paying more attention to her than to his game.

He could ride the few miles to Dobytown where the saloons would be full of drunken soldiers and transients who might not be so cautious with their cards. He glanced again at Mercy. Most of the soldiers had sense enough to keep their distance from her. It was clear she wasn't in the mood for a sing-along.

Only Captain Jamison seemed unable to take the hint. He'd approached her twice, apparently trying to strike up a conversation. She'd dismissed him without even looking up. Thad watched as Captain Jamison made a third approach. This time he waited for a pause in the music. She looked up, shook her head, closed the piano and walked away.

Thad was tempted to follow her, but he was afraid

he'd get the same reception Jamison had. He considered whether he ought to remain in the game. Maybe he'd go visit Harold. Miss Miranda could no doubt use the break. He turned toward the door just as a familiar figure entered.

"Well, Buchanan. Fancy meetin' you here?" O'Reilly's grin was as obnoxious as ever. "Ready to return some of me money, are you now?"

It was definitely time to cut his losses. Thad picked his remaining money off the table and exited while O'Reilly laughed.

Instead of heading toward the hospital, Thad decided to search for Mercy. He found her in the stable feeding Annabelle an apple.

"When was the last time you ate something?" he asked.

She threw him a scowl and returned her eyes to the horse. "I don't know. Earlier today."

"Didn't see you at breakfast, or lunch." Why he should worry about her, he didn't know.

"I wasn't hungry. I had an apple."

"How much of it did you eat, how much did Annabelle get?"

"You sound like my pa." She stroked Annabelle's muzzle, then turned to him. "Will you walk with me? We need to talk."

He nodded, following her out of the stable and along the row of houses built for soldiers' families.

"I shouldn't have agreed to guide you," she said. "I've put you in danger."

"We talked about this before." Thad turned to look at her as they walked. "There are random attacks all the time—"

"I don't believe it was random." Her gaze penetrated his.

"Because of the cattle sale money." He shrugged. "But no one here knows—"

"O'Reilly knows." She looked back toward the large brick building in the center of the fort. "Come to think of it—you saw what happened in Abilene."

Thad remembered the way O'Reilly had threatened the two women in Abilene, but he also recalled Mercy hadn't needed any assistance in fending the drunk off. "O'Reilly's here now."

"Yes, he just greeted me as I walked out of the dining hall."

Thad studied Mercy. She was hatless, her hair gleaming in the sunlight.

"I'm going to speak with Captain Jamison," she said. "See if he can arrange another guide for you. I'll return your fee, of course."

"No. I'm not leaving you." He gripped her arm. "Sorry." He let go, expecting her to scold him, but she said nothing. "O'Reilly's a stout fellow. Those two were both slender."

"I thought of that." She heaved a long tired sigh. "But that doesn't mean they weren't working for him."

Thad examined her face while he had the chance. Her eyes were a bit red, the hollows below them dark. She hadn't been sleeping any better than he had. All this worry over Harold and keeping her money safe. If only she didn't insist on carrying the whole burden herself all the time. He'd help her in a minute, if she'd allow it.

She had a point about O'Reilly, though. The Irishman would have others doing his dirty work. "O'Reilly doesn't scare me, nor you as I recall." That comment won him one of her rare smiles.

"No. That buffoon doesn't frighten me. But men with Winchesters . . . I'd be foolish not to worry."

Thad nodded. "I'll take my chances with you. You scared off those two gunmen—"

"Not nearly in time for Harold."

Thad shrugged. "We both might've kept a closer eye on the boy. No point punishing ourselves for that now." He could see she wanted to argue, but he wasn't about to let her. "I trust you. Even if you're right about O'Reilly or someone else being after you, that doesn't guarantee that I'd be any safer if I were on my own, or with another group."

He thought she'd continue to protest, but she nodded. "Truth is, I've got my sister to worry about. I won't have her hurt, or . . . worse. I can't protect Miranda alone. I'm grateful for your help."

He should probably just accept her gratitude, surprising as it was to receive, but he couldn't let her continue to take the blame. "Not everything that happens is necessarily your fault."

She gave him a wistful smile. "I agree with your logic, Thad. But my heart tells me different."

They walked in silence for a moment until they were nearly bowled over by a yapping puppy with two young boys chasing after him at breakneck speed. The dog, a wiry black and white terrier, was carrying a lady's hat, which the boys seemed determined to retrieve. Thad and Mercy both laughed at the spectacle. He turned to face her.

"Hope they get the hat back before their mama realizes it's gone missing."

Mercy pointed to a hatless woman marching down the street, fists clenched tight and face glowing apple-red. "Too late, I fear."

Thad shook his head. "We'd best head back before things turn violent."

Mercy chuckled and turned back toward the center of the fort.

"Mercy . . ."

"Yes?"

"I . . . I've been meaning to ask you . . ."

Mercy raised her eyebrows. Why was he suddenly nervous?

"Before I left home, I had a letter from Clarisse." They resumed their stroll. "She mentioned a young widow in Fort Victory."

"A widow?"

"Yes. One who might find me . . . compatible."

"Oh." Mercy chuckled. "Clarisse is matchmaking, is she?"

"I suppose. She knows I'm anxious to settle down. Well, I just wondered if you know who the nice widow lady might be."

"She lives in Fort Victory?" Mercy couldn't think of many widows in town.

Thad nodded. "I believe so."

"Hmm. Do you suppose she could mean Rita?" Mercy shook her head. "I reckon she'd be compatible, but . . ."

"Tell me about her?"

"She owns the saloon in town. Runs a poker game— I'm sure you'd enjoy that." Mercy looked up into Thad's face. "I think she's older, though."

"Older?"

"Older than you, I mean. How old are you anyway?"

"Twenty-three."

"Really? I thought you were closer to my age."

It was Thad's turn to raise eyebrows. "I hardly think I'm younger than you. Am I?"

"I was twenty-seven last spring."

"Twenty-seven?" Thad scowled. "And Rita?"

"I reckon she's thirty. Lovely woman, though—you'd like her."

"I don't mind older, though I was hoping for . . . um,

children." Thad didn't seem to be able to look at her. "She doesn't sound exactly like the woman I'm looking for."

"If you have a certain type of woman in mind, you'd be better off looking in the Eastern states where women are more plentiful. Colorado Territory has too many men."

"So I understand. But, Clarisse told me to come—that I'd find my match in Fort Victory." He removed his hat and ran his hand through his hair. "She maybe didn't mean right in town."

Mercy bit her lip, thinking of all the women in the area. "Tell me about this ideal woman of yours. What is she like?"

"That's easy, I have a clear picture of her in my mind. She's thoughtful and considerate. Warm-hearted. She smiles all the time. And she's dedicated to making a home for our family."

"You said it was a picture, but you haven't described her appearance at all."

"Do I have a choice about that, too?"

"I've already said you have very little choice of anything if you're searching for a wife in Colorado."

"Then I reckon I'll worry about her heart and take whatever face comes with it."

"You're an unusual man, Mr. Buchanan."

"I wouldn't complain if she has a pretty face, mind." He gave her a wink, which made her smile.

"You'll have to stop that sort of behavior when you find your wife, you know."

"What behavior?"

"You are a flirt, Thad Buchanan. I'm not sure your future wife will appreciate that."

"She won't mind if I save all my flirting for her."

His mustache flicked and that dimple sprang to life

again. It would take a strong woman to resist that. She turned her attention back to the question at hand. "Children?" she asked.

"I hope to have a large number of them."

"I mean, do you mind if your widow has children?"

"Mind?" Thad's grin widened. "I wouldn't mind at all. It'd be nice to have a family ready-made."

"Then perhaps Ingrid Hansen."

"The widow?"

Mercy nodded. "Ingrid has two little girls and another babe on the way. Her husband was killed a few months ago." As difficult as Hansen's death had been for his wife, she hadn't had an easy time of it when her husband was alive.

"Killed?"

"A dispute over a mine claim."

Thad shook his head. "That's a shame. And he left her with two girls?" He spoke the words almost reverently.

"And another child very soon."

They reached the parade grounds and Mercy hesitated, wondering whether to go to the hospital or the stable. Neither activity would get her one inch closer to home. She must talk to Miranda about leaving tonight.

"Have a nice afternoon." Mercy started to walk away, then looked over her shoulder. "By the way, Ingrid's quite pretty. You'd have beautiful children with blond hair and blue eyes."

His eyes drifted away and Mercy imagined he was picturing his ideal family. "Thank you," he said.

"But you'll have your work cut out for you getting that farm in shape."

"She has land?"

She nodded. "Her husband's gold fever kept him from it. It will need a lot of work."

"To work the land again and have a family . . ."

"You still have to win her," she warned. But he didn't seem to hear her.

Mercy sighed and turned away from the sight of him dreaming. She marched on to the stable, thinking of Thad Buchanan bouncing the Hansen girls on his knee. It was a charming picture, and completely wrong.

"We've lost a week already," Mercy reasoned with her sister. "We can't afford to stay here any longer."

It was one of those rare times when Miranda had agreed to leave Harold's side and use the bed for which Mercy was paying so dearly. Mercy wanted to let her sister get some sleep, but they needed to have this conversation first.

"But Harold isn't strong enough to travel yet." Miranda sat up under the blankets, looking at Mercy who sat with one leg under her, at the foot of the bed.

"I know." Mercy watched her sister by the flickering light of a single candle. She looked tired and drawn— she hadn't slept or eaten properly since they'd arrived at Fort Kearny. "We'll have to leave him here. When he's strong enough, he'll take the stage back to Abilene. I'll make sure he has enough money to see him through the winter if necessary."

"No."

"We have no choice," Mercy rubbed her hand against her sister's knee. "I know the ranch isn't important to you, but it is our livelihood. Even leaving now, we'll barely make it back in time to pay Lansing."

"You go then. I'm staying with Harold."

"You're nineteen years old. I am not leaving you alone in the middle of an Army camp."

"But you're willing to leave Harold?"

"He's not a beautiful young girl." Mercy shook her

head. "Truth is, I don't want to leave him either, but I don't see any other option."

"Go then." Miranda crossed her arms in front of her chest. "I'll take care of Harold."

Mercy shook her head.

"I've spoken with the camp laundress," Miranda said. "She'll let me stay with her in exchange for work."

"Miranda—"

"No," she interrupted. "I need to tell you . . . Harold and I were talking about getting married when we got to Fort Victory. I think maybe now it would be better for us to go back to Abilene—we can work in his father's store."

"You never told me you were considering marriage."

"I already explained. I didn't know how to tell you about Harold and me." Miranda bent forward and put her hand over Mercy's. "I didn't want to cause you pain."

Mercy turned her hand and squeezed her sister's. "Are you sure about this?"

Miranda nodded. "I love him, Mercy."

"And he feels the same way about you?"

Miranda nodded.

"Even now? Does he want you to stay?"

"Harold doesn't know what he wants just now." Miranda sat up, pulling her hands out of Mercy's grip. "He's scared, Mercy. He doesn't understand any of this."

"He's going to need time to heal—not just his leg. He may never be the same on the inside."

"You don't expect me to abandon him just because he's lost his leg."

"No," Mercy slid up next to her sister and slipped an arm around her. "Of course you wouldn't. Not the Miranda Chase I know and love—she's loyal through and through."

"Harold's not strong like you are, Mercy. He needs people. He needs me."

Mercy sighed, thinking of O'Reilly and other threats that might be awaiting them. Perhaps Miranda would be safer here than on the trail to Fort Victory. "I hate the idea of missing your wedding."

"You'll let me stay then?"

"I'll *let* you stay." Mercy touched her sister's cheek. "As though you were giving me a choice."

Miranda threw her arms around her and Mercy squeezed tight. Luckily, in the darkness, Miranda couldn't see the tears pooling in Mercy's eyes.

Then she had another thought. *Hellfire! A week on the trail alone with Thad Buchanan.*

Two days later the parting was even harder than Mercy had expected.

"I can take care of myself." Miranda gripped both of Mercy's hands. "Don't you worry about me."

Mercy squeezed her sister's fingers. "I know you can. I just wish you didn't have to." Mercy looked around the open square that formed the center of Fort Kearny. Annabelle and Clover stood nearby, packed and ready for the trail. Mercy was ready, even anxious, to be on her way. She watched the men milling about the open square, heading to their assigned posts. Men everywhere with a few wives and a handful of other women. "I don't like leaving you in this place." She pulled Miranda close and wrapped her arms around her. "But I know you can handle yourself."

Mercy released her sister, placed her hands on Miranda's shoulders, and looked into her eyes. "You've got your Colt." Miranda nodded, slapping the thirty-six caliber Colt strapped to her hip. It was smaller than Mercy's forty-four, but deadly in Miranda's skilled hands.

"And you've got the money stashed in a safe place?" Her sister nodded again. "You don't put up with any nonsense from these men."

"I'll be working, or staying with Harold all the time. Once the men realize I'm engaged to Harold, they'll leave me be."

Mercy shook her head. "I'm afraid it's not that simple. The men won't just stay away. You've got to make them respect you."

Miranda nodded again, but her expression was different. Scared? Mercy hugged her sister close again. She blinked, refusing to let Miranda see her tears.

Miranda sniffed. "I didn't want you to see me cry," she said, her voice cracking.

Mercy smiled and wiped the tear rolling down Miranda's cheek. "I'll miss you."

"I'll write often."

"You'd better." Mercy brushed a kiss on Miranda's cheek, straightened her hat and turned to see Thad leading Zeus. Both man and steed were striking.

"And Mercy?"

She turned back to her sister.

"Be careful of Thad."

"What do you mean?" The last thing she wanted was for Miranda to notice her admiring Thad. Miranda would not understand that Mercy could enjoy his appearance without having any feelings for him.

"I mean be nice to him."

"Nice?" *That could be dangerous.*

Miranda laughed. "It isn't such a hard thing, big sister. I know you don't like him, but he is a good man— very thoughtful. Do you know, Harold told me he bought a new shirt to wear when he sees his sister. It's a small thing, but how many men would think of it?"

Mercy nodded. She had come to appreciate Thad. Especially the way he had protected Miranda. But her appreciation had definite limits and she intended to keep it that way.

"You'll try to be nice then?"

Mercy nodded again. "I'll do my best." *I'll do my best to be polite, kind and aloof.*

Thad stood next to her now and Mercy turned to greet him. He was clean and smooth shaven, emanating the spicy aroma of bay rum.

"What's that?" Mercy pointed at a large leather satchel strapped behind Zeus's saddle.

"Guitar." Thad grinned. "Last night's poker winnin's."

The man's a gambler, Mercy reminded herself. Another good reason to avoid further entanglements with him. Not that she needed another reason.

"Don't worry," Thad assured her, "Zeus won't have any trouble with the extra weight."

Mercy glanced at Thad—apparently he'd misinterpreted her silence. She moved closer to examine the bundle attached to Zeus. "Looks like your lashing job will hold well enough," she allowed.

"Thank you." Thad seemed to be suppressing a chuckle.

Mercy glared at him. "It's important the pack doesn't shift around. The last thing we need is a sore horse to nurse."

"I'll take care of my own animal." He winked at her. *Infuriating!*

Thad turned to Miranda. "Miss Miranda, I hope we'll meet again soon. You take care of Harold now. I expect with you nursin' him, he'll recover in no time."

"I hope so," Miranda said.

Thad tipped his hat and mounted Zeus.

Mercy pulled Miranda into another embrace before turning to mount Annabelle.

Annabelle and Clover started walking when Mercy

clucked her tongue. She threw a last glance over her shoulder and Miranda waved. Thad trailed behind on Zeus and he smiled when Mercy's eyes met his. She turned to face the river they would follow for the next two hundred fifty miles and urged the horses a little faster. They had a long way to go.

Chapter 12

Mercy surveyed the empty plain. The sun was past its zenith. They'd been riding for hours in silence. Miranda was now miles away, truly on her own for the first time.

"You having second thoughts about leaving Miranda behind?" Thad's voice startled her. "It was the right thing to do."

Mercy smiled, then wondered why his reassurance meant so much.

She picked up the pace as much as she dared. The afternoon sun was hot and the horses would tire quickly. They'd cover more ground if they moved slowly all day long. They would get back to Fort Victory in time. She couldn't miss this deadline.

"You could be in a traveling show with your mind-reading abilities," she said.

Thad returned her smile. "It doesn't take a wizard to see how much you care about your sister. I know it was difficult for you to leave her at Fort Kearny, but Harold needs her." Thad turned back to the trail. "I think maybe they need each other."

Before he turned away, Mercy saw the pain in his eyes. She was certain Thad felt as responsible as she did for Harold's injury. The difference was Harold was her responsibility. She felt another pang of guilt, thinking about his leg.

"It won't be easy for him . . . the loss of his leg." Thad read her mind again. "I knew several men back home who have been through an amputation. It wasn't easy for any of them, but those with someone who cared for them . . . With Miranda's help, Harold will walk again— and joke again, too."

"I believe you're right. Harold does need Miranda right now. And . . . she'd have fought me if I'd tried to force her to go on without him. I am nearly a foot taller and I weigh more, but I wouldn't wager that I could win that fight."

"I reckon you could have made a fortune selling tickets to the bout," Thad laughed.

Mercy shot Thad a quick grin and watched his thick mustache twitch as his eyes lit up with a smile. It was getting harder and harder to remember why she'd tried so hard to hate this man.

"I keep telling myself she'll be fine. Happy . . ."

"But you can't be certain."

Mercy shook her head. "No. I can't be sure that Harold will recover—"

"He will." Thad cut her off.

"I mean. This is bound to change him, isn't it? I wasn't sure he was right for Miranda before, but now . . ."

"We don't even know what's beyond the horizon." Thad lifted his chin to point ahead.

Mercy sat taller. "I'm ready for anything that may come."

"Are you?"

She looked into his eyes—no hint of teasing now.

"Sometimes we just have to take a chance, is all I'm sayin'." Thad held her gaze. "Miranda knows what she's risking."

Mercy thought of all the pain that had come out of her marriage. "I'm not sure she does, Thad."

"I expect you've taught her a good bit more than you give yourself credit for."

She wished she knew for certain that she'd done everything she could to prepare Miranda. Mercy thought again of the hopeful look in her sister's face when she announced she was in love. Miranda might know she was taking a chance, but she couldn't know the price of failure. She sighed. Perhaps her sister would be one of the lucky ones.

Mercy scanned the horizon for some break in the broad expanse of open plains. She reined Annabelle in and glanced over her shoulder to be sure Clover slowed as well. Thad and Zeus matched the slower pace. Up ahead, dust swirled, sagebrush stirred. After a long, still day, the breeze was welcome, but surprising. Annabelle's ears flicked, back and forth. Mercy looked around.

"What is it?" Thad asked.

"Thunderstorm." Mercy pointed to the left, bringing Annabelle and Clover to a halt.

Thad pulled up. Purple and black storm clouds churned on the western horizon. A streak of lightning flashed through the dark, billowing mass.

"We've got to get back to that gully we passed," Thad said.

"No." Mercy shook her head, scanning the plains. "There!" She pointed to a bump to the north. "We're heading that way. Move!" She squeezed her heels into Annabelle's side and the horse shot forward, Clover following at the same pace.

"The gully's closer. We'll never make it that far," Thad shouted after her.

"Trust me," Mercy shouted back at Thad. She could see Thad wanted to argue with her, but they didn't have time. She pulled on Clover's lead and urged the two horses into a gallop as the wind picked up dust all around them.

The sky darkened. Bright blue became gray, then purple. Thunder rumbled in the distance. The first light drops of rain bounced against the brim of her hat. Mercy drove the horses forward. Thad was shouting something behind her, but she ignored him, hoping he would follow her, hoping the distant bump was the cabin she remembered and that there was enough of it left to provide some shelter for them.

Mercy leaned forward, keeping her head down, her eyes focused on the bump, larger now, but more difficult to see in the indigo sky with wind-driven rain pelting them. Light flashed around them, followed by a clap of thunder. Clover pulled back, whinnying loudly in protest. Mercy turned to her.

"Almost there, girl," she shouted over the rain and wind. "We'll be out of this soon." The sky lit up again and a crack of thunder followed. Another burst of light and more crashing thunder.

The old sod cabin was visible now. Mercy turned to see Thad struggling to control Zeus. She urged Annabelle faster and Clover followed. When they reached the soddy, it was clear that no one had lived there in some time. The roof was largely missing on half of the ramshackle building, but appeared to be solid on the other half, where it extended out to form an open shelter for the horses.

Another flash. Mercy leaned forward against Annabelle's neck. *Boom!* The lightning was nearly on top of them. Clover froze. Annabelle, raised her head, shifting from side to side.

"Let's get under. Come on, girl."

They could leave the horses out in the rain, but al
their things would be soaked. The shelter would make
it far easier to unpack. Besides, anything standing in the
open might attract that lightning.

Mercy slipped off Annabelle's back but Clover re
fused to move.

"Come on, girl." Mercy soothed the frightened horse
She held Clover's lead firmly, but didn't tug, not want
ing to frighten the horse more. She pulled her hat of
and used it to shield Clover's eyes, hoping the horse
would be less frightened if she didn't see the flashing
The ruse worked, as Clover blindly followed Mercy.

Outside, Thad was still more than twenty yards away
Zeus was side-stepping and turning in place, refusing to
go any closer to the cabin. Mercy ran out into the storm
to help Thad coax Zeus.

Annabelle and Clover stomped the ground restlessly
but Zeus was completely out of control. He reared back
when he came under, kicking his hooves against the sod
wall, and bumping the roof with his head. Mercy feared
he would knock the crumbling building down around
them.

Thad pulled Zeus's reins, trying to regain control,
but his considerable strength was no match for the
frightened horse.

"Easy there, big fella." Mercy meant her words as
much for Thad as his horse. Zeus wasn't going to calm
down with Thad fighting him. The horse turned to look
at her, his eyes wild with fear. She stepped forward, gripping the bridle.

Boom! Zeus stepped back, whinnying loudly.

"It's all right," Mercy reassured him, rubbing one
hand under and another over his muzzle. She looked
into his frightened eyes. "It's all right, boy." Zeus nuzzled Mercy's chest.

Mercy turned to Thad, relieved that they'd reached shelter, and smiled.

"What were you thinking?" he shouted above the sound of rain pelting the wooden roof. "We could have been killed by that lightning. Why wouldn't you go to the gully?"

Mercy stepped away from Zeus, her hands placed firmly on her hips. "You're welcome to go there if you want! Good luck to you. If this storm brings a flash flood, any man or beast in that gully would be washed away. They wouldn't have a chance."

"Flash floods?" Although he no longer shouted, Mercy couldn't mistake the ring of anger in his voice. "You might have said something about flash floods."

"We didn't have time for a discussion out there." Mercy worked to calm herself. "I asked you to trust me." *Not that I care whether you do or not.*

She glared at him. He glared back.

"I'm in charge of this expedition," she hissed. "I don't have to explain every decision to you."

Just because the man couldn't admit he was wrong didn't mean she had to stand around shivering. She'd care for the horses, then get inside the cabin.

Thad watched her working. *Mule-headed woman—always bossing. It never occurred to her a man might have some pride.*

He removed Zeus's saddle, then went inside himself to survey the situation. Rain poured in where the roof had collapsed. Already the floor on that side had become a small pond. In the center of the room was the smallest pot-bellied stove he'd ever seen. Thad doubted the rusted chimney worked, but with the gaping holes in the roof that might not matter. There was a small stack of wood and a large pile of buffalo chips on the dry side of the stove. Looking more closely he could see that the wood was salvaged mostly from crates and possibly furniture. There wasn't a table or chair in the room.

Mercy stomped into the room, dropping her saddlebags on the dirt floor. She removed her jacket and hung it in on a peg in the driest corner.

"I'll try to get a fire goin' in this old stove," Thad said.

Mercy nodded. He could see she was still seething. What had he done to deserve her silence? Perhaps silence was better than shouting. Wind whipped through the cabin, driving rain through the empty window frame and through yawning holes in the door. The occasional clap of thunder punctuated the steady rhythm of the pouring rain.

Thad removed his soaked jacket, hung it, then went to work on the fire. He used the end of a ladle to pry open the door to the stove, then reached toward the woodpile.

Ssssss. Thad froze, staring at the snake.

"Get back!" Mercy shouted.

Thad jumped, then slowly backed away. By the light of the open window he watched the huge snake peering up from the woodpile, its mouth gaped open, revealing large fangs. The snake stretched taller, its rattle sounding as its tongue flicked and its head darted toward Thad. He took another step back.

Mercy inched closer, her gun held in both hands. She aimed, then squeezed the trigger.

The blast of Mercy's Colt filled the room, followed by another dull burst of thunder outside. The snake collapsed and lay still, most of its head gone.

Mercy holstered her gun and turned to Thad. "Are you all right?" She placed her hand on his arm. He noticed she was trembling. "Did he get you?"

Thad shook his head, embarrassed that he hadn't

thought to pull his own pistol. "Do you suppose there are any more in here?"

Mercy smiled, the rigid lines of her face softening as her fingers tightened around his arm. "It wouldn't hurt to look around to see if that ol' rattler has a family in here."

Thad nodded, amazed at the transformation that smile wrought—from cattle boss to tenderness. Her fingers slipped away from his arm and they searched the small room. Not too many places a snake could hide. Thad peered into the stove, while Mercy poked around the woodpile. After a thorough search, they determined there were no more rattlers.

Thad went back to building the fire while Mercy made a dry nest. Her rain-soaked shirt clung to her, leaving little to his imagination. Her splendid body was mighty tempting. And as dangerous as a flying cannonball, he reminded himself. Mercy was quick to judge. Quick to condemn. She held a grudge better than anyone he'd ever met. But Lord help the man, or snake, who threatened someone she cared about. Not that she cared about him. She felt responsible because he'd hired her to guide him.

The fire caught and much of the smoke poured into the room instead of up the chimney, but it soon found plenty of chinks, cracks, and gaping holes though which to escape.

Mercy looked through the food they'd purchased at Fort Kearny. Selecting an apple, she cut it and gave Thad half. "I'm afraid I'm not much of a cook. I always leave that to Miranda. I guess we have fresh meat, though." She nodded toward the dead rattler.

Thad felt a chill slip down his spine. He finished the apple, trying to appear casual while he looked over the rest of the supplies Mercy had laid out. "I might could rustle up some biscuits and use some of this bacon to fry up that . . . uh . . . snake meat."

"Could you really?"

Thad laughed. "You don't believe me?"

"It isn't that . . ."

"I've been doing all the cookin' for me and my mama these past three years. A man's gotta have more'n coffee to survive."

Mercy smiled. "Well then, I'll do the wash-up if you'll do the cooking."

"I accept that bargain." Thad reached out and Mercy shook his hand. He clasped his second hand over hers.

Mercy nodded, jerking her hand away. He thought he saw her face color, though he couldn't be sure in the dim light.

"I'm sorry," Thad said.

"What for?"

"You were right about coming here instead of the gully." Thad dug the bacon out of its flour sack wrapping. "I shouldn't have yelled at you."

"No matter." Mercy shrugged, pulling out plates and utensils for their meal.

Thad let out a long breath. "It does matter. I've apologized, I'd like to hear you forgive me." Why couldn't she have a civil conversation with him? Just because they were wet and cold and miserable was no reason to be irritable.

"What difference does it make?" Mercy snapped.

"It makes a great deal of difference." Thad worked to keep from raising his voice. It was easier to collect water in a sieve than it was to talk to her sometimes.

"I don't think so. There's nothing to forgive—you didn't know about the dangers of flash floods."

"No. You're angry and I don't deserve that. All I've done is apologize."

"It's forgotten. No need for apologies."

"For a person named Mercy, you know precious little about that quality."

"Of course I know. Just because I didn't go to any fancy school doesn't mean I'm not educated."

"I'm talking about something you can't learn from a book." Thad tried to look into her eyes, but she wouldn't meet his. "I didn't mean to offend you. I know you worked hard for your education—mine was given to me."

She looked up at him then. "You went to college, didn't you?"

He nodded. "College of William and Mary."

"That's in Virginia, isn't it?"

"My mother was from Virginia. Her grandfather and father went to William and Mary. She was proud to send all of her sons there. I only had a year before the war." Thad threw the apple core into the fire. "It was just as well, I wasn't much of a scholar." He started digging through the packs for the pots and utensils he would need.

"Clarisse told me a lot about your family." Mercy knelt next to him. "I remember she said your mother was sick for quite some time."

Thad nodded. "She was always frail." He relaxed, shrugging his shoulders to try to loosen the knot that had formed between them. "The war killed her by littles. Losing Papa and my brothers was the final blow, though she lived for months after that, confined to her bed most of the time."

She placed her hand on his arm again, her eyes penetrating his. "I imagine it was difficult for you. Clarisse told me food was scarce."

Thad could swear he saw tears pooling in her eyes. Most likely it was the smoke.

"I couldn't help thinkin' if I worked harder somehow I could have kept Mama alive."

"It wasn't your fault."

He shrugged. "I had to move on." He glanced at the snake's body. "You ever skin one of those things?"

She nodded, reached for her knife and chopped off the remains of the snake's head.

"I . . . I accept your apology," Mercy said stabbing the head and tossing it into the fire.

"Thank you."

Thad untied the string holding the flour sack closed.

"How'd you end up in Colorado Territory?" Thad asked her as he mixed up the biscuits and placed balls of dough in the Dutch oven.

Mercy pulled two flat boards from the woodpile to use as a cutting surface. "My Uncle Jake went looking for gold. He wrote to Pa and told him about the land. Next thing I knew we were headed west again."

"From Kansas?"

She nodded. "We were farming next to Will and Emily."

"Your Uncle Jake find his gold?"

She shook her head and blinked. "He joined the army. Died in a prison camp." She put cleaned snake meat on a tin plate and looked around for something to wipe her hands with.

"I'm sorry about your uncle." The words weren't enough, Thad knew.

She stepped over to the window and held her hands outside, scrubbing them in the falling rain. It was a few minutes later when she turned back to him.

"I know from Clarisse that your family had many losses too. It was hard on her. Being so far away."

Thad cut a thin slice of bacon. "I know she wanted to come help with Mama."

"Wendell pretty near had to tie her down to keep her from going."

A great clap of thunder shook the soddy. They both

turned to the window, watching the gray sky. The next flash came a few seconds later, but the roar of thunder was more distant this time.

"I was sleeping in a warm bed when my brother was cut down—younger than I am now."

"You were home recovering from your own wounds."

Thad shrugged. "That doesn't change the fact I missed the battle that killed my father and brothers. One brother died instantly on the battlefield, like my father. My oldest brother wasn't so lucky. He lingered for days. Word came to us that he was wounded and my mother and I set off to find him. The casualties were terrible when the Yankees took Nashville, dead and wounded everywhere. It was hard to find a particular man. But we did and we brought him home." He took the small Dutch oven and set it over the coals.

"At first we thought he would live. He hung on for so long. Then the fever came fierce and he just didn't have the strength to fight it." Thad tossed the bacon into the hot pan. It sizzled and sputtered as he rubbed it around the pan with his knife. "Mama took ill after that and never recovered."

Mercy rested her hand on his arm again. The sizzling of bacon grew louder than the pitter-patter of rainfall. She held his gaze and this time he was certain there were tears pooling in her eyes. The bacon started to burn and he turned back to the pan. Mercy sat about a yard away from him with her head resting on her knees. He hadn't meant to cast such a somber mood on their evening.

"But I still have some family. I'll be meeting my three nephews soon, thanks to you."

Mercy lifted her head. Her smile sent a warm rush deep inside his chest. He had to remind himself to breathe.

"They're wonderful boys." She grinned. "Not that they don't get into their share of mischief."

"Like what?"

"I got caught in town once when there was a big storm and Clarisse invited me to stay. When I got up in the morning, I found a lizard in my boot."

Thad grinned, knowing the boys' prank wouldn't frighten Mercy.

"Nothing dangerous, mind. But I'm glad I checked before I put my boot on." She shuddered. "Imagine trying to remove a crushed lizard from your boot."

"I'd rather not."

The corners of her lips hinted at a smile. "The worst prank was the time they decided to put sugar in my coffee."

"That doesn't sound so bad."

"There's three boys and they each put in two spoonsful. I hate sweet coffee" Mercy made a face like she'd bitten a bad lemon. "I nearly choked." She laughed. "I drank it, of course. Even so, Clarisse found out about it and she was furious. Coffee and sugar were so hard to come by during the war . . ."

The mention of the war turned her somber again.

"Dinner's ready," he said, poking the snake meat. "If we dare risk it."

Chapter 13

After dinner, Thad pulled his new guitar from its leather satchel while Mercy washed up. He played, quietly humming a tune that Mercy didn't recognize. She watched him play, his eyes closed as he moved from one chord to another, sometimes pausing to adjust the tuning pegs.

He opened his eyes. "Sing with me."

"I don't know the song," Mercy said.

"Oh, that wasn't a song. Just strum and hum whatever moves me. You know this one?"

He started a bright tune about a drunken sailor. Mercy caught on readily and sang with him. Cleaning the dishes went quickly as Thad segued from one song to another. She loved to sing, especially with someone who could harmonize as skillfully as Thad.

She stopped to listen when he sang "Beautiful Dreamer." His voice was resonant—alive, vibrant, not like so many bass singers she'd heard over the years who were all rumble. Because so much of the room's floor was now mud, Mercy sat close to him. The sound of his voice filled her as she inhaled his warm, masculine scent.

Thunder cracked above them, yanking Mercy out of her trance. She looked out the window. It had grown dark.

"We'd best get some sleep," she turned back to Thad. "We'll have to get moving early to make up for our short day today."

Thad rested his fingers on Mercy's elbow. Another crack of thunder—electricity shot through Mercy's arm. Not lightning, she decided, as her breath caught in her throat. She ignored the sense of danger that struck her as she tried to find her voice.

"Hmm?" she managed.

"Mind if I ask a question?"

"Mmm-hmm." Mercy nodded, pretending she could make sense of his words. She moved her arm back away from his touch, hoping her movement wasn't too abrupt. She couldn't let him believe the contact affected her. After all, it wasn't him. It was only that she'd been so long without any touch from a man.

"I've never seen anyone talk to her horse so intently." Thad grinned.

"I suppose you think it's funny." Mercy's voice returned.

"Maybe not. When we were out in the storm—Annabelle was the only horse to stay calm." He pulled the leather satchel around his guitar. "Could be all that talkin' helps the animal to trust you in a frightening situation."

"That's part of why I do it."

"Why else?"

"It's silly." She pulled the ribbon from the end of her braid and shoved it into her pocket.

"No, tell me."

"When I talk to her, I can work out my problems."

"I see." Thad scratched his head in the shadows and she reckoned he didn't understand at all.

Mercy turned and rolled her jacket into a pillow. She clenched her teeth, realizing her bedroll would have to be next to his. There wasn't enough dry space for a decent amount of separation. She ran her hand over her hair, forcing herself to relax. She wouldn't give any sign that the sleeping arrangements troubled her. After all, theirs was a business arrangement.

"So, when you can't find a solution on your own, you turn to your horse. I don't suppose it occurred to you that she isn't really going to provide an answer for you."

"I know it doesn't seem logical, but . . . she's so calm about everything and it feels like she provides . . . maybe not answers but a kind of wisdom. Couldn't find the solution without her help."

"Well now." Thad hesitated. "First time I ever hear you admit you need anyone and it turns out to be your horse. Why am I not surprised?"

Fuming, Mercy pulled her blanket a few more inches away from Thad and closer to the mud. "Sleep!" She sat on her bedroll. "We've a long day ahead of us tomorrow."

She loosed her hair from its braid and began her nightly ritual of brushing it out. As the last embers of the fire died, the blaze within Mercy grew hotter. Pulling hard on the brush, she tried to numb herself with the repeated motion. But it was no use—even through the smoke, she could smell him. One touch from him would melt her.

Even if she could manage to sleep tonight, she didn't dare.

The sight of Mercy, silhouetted against the amber light of the remaining embers, mesmerized Thad. Each night she loosened her hair from the thick braid and brushed it out. Then she wove it into two braids. In the morning, she would reverse the process, turning the two braids into one. The entire routine baffled him, yet watching her was strangely arousing. He couldn't help wondering what it would be like to bury his head in her hair, to find her neck beneath the dark curtain and cover it with kisses. He wasn't exactly sure how she'd react, except that she would be passionate.

Would she return his kisses, or just shoot him? Making a move was definitely too dangerous to risk.

He pretended to sleep while she finished with her hair. When she stood and left the cabin, he realized it had stopped raining. It should only take her a moment to check the horses sheltered next to the soddy, but she didn't return for several minutes. In fact, he heard no sound. He reached out and touched the hard surface of Mercy's gun under her pillow. A tight knot formed in his stomach—she was defenseless out there. He pulled his own pistol, inched over to the window and peered out. Keeping low, he made his way out the door, cursing silently when the hinge creaked as he opened it.

He froze. The only sounds were the quiet murmurings of the resting horses. No sign of Mercy, or of anyone else. He crept out of the shadow of the cabin until he saw her sitting several yards away. He released the breath he hadn't realized he'd been holding, shoved his revolver into his belt and strolled over to sit next to her.

He thought he heard her sniff as she brushed the back of her hand across her face. His stomach twisted at the thought of Mercy crying. Couldn't be tears, though. More likely the damp weather had caused her nose to run.

"Having trouble sleeping?" she asked.

"I was about to ask you the same question."

"I was checking on the horses."

"Well, they're behind you." He tilted his head back toward the small shelter where the horses were tied.

"The sky cleared and I was caught up in the show." She pointed up.

Above them, the sky shone with countless stars. It was beautiful. Then he saw a quick flash and another. "Meteor shower," he said.

She made room for him on the oil cloth she carried rolled behind her saddle. They sat shoulder to shoulder to avoid the mud.

Mercy sighed. "Imagine what it would be like to be riding on one of those?"

"A shooting star?" Thad sounded skeptical. "Might be a wonderful ride, but seems to me it's over too fast."

Mercy tilted her head back up and sighed. "Perhaps it isn't possible to make such a ride last for long."

"Why not?" Thad brushed the dust from his knees. "Don't you think we're meant to be happy? In the long run, I mean?"

"Really happy?" Mercy shook her head, still watching the sky. "Happiness comes in little bursts, like those shooting stars. Then it's over and all that's left is darkness."

"What about all those stars that stay up there, night after night? They blink from time to time, but the light comes back."

Mercy shrugged.

"You don't have to deserve it."

"What?"

"Everything. Happiness. Life." Thad took a slow breath and released it. "Took me quite a while to figure that out." Mercy sat motionless as words he thought he'd never tell a living soul spilled out of him. "I told you before, I was shot in the war. I make light of it, but the fact is I should have died. Two bullets hit me at close range. Here." He touched near his right shoulder. "And here." He touched his left side. "Why did I live when my brothers didn't?"

"Life is a game of chance, not skill." Mercy mocked his words.

Thad nodded. "There's some chance in everything. But there's more to it than that." He pulled his father's pipe out of his pocket. "When I was wounded, Papa gave me his pipe to take home for him. Said he was afraid it would be damaged." Thad felt the comfortable weight in his hand. "Truly, I believe he knew he was never coming home . . ." He looked up at the sky for a moment. "The last time I saw him, Papa told me his sons were his future. We were the ones who would carry on the family name, build the farm back up." He stuck the pipe back into his pocket. "When Mama died, I wanted to be buried with her. To just give up. Until I remembered my father's words. My brothers were gone. I was all that was left of his dream for the future."

They sat in silence watching the display above.

"I worked harder than I ever have," he continued. "But I lost the farm. I talked the bank into a year's extension, but I couldn't pay the mortgage even then. A Yankee banker came in and took over. That hurt." He shifted so that his leg rested against hers and she fought the urge to put her hand over his. "I didn't know what to do. Thought about a lot of things. Even thought maybe Jesse James and his lot had it right—robbing the Yankee banks that had stolen everything my family had."

Mercy flinched.

"I wouldn't have." He shoved his fingers through his hair. "I don't condone violence and thievery, but angry as I was, part of me thought there was some justice to it." He sucked in a deep breath and slowly released it. "I was getting desperate when Clarisse's letter came, inviting me to come west and start over. I knew I had to take a chance."

"Take a chance on happiness with the nice widow," Mercy teased.

"I owe it to Papa to start over. Build a farm. Have sons."

"And it wouldn't hurt any if she happens to be pretty."

Thad chuckled. "I wouldn't mind, no."

Mercy leaned back and laughed, giving Thad the strange desire to take her for a ride on a shooting star. Then she wrapped her arms around her legs, resting her head on her knees.

"It's different for me, Thad. It's my fault my husband died."

"Harold told me it was a bull—how is that your fault?"

She pulled in a deep breath and released it. "Nate was never meant for ranch life. He should've been a lawyer. His father had a law practice in Chicago. No loose bulls in that office, I'm sure. If it hadn't been for me . . ."

Thad kept silent, knowing there was more she needed to say.

"My last words to him were, 'we'll talk later.' Not 'I love you,' or 'I'm sorry.' " She turned away and wiped a tear from her cheek.

Thad cupped her chin and turned her face back to him. "You've lost the one person who was closest to you in your life. No one will think less of you for cryin'."

She shook her head, blinking back tears. "You don't understand the West, Thad." She set her jaw so her whole face seemed stiff—more like a bronze statue of a soldier than a warm, living woman. "I'm a female trying to run a cattle ranch—I'm not allowed to cry. If I show any weakness, no one—not buyers or ranchers or bankers— will take me seriously."

He couldn't just let her lock herself away again. "This isn't business." He placed his hand over hers and felt a shock of electricity to rival lightning. "This is you and me, alone."

Mercy looked around, as if she expected a crowd of onlookers.

"There is no 'you and me,' Thad." She looked into the darkness. "We are colleagues, not . . . not friends."

"You're mistaken, ma'am. After what we've been through together, we are most definitely friends."

She hugged her legs again and he was afraid he'd lost her. Then she lifted her head. "Then tell me, friend. If happiness can come without us earning it . . . how do we find it?" Her face was so close he could see the dampness on her eyelashes. He drew his finger from her cheekbone down her jaw.

"Be ready for the opportunity." He leaned close until his nose nearly touched hers. "Take a chance."

His lips brushed against hers and he drew back an inch, waiting for her to pull away and storm off. Or perhaps more likely haul off and punch him. She didn't move. He touched his lips back to hers, nibbling experimentally. She drew her arms around him and pulled him closer, deepening the kiss.

Her breasts pressed hard against his chest and her tongue explored his mouth with abandon. He heard a groan, which might have come from either of them as the kiss turned hot as rocks under the July sun. When she released him and drew away, the cold night air chilled him through.

"I . . . I'm sorry . . . Thad. I shouldn't have . . . I don't want you to think—" She shoved herself to her feet. "That should not have happened!" She stomped off to the cabin leaving Thad painfully aroused and confused.

Chapter 14

Mercy marched away from Thad and stumbled into the dark soddy.

"Damnation!" she muttered as she tried to find her blanket and disentangle it from Thad's. "Idiot. I'm an idiot."

She remembered again that she'd have to sleep inches away from him. She'd gone outside to avoid him and ended up confessing things she'd never told anyone. He had seen her cry. And she'd let him kiss her.

Let him? She'd practically thrown herself into his arms.

Thad walked in and nearly fell over her. "Sorry," he mumbled. "I was just lookin' for my bedroll."

"Here, I think." She held his blanket up to him.

"I'll sleep with the horses." Thad started toward the door.

"No." Mercy said. "Don't be silly. It's all mud and there's not much space. Zeus is likely to step on you. There's plenty of room here." She'd lost her mind and her mouth had nothing left controlling it.

"If you're sure?"

"Of course." Mercy kept her tone light, she hoped.

She needn't be concerned; Thad was a perfect gentleman. If she were honest, that was exactly what did worry her. Their kiss echoed in her mind and she felt heat radiate through her again. She could ignore that feeling. She would.

Her body felt rigid as she settled her head on the pillow she'd made from her buckskin jacket. She turned her back to him, vowing not to roll an inch closer. If she touched him . . . Her tongue swept across her lips as she imagined another kiss. And much more than kisses. She crossed her arms over her chest and squeezed tight.

He moved quietly, spreading his blanket next to hers. Something warm brushed her back.

"Sorry," he mumbled and scooted away from her.

She stared into the blackness, her eyes wide open, every muscle tight. She inhaled and forced her lids shut. *Calm.* She wouldn't sleep, but at least she could try to rest. Her eyes wouldn't stay shut.

Thad rolled over. She could almost feel his tension. No doubt, he was suffering as much as she was. More. Wasn't this sort of thing supposed to be more difficult for men? No. It couldn't be worse for him.

She thought of all they'd shared this evening before that kiss that had ruined everything. Except the kiss hadn't spoiled the evening, it had been . . . right. Her tongue strayed across her lip again as she remembered his taste.

She ached to touch him again, to feel his solid chest, and twine her fingers through his hair. She needed him close. Surely, there would be no harm in just one night . . .

She couldn't think of any damage it would do. The problem was she couldn't think at all. His touch had unleashed some sort of madness.

She rubbed her thumb across her wedding band, old

mistakes pushing at the edge of her mind. This was different. She didn't intend to give Thad her heart.

She rolled onto her back, her shoulder brushing against him. He wriggled away.

"Move any further, you'll be sleeping in the mud." She swept her hand along his arm and felt him tense. "Thad?"

"Hmm?" His voice was too high.

Good. He *was* suffering.

"I don't think it would be wrong if, just for tonight, we held each other." She swallowed. "And . . ."

He rolled onto his back and she leaned over him. She couldn't see his face, wasn't sure what he would think of her, but she decided to take a chance.

"I don't want you to think I make this offer to a lot of men—in fact, I've never . . ." Her mind flitted again to Nate. He'd be shocked to see her so bold. But she needed this—they needed each other. Just for one night. And she knew Thad was far too much of a gentleman to suggest it.

He lifted his hand, caressing her face before weaving his fingers through her hair and pulling her down to him. As their lips melted into each other, fire ignited deep within her. Even through layers of clothing, her nipples throbbed as they rubbed against his solid chest to the beat of a song she thought she'd long forgotten.

A moment later she came up for air, gasping before she buried her face against his neck, nibbling, tasting the salt of his skin, and breathing deeply of him. His groan echoed the hunger she felt—an emptiness that had waited far too long to be filled. He rolled them both over and she could feel the strength of his arousal as he straddled her.

He kissed her again, then retreated.

"Thad?" She watched his shadow kneeling above her, tugging at the waist of her pants. "Oh." She smiled as he unfastened her pants, pulling them down ever so slowly. She helped him, lifting and wiggling her bottom, but he continued to move with glacial speed. He pulled her trousers down to her thighs, then stopped.

"Shoot," she muttered. "Why are you stopping there?"

He chuckled. "These legs deserve a proper unveiling." He caressed her thigh. "Wish we had some light."

"Flattery is hardly necessary—"

"Ah, ah," he interrupted. "There's a right way and a wrong way to do everything. And I'm gonna do this right."

He continued slowly, fondling her legs as he dragged the fabric over her knees. She wrenched one leg out and kicked the pants away. Finally, they could get on with it. She was desperate and he was wasting time with unveilings.

"Patience," he whispered.

"Oh!" She blurted as he bent to kiss her ankle. His warm lips inched up to her calf. It was nice. It was wonderful, but she wanted him, needed him a good bit higher. She wanted to touch him, couldn't reach, and somehow couldn't think what to do about that.

He had kissed his way to her knees when she finally thought to sit up and reach for him. She massaged his shoulders, reveling in the firm muscles beneath her fingers.

When he reached her inner thighs, the hot, wet strokes of his tongue erased every thought except one—she needed more.

"Please." Her voice cracked on the only word left in her mind.

Thad moved on up to the buttons of her shirt. She helped him finish and shrugged out of her shirt.

"No need to rush." He wanted to make this last.

He slipped his hands under her chemise, sliding over her flat belly until he found her breasts—supple as a pair of ripe peaches. He discovered her nipples with his thumbs and she moaned with pleasure. Just for to-night—he'd take her on one of those shooting star rides. A short burst of joy was just what they both needed. They'd worry about tomorrow when the sun came up.

He lifted her chemise and bent to suckle one breast—soft as velvet and smelling honeysuckle sweet from the soap she favored. Too bad the night was so dark—his eyes were missing the feast. Lord, he'd never thought to find a woman built like this. He drew a hand from the curve of her hip to her luscious breast. He'd felt a few feminine bodies and imagined many more. Before meeting Mercy he thought women were supposed to be delicate—fragile. Yet the sleek muscles in her legs, her back and arms were fueling his lust as much as her soft curves did.

He ached to be inside her, but hated to end his exploration. He bent his tongue to her navel and nuzzled her belly, then tracked kisses back up to her breasts, delighted with the compact form beneath his lips.

Mercy started to open his pants, reminding him of the painful desire trapped behind the buttons. As she worked to free him, he captured her breast again, memorizing the taste and feel—the pliancy of her breast and the tiny, hard nipple erect and very sensitive, if her writhing was any indication.

"Ahh," he groaned as she pulled his pants down and captured him with her slender fingers.

"Come inside me." Her voice was urgent, pleading.

"I . . ." He lost the thought as she squeezed again, massaging, sending jolts of pleasure through him. "I don't want to make a child."

She pulled her hands up to his chest, leaving him naked and even more desperate to bury himself inside her.

"It's not . . . possible," she said. "I mean, ahh—"

He was still kneading her breast. He stopped. In a moment they'd both be beyond reason and it was important they understood what they were doing.

"I can't . . . have children. No need to worry."

"You're sure?"

"I was married nearly five years. I'm very sure."

"I mean, are you certain you want to do this."

"Yes." She nearly screamed it. "I want this."

He noticed she didn't say, "I want you." That was good, wasn't it? This was all physical. Just two adults needing each other. A game of skill, not chance.

When he didn't move, she took hold of him again. Caressing. Inviting. She drew her hands around his bare bottom and guided him down to her.

He pressed against her. She was wet and ready, but tight when he thrust inside her.

"Oh!" she cried.

"Sorry, did I hurt—"

"No," she gasped. "Been a long time is all. It's good. Nice."

"Mmm," he agreed, losing himself in the feel of her around him.

Thad settled deeper inside her and she shuddered under him. He bent to kiss her. Their tongues danced playfully together as she wrapped her legs around him, binding them into a knot that seemed unbreakable. He palmed her breast and they rocked, finding the beat together until they were both soaring.

She was hot—on fire. A shower of sparks exploding inside her core. No thought. No memories. She felt his pleasure as though it was a part of her and another shooting star carried them to oblivion together.

It was over too soon.

He relaxed and withdrew from her and she felt the hollow emptiness again. But before she could curl away from him, he wrapped his arms around her, pulling a blanket over the two of them. He nuzzled the top of her head and held one breast in his immense hand.

"Perfect fit," he mumbled against her shoulder. He pulled her to his chest.

Perfect. Except they couldn't be. She couldn't bear him the children he wanted so desperately. It was exactly how she'd lost Nate, only this time would be different because she didn't love Thad. She wouldn't be foolish enough to offer her heart to any man again.

In a little while, she felt his sleeping breath steady against her neck. Mercy allowed her eyes to drift shut, dreaming of those few moments of delight. Perhaps it was a good idea to take a chance now and then.

She snuggled against Thad, feeling warm and secure in his embrace—but not for long. Her eyes flicked open. The shelter of a man's arms was more precarious than the ramshackle roof overhead. She sure as hell was not going to allow herself to get used to this.

Mercy pulled out of Thad's grip and squirmed away from him, shivering with the loss of his warmth. She tucked a blanket around him, then rolled into her own. His steady breathing seemed miles away as she stared into the pitch black. She stifled a sigh.

It was as she'd said before—joy came in short bursts. She couldn't be truly happy any more than she could remain within Thad's arms. She curled into a tight ball, making her own shelter.

Chapter 15

One by one he teased open the buttons of her shirt before brushing his thumb along her collarbone, then into the hollow of her neck. He traced a circle with his thumb and bent to kiss her. She shivered with anticipation. She wanted to shout at him to get back to the buttons, but her voice caught in her throat when she felt his tongue warm and wet against her neck. He was so close, her senses were flooded with his heady aroma. Intoxicating. Or, perhaps it was his eyes boring into her with such intensity she thought she'd catch fire.

She inhaled his spicy fragrance again—and felt his heart beating, or was that her own?

The sound of a throat clearing woke Mercy. She sat up, pushing away from Thad and grabbing her blanket to cover her chemise. Her heart pounded. She'd fallen asleep half-naked.

She realized with horror that she'd been curled up against him, though she recalled taking great pains to stay away after they'd . . . Oh hell, the dream was nothing compared to what they'd actually done last night. She swallowed.

He was watching her, amused. The golden hair on

his bare chest reflected the sunlight streaming in through the window. Her first view of the ragged scar on his shoulder did nothing to diminish the urge she felt to touch him—to rest her head against his chest and feel his arms around her again.

"Thad!" She meant to sound indignant, but her voice was hoarse with sleep.

He raised an eyebrow, then, still reclining, stretched. The blanket fell to his hips and the muscles on his abdomen rippled as he moved. Damn, the man was cocky. It was her fault for throwing herself at him last night. Unless somehow he knew he'd been in her dreams. She tried to read his eyes, wondering whether she'd spoken in her sleep.

"You were staring at me!" This time she managed to sound indignant, though he still looked amused.

"I was enjoying watching you sleep." He placed his hands behind his head, leaning back, watching her. "The morning sun brings out the gold in your hair."

She pulled on her shirt, fumbled with the buttons and left it hanging open as she looked around for her pants. When had she taken those off? No. It was him. Thad had removed most of her clothing, though she'd certainly helped.

"I'm sorry." Thad sat up. "Didn't mean to embarrass you."

She shook her head. "I was just surprised, is all." She glared at him.

What did she expect? She'd been too caught up in her desires to consider the consequences of her actions last night.

"I didn't get a chance to see you last night." He flashed his dimple, but she resolved to ignore it.

He sat up and reached a hand to her face. She drew back, pulling the blanket up around her again.

"Why are you angry?" he asked.

"A gentleman wouldn't be staring at a lady."

"Even a gentleman can't help wanting to see what he's touched and kissed."

"Last night was last night. It's over. We had an agreement."

"I don't remember agreeing—"

"I said, 'just for tonight.' Don't you remember?"

Thad nodded. "Yes." He captured her hand in his. "But I think perhaps . . ." He leaned forward until his lips brushed hers, sending sparks shooting down through her body and on to her toes. She stretched her arms around him, feeling the solid muscle of his back, her right hand fondled his naked bottom. The blankets dropped and there was nothing between them but her chemise and he was lifting that, finding her breast. Her insides were softening like wax melting in a flame.

"No!" She pushed him away. "Not again. It was only that we needed each other last night . . ." She bit her tongue, lest she admit how much she needed his touch still.

She turned away from his beautiful naked body and reached for her pants. One cuff was wet from sitting in a mud puddle. She had thrown them without thinking. Another sign that she'd completely lost her senses. She squirmed into her pants under the blanket. She glared at Thad, but he didn't turn away. He sat there shamelessly watching her. And . . . his blanket did little to hide the fact that he was fully aroused. She fought an instinct to reach for him.

Instead, she pulled her pants up, then stood with her back to him to find the buttons. "It was just for one night. I won't . . . I can't make a habit of . . ."

"Of what? Enjoying yourself?"

She kept her back to him to hide the fact that she was blushing. She could hear him dressing. At least she hoped he was covering himself, because there were limits to a woman's resistance. Suddenly he was next to her, his hand on her shoulder.

"Mr. Buchanan," she snapped, then turned to him, sucking in a calming breath. He didn't deserve her wrath. She was only angry with herself.

He'd put his pants on. That was some help. "Thad. Please, just keep your distance in the future."

He placed his hand on her elbow. "Did I offend you in some way? I mean, last night you seemed so sure, so willing—"

"You don't understand, this has nothing to do with last night." She couldn't stand the hurt look in his eyes. "Sorry. I'd forgotten the importance of male pride. You were perfect last night. Very manly. I'm most grateful. Now, I just want to forget it ever happened."

He squeezed her shoulder. His face twisted into an imitation smile. "Can't say that'll come natural to me."

She shrugged away from him. "Nevertheless."

Thad nodded. "As you wish."

Too bad she wasn't certain what she did wish.

Once again, Thad watched Mercy's braid swishing across her back as she rode Annabelle. He'd put all his chips in on one big hand and lost. That was all. It had happened to him plenty of times. Take a chance on a pair of queens and another player comes up with three of a kind.

It's not as though he wanted marriage to Mercy. A maternal woman like the widow Hansen would suit him better. He knew that without even meeting her, just from Mercy's description. She was kind-hearted and loved her children. She could give him the sons he needed to carry on his father's name. Mercy said she was pretty too. And she had land.

Not that he'd marry a woman for her farm. He'd

been building a stake slowly at the poker table, wouldn't be long before he had enough to buy some property. That was part of the reason Thad had come west. He aimed to build a farm, even if he had to start with land that had never seen a plow. It wouldn't make up for losing Papa's farm. But it was a start.

He stared at Mercy's back, remembering the curves her jacket hid so well. He would have to bury the memories of Mercy's luscious flesh if he was going to be a faithful husband. That wasn't going to be easy. Her ripe breasts, round hips and supple legs. *Damn.* It was going to be uncomfortable sitting in the saddle all day if he didn't find something else to think about.

He moved Zeus up next to her. "Weather's surprisingly fair after that big storm."

She glanced at him with the determined face of a granite warrior. "So you said earlier. Twice."

"Truth is, I'm afraid to talk about anything but weather."

"Why talk then?"

"Because we have six or seven days left on the trail and . . ."

"And silence is uncomfortable?"

"The silence leaves my mind to . . . wander."

Though the shadow of her hat obscured her face, he somehow knew that she understood exactly where his mind was wandering.

"Do you want me to tell you more about Ingrid Hansen?"

"What I want is . . ." He wasn't certain. He might like to stop the horses and smother her with kisses. No. He wanted to get to Fort Victory and find the right woman for him. "I'd just like to go back to yesterday when we were able to talk easily."

She made a show of scanning the broad expanse of plains around them. In another day or two, the mountains would be visible in the distance. Now there was nothing but flat grassland in every direction, except where the meandering river occasionally came into view to the north of the trail.

There was nothing to see around them, but she couldn't look back into that face without thinking of his lips on hers. And the hundred other places his lips had touched. Places he would never touch again—no matter how much she wanted him. He needed a woman like Ingrid Hansen. A woman who could give him children. The family he dreamed of having.

"You're right. We mustn't let . . . the events of last night change things between us," Mercy said. But how things had changed.

"We were becoming friends, I think."

She had to turn then, to show him the smile she'd practiced for so long. "Of course we'll be friends, Thad." She turned back to the trail. "Not that I have a lot of time for socializing with the ranch to run. You'll see me at church and . . . there are so few women around Fort Victory we are all good friends. I'll be calling on your wife from time to time . . ."

"My . . . wife?"

"Once you find one, I mean."

She squinted ahead. There was a wagon with people moving around it. Still too far to make out how many people, but it didn't look like a crowd.

"And I suppose . . . you may find a husband—"

"No." Her voice was too loud and she bit her lip, taking a moment to regain control. "I don't intend to remarry. I like my independence."

"Independence?"

"Of course. You've no doubt noticed that I'm not like other women. I like to take charge, make the decisions."

"And your husband didn't let you."

"Let me?" She choked out a laugh. "He had no choice. Do you suppose he would have sent to England for those Hereford bulls? That was my idea."

"Of course. I should have realized," he said. "Lucky you didn't have any children then."

"Lucky?" The invisible vise squeezed her heart until it ached, but she kept her smile in place.

"I mean, I reckon it would have been harder with children to raise . . ."

"Yes, lucky." She swallowed, but couldn't get rid of the lump in her throat. "A bunch of squalling brats would have made things difficult. No time for that sort of thing." She needed a distraction. "Is that a wagon?"

Thad squinted in the direction she was pointing. "Yes. And something isn't quite right . . ."

They approached the wagon cautiously until they spotted the children playing chase around it. A woman was hanging laundry over a line, while a man sat nearby hacking at a log with an ax. The family appeared to have been camped on this spot for some time. One look at the wagon provided an explanation for that. It rested at an angle—the rear end sat over wheels as it should, but the front was flat on the ground.

The man stood as they approached and walked over to them.

"Afternoon, sir," Thad said as he dismounted. "Looks like you could use some assistance." He turned to the woman who wiped her hands on her apron as she walked toward them. "Afternoon, ma'am."

"Praise the Lord," the woman said. "Albert, I do believe these are the very folks we've been praying for."

"I believe you're right, Martha." The man spoke with a distinctive New England twang. "Axle broke a few days

ago. We're carrying a spare, but I'll need help to mount
the wagon upon it. And you're the first folks to come
along." He shook his head and extended a hand. "Sorry,
we've been stuck here for so long, I've forgotten my
manners. Name's Sanders."

Thad reached out to take Mr. Sanders's hand, but
froze when Mercy leaped forward. Everyone turned to
watch her snatch a toddler who was reaching for the
cauldron that hung from a tripod over the fire.

Mrs. Sanders gasped and the little one started screaming.

Mercy handed the child to her mother. "Sorry. I was
afraid she would burn herself."

"Don't apologize. I . . ." Mrs. Sanders was looking
very pale and her husband helped her sit down. "I know
better than to turn my back on this child." Mrs. Sanders
started crying.

"It's all right, Martha. Liza's fine." He patted his
wife's shoulder. "Don't get yourself riled up now, 'tisn't
good for the baby."

Mrs. Sanders put her hand over her belly then and
Thad realized she was carrying another child.

Sanders looked at Mercy. "We owe you a debt, Missus . . ."

"Clarke." Mercy nodded and offered one of her rare
smiles. "Mercy Clarke."

Sanders glanced over at the two older girls. "Come
sit here with your mother," he ordered.

The two little girls came forward, cautiously keeping
their eyes on Thad. He smiled, but they both continued
their wide-eyed stares.

Sanders looked at his wife. "Do we have some re-
freshment to offer our visitors?"

"I could make some coffee." She swiped a handkerchief over her eyes and blew her nose, holding Liza as
close as she could to her protruding belly.

"That won't be necessary, ma'am," Thad said. "Why don't we get to work on that wagon?"

"I appreciate your help," Sanders said.

Mercy was getting very tired of singing "London Bridge," but the little girls were enjoying it. She might be able to think of another song for them to sing if she weren't so distracted by the sight of Thad Buchanan, shirtless in the afternoon sun. Damn, he was fine. Watching him work—pushing and lifting the wagon only emphasized the power of his arms—the way his broad shoulders tapered down to his waist, the ridges on his solid stomach. Her fingers ached to touch him again—hell, not just her fingers.

"One more time?" the middle girl—Mary—asked.

Mercy smiled and began to sing, "London Bridge is falling down" . . .

Beads of sweat rolled down Thad's face and neck. He took a swig of water, allowing the cool liquid to sit in his mouth before it spilled down his throat. They'd been working for hours and had finally managed to lift the wagon onto its axle.

"I'm mighty grateful to you for your assistance," Sanders said.

"You're most welcome, sir." Thad's right shoulder protested as he lifted it to release some of the tension from his muscles. "Glad I could help."

It was clear that the diminutive Sanders would never have been able to lift the wagon and his three young daughters and pregnant wife would not be of much assistance.

"What brings you out to this wilderness, Mr. Sanders?" Thad was too polite to add *alone*.

"Hoped to bring the Bible to some of the minin' camps in the Rocky Mountains, then maybe move on to California."

"Then it's Reverend Sanders?"

"Didn't I say?"

"I reckon I missed that in the confusion."

Thad and Sanders crawled under the wagon to inspect the new axle they had installed.

"Looks like she'll hold," Thad commented.

"Yep. Stronger'n the original, I expect." Sanders patted the axle proudly.

Thad shrugged back into his shirt and rubbed his aching shoulder.

"War wound, is it?" Reverend Sanders asked.

Thad nodded and dropped his hand.

"Infantry?"

"Yes." Thad busied himself with the buttons on his shirt.

"Sorry, didn't mean to pry." Sanders slapped his hip. "I've still got a bit of lead here to remind me of the war. Served in the 20th Maine Infantry myself."

Thad stared at the wagon.

Sanders glanced over at the women. "My wife says I talk over much about near everything, but I have no desire to recount the war—rest assured."

Thad took a deep breath. "I'm from Tennessee, Reverend Sanders. Confederate territory—at least my family . . ."

"I had kin in Georgia." Sanders placed a hand on Thad's elbow. "Sometimes wondered if I was shooting at a cousin. Then I realized we're all cousins." He cleared his throat. "Forgive me—it's been a while since I've been in a pulpit, so I find myself sermonizing at the most inappropriate moments." He pulled a handkerchief from his pocket and wiped his brow. "You and Mrs. Clarke will have supper with us, won't you? We have fresh meat—snagged an antelope this morning."

Thad glanced over at Mercy who bounced little Liza on her back and led the others in singing nursery rhymes. Mrs. Sanders sat nearby, one eye on the supper cooking over the fire, the other on Mercy and the girls. Thad suspected both parents were glad of a little adult company.

"We'd be pleased to stay. That's very kind of you."

"Well then." Sanders crawled out from under the wagon with Thad following. "There's a swimmin' hole downstream a ways. How 'bout we drift down there and get ourselves cleaned up. I dare say the wives will appreciate us more when we smell a little better."

Wives?

Thad stared at Sanders's back. He opened his mouth to correct him, then hesitated. He thought back over the afternoon. With the confusion over the baby and the fire, had his name been confused? Or perhaps Mercy had told Sanders they were married. He had spoken with Mercy alone briefly, while Thad was filling his canteen. It seemed safest simply to keep his mouth shut. After all, it was just for the one night.

"It's the most beautiful place on God's earth," Mercy said. "Our ranch is high up, but most of our land is flat—perfect grazing country. The mountains just shoot straight up from the plain, like giant soldiers guarding us."

"Are we going to see those giants, Pa?" the oldest girl asked.

"Yes, missy," Sanders said. She moved behind her father and peered at Thad over Sanders's shoulder. "Are they bigger'n him?" she whispered loudly enough that they all heard.

Mercy laughed, a musical sound that made Thad's heart skip a beat.

"Yes, child," she said. "Those mountains are even bigger than Thad."

Their eyes locked and it was as though she had touched him. Warmth shot through his chest. He leaned toward her, nearly forgetting dinner, Sanders and all.

"Mrs. Clarke is talking about mountains, sweetheart." The reverend's words brought Thad to his senses. "You know what those are." The little girl nodded. "We're going to see those mountains and cross over them too."

Mrs. Sanders placed a hand over her belly. "We may not be able to cross them before spring."

Mercy nodded. "Winter comes early to the mountain passes. You don't want to be caught by a storm up there this time of year."

Sanders turned to Thad. "What do you think?"

Thad glanced at Mercy. "Mercy's the expert. She's more familiar . . ." He remembered Sanders thought they were married. "I mean, she knows some folks who made the crossing. Don't you, Mercy?"

"I know several. Including your sister, though she and Wendell crossed west to east—from San Francisco to Fort Victory."

Mrs. Sanders bent to cut a bit of meat for the little one. While the Sanders had been camped here, they'd seen no game until this morning. Parents and children were excited to have fresh meat. Thad reckoned the antelope was more welcome than the rattler he'd discovered in the cabin yesterday. Had that been yesterday? He glanced at Mercy. It seemed like a lifetime ago.

"It's a blessing you folks happened by when you did," Sanders said. "An answer to our prayers."

"Glad we could help." Thad, realizing he was rubbing his shoulder again, put his hand in his lap.

"Albert, perhaps we should ask these folks to join us as far as Denver?"

"We'd be—" Thad started.

"No!" Mercy said. "I mean, I'm sorry—we can't. I have to get to Fort Victory before the fifteenth of October and we've lost a good deal of time already."

Thad had forgotten about Mercy's deadline. He cleared his throat. "I'm afraid Mercy's right. We must move on."

"I'm sorry we delayed you folks," Sanders said.

"Please, I didn't mean to make it sound as though . . . we are glad to have been able to help." Mercy's voice was calm again. "We have a week which should be plenty of time." She worried her lip. "Only, I'd rather be home ahead of schedule. If we go through Denver and—"

"And with the wagon and the children slowing you down," Mrs. Sanders said. "We understand."

"Quite sensible," Sanders said. "We have no reason to rush, but you do. Again, we thank you for taking the time today. You've both been very kind."

The adult conversation flowed between demands from the girls for help cutting food, more water, and a story before bed. The youngest finally abandoned her plate altogether and settled on her mother's lap where Thad was surprised to see her snuggle under her mother's shawl to nurse. Thad turned to Reverend Sanders who was smiling, obviously used to all the activity.

"You don't have children?" Sanders asked.

"Don't be silly, Albert. Can't you see they're newly-weds?"

Thad looked at Mercy and saw she was blushing. The look on her face told him, it had not been she who'd informed the Sanders they were married. He realized Mrs. Sanders had asked him something and turned to her.

"You are newlyweds, aren't you, Mr. Clarke?" she repeated.

He glanced at Mercy again, but she was looking down at her plate and offered no assistance. "Well, it's fair to say we haven't been married for long."

"See, Albert. I knew it. Only newlyweds look at each other the way these two do. A woman can always tell these things."

He saw more than surprise in Mercy's eyes, but he doubted it was the adoring look of a newlywed. More like the warning glare of a woman with a whip.

Chapter 16

After supper, Thad suggested a sing-along. He tuned his guitar and started the music before Mercy could pull him aside to lecture him. If he could get Mercy singing, there was some chance she wouldn't kill him. He'd discovered at Fort Kearny that music calmed her as nothing else could.

Soon everyone was in a festive mood. The girls wanted to sing silly songs like "The Blue Tail Fly" and "Listen to the Mockingbird." Thad was happy to oblige. Anything to keep Mercy from glaring at him.

When Liza returned to her mother's lap to nurse, the older girls snuggled up to their father, but after a moment one of them crawled over to Mercy and curled into her lap. Thad was surprised when Mercy opened her arms and didn't try to send the girl back to her father. Thad switched to quiet ballads. Harmonizing with Mercy felt so natural, it was as though they'd been singing together forever.

The girls were soon dozing. Mercy cradled the oldest, who was likely no more than five years old. Mercy smiled, her eyes focused on the child's face, her long, graceful fingers stroking the girl's hair. All afternoon and evening she'd spent time with the children, laughing and playing as though it came naturally to her. Perhaps she didn't object to "squalling brats" so long as they weren't on her ranch.

Mercy turned to Mrs. Sanders. "Can't believe she fell asleep so quickly."

"That's my Dotty. Ball of fire one minute, fast asleep the next." She yawned. "Best get these children to bed before I fall asleep."

Sanders helped his wife to her feet and they each carried a child to the wagon. Mercy followed with Dotty in her arms.

"Won't be long before you have your own little ones, I expect," Mrs. Sanders said to Mercy.

Thad strained to hear her response, though he wasn't sure why.

He slipped away to sit near the creek. He wasn't avoiding Mercy exactly, just hoping she'd keep her distance. A vain hope, as it turned out. A few minutes later she marched over to him.

"Why did you tell them you were my husband?" Mercy hissed, as she dropped to the ground next to him.

Thad turned to face her. "I didn't. I thought you did to protect your reputation."

"My rep . . . ?" Mercy shook her head. "My reputation would have been just fine if you'd corrected them in the first place."

"So why didn't you?" Thad studied her face in the fading light—so beautiful and so near. If he leaned just a little, his lips could touch her cheeks, her forehead, her lips—now drawn into a tight, angry line. "I waited for you to say something."

"How could I? With the children there and everyone obviously thinking . . ." Mercy turned to gaze at the Sanders's wagon.

He leaned closer, betting she wouldn't punch him with the Sanders so near.

His gamble paid off. He brushed her lips with his, once, twice, then lips parted, she met him full force. Her sinewy arms fit around him perfectly. As though she were made for him.

When their tongues met it set off a conflagration— heat spreading out from his belly, the flames causing a throbbing ache that made him want to strip her clothes off and bury himself inside her.

Mercy pulled away, but gently and not far. He touched his lips to her forehead before pulling back enough to see her face. She was smiling. He knew he was grinning broadly, but he couldn't help it. So much for all his best intentions.

"That's all you're getting of your marital rights tonight, Mr. Clarke," she mocked, but her smile remained as she walked away.

Thad sucked on his pipe, though it wasn't lit. His heart was still pounding. She was completely wrong for him in every way but one. He should put her out of his mind, should avoid her kisses and he definitely shouldn't make love to her again. Yet, when she was near him . . .

He wanted a quiet, domestic life. Mercy wanted her ranch and her independence. She didn't want a husband or a family. Still, she had allowed him to come along with her and he'd be ever grateful to her for that. He let out a long breath. How easy it would be to convince himself he could show gratitude and indulge his own longing for her at the same time.

That would be wrong. He must offer her the hand of friendship. They could be friends even after they reached Fort Victory and he found himself a bride. She had tried to tell him so this morning and he'd misunderstood. He'd been so caught up in his own burning desire for her that he couldn't think straight. Well, he was thinking now and he knew what he needed to do.

Mercy sat on her blankets trying to decide whether to take off her boots. No point. She'd never sleep with memories of that kiss circling round her mind. Once again she had allowed him to befuddle her. She punched the saddle next to her, then flexed her fingers as the pain brought her back to reality.

The campsite was quiet now that the children had settled. The parents spoke in whispers on the other side of the wagon. Standing, Mercy looked up at a sliver of moon and countless stars decorating the black canopy above her. It was an awesome sight that never failed to move her. She couldn't control the stars, but she could depend on them to be there. The same stars, the same moon, night after night. Even when clouds covered them, she knew they were there. She'd always found that comforting.

Returning her gaze to earth, she caught sight of Thad still sitting by the water. She had thought it would be simple to keep her distance from him. And it had been easy while she believed he was merely an arrogant rogue who claimed poker was a game of skill. Just her luck, he turned out to be a good man. *And a mighty fine kisser.* She pressed her finger to the place where his mustache had tickled her face. Pushing to her feet, she walked to the edge of camp.

She didn't need a man. All she wanted was to return

quickly to Colorado, pay Lansing, and get on with running her ranch. To keep warm at night, she'd get a dog. Men were far too risky.

She strolled through the cottonwood trees along the creek. Rubbing her thumb along her wedding ring, her thoughts turned to Nate. She would never marry again. It was best for her and her family if she remained single. Besides, she never wanted to love again, to feel the pain of loss, the helplessness of inadvertently hurting the one you love. Her decision had been easy and she'd never had second thoughts about it. Until her body had betrayed her, hungering for a man against her will.

Mercy moved deeper into the trees. The night air near the creek was moist and almost chilly, a pleasant change from the blistering day. Mercy inhaled deeply, her eyes closed as she listened to the chirping of crickets, the rustling of small critters in the brush. Her widowhood had made her free. Being unable to have children should give her an added measure of freedom. She smiled at the irony that something good could come from that painful fact. A wild horse would never walk into a corral and close the gate behind itself, yet Mercy had built this corral herself. It was time to open the gate and run free.

A footfall snapped her back to reality. Her hand flew to her Colt.

"Mercy?"

She released her breath at the sound of Thad's voice. "I'm here," she said, holstering her gun and stepping toward his voice.

"Thought you might like some company."

"I was just enjoying the cool evening air."

"It is pleasant." Thad was so close the brim of her hat skimmed his chin.

He removed her hat. "A penny for your thoughts," he whispered.

Mercy swallowed. "My thoughts are a good bit more valuable than that." She retrieved her hat and slipped away from him.

He followed, snatching her hat again. She turned to look at him in the shadows. "How much?"

"Priceless."

He chuckled. "Everything has a price."

"Ten dollars, then."

He hesitated. "Too dear."

"Suit yourself." She walked away.

"Wait!"

She turned back to him. "I'll pay you five now and another five if your thoughts prove to be worth the price."

Mercy held out her hand and felt him place a coin in it.

"I was thinking how foolish I was to let you kiss me just now." She smiled, knowing her words were very nearly true.

"No."

"What do you mean, 'no'?"

"No, you don't regret kissing me."

Mercy drew a quick breath, but Thad continued. "Don't try to deny it, you enjoyed that kiss and would like another."

"You'd like to think so!" The man was dangerous—he read her too well.

"It's true." Thad drew closer until she could feel his breath against her forehead, he traced his index finger across her chin, rubbed his nose against hers, then brushed his lips against her nose. Mercy leaned forward, lips parted. She nearly lost her balance when he stepped back. "I rest my case."

"That wasn't fair!"

"I was simply trying to prove a point." Thad held his hand out. "Now, I believe you owe me a full refund."

Mercy placed the coin in his hand. "Thank you," he said, pocketing the money.

"Now, you owe me something." She wrapped her arms around his neck, lacing her fingers through his hair.

Their lips met in a surge of energy that released the last of her inhibitions. She slipped her arms around his waist, pulling him against her. His hands roamed under her jacket, inching slowly up her back while his tongue explored her mouth. Mercy's hands found their way under his jacket. Even through his vest and shirt, she felt the solid strength of his chest.

She pulled open the buttons of his vest and began working on his tie—all this clothing was in the way. Without releasing her lips, Thad shrugged off his jacket and threw it on the ground, pulling her down on top of it. She tore off her own jacket and soon had his shirt opened, her fingers kneading the solid muscle over his ribs. Somehow he'd loosened her braid and was now pulling his fingers through her hair as he kissed her, endlessly kissed her, his mustache tickling her lip, his tongue probing deeper and deeper.

He pulled his mouth away from hers. His breathing was ragged. "We can't do this."

Mercy sat up. She hadn't noticed the top buttons on her shirt were open. She was panting, her heart pounding. Why had he stopped? She caressed Thad's face. His cheek was rough with two days' growth of beard. Her lips tingled from rubbing against that face. She wanted so much more.

He pulled her hand away. "No more."

"Why . . . why not?"

"It's not right. We had an agreement to be friends."

"We can still be friends. I'm not looking for marriage—"

"But I am."

"And I won't stand in your way. Once we arrive at Fort Victory and you find your bride, I'll step aside. Until then—"

"No." He stood up, towering over her. "It was pleasant enough for one night, but I can't indulge your . . . your desires again. There are limits to charity, my dear."

"Charity?" She pushed to her feet.

"Certainly. You didn't think there was anything special between us, did you?"

"No," she whispered, "of course not."

"Glad we understand each other." He took in a deep breath. "I won't play a hand when I know for certain I'm gonna lose."

She stepped away quickly, pulling her jacket tight against the sudden chill she felt.

Chapter 17

Mercy sat near the fire, pulling her brush slowly through her hair until she lost count of the strokes. She had to numb her brain and keep from thinking of Thad's rejection. It was for the best, but the truth was, it hurt. Charity, he'd called it. She had thought he felt the same attraction she did. But then, she'd thought the same thing about Nate. Though perhaps her husband had felt something at first.

The fire was nearly dead, but her eyes had adjusted to the darkness now. Thad hadn't emerged from the woods. The shadow of the Sanders's wagon was silent except for the sound of Reverend Sanders snoring. At least she assumed the snoring was his.

She pulled her jacket tight around her, reassured by the extra padding. Even after the expense of staying at Fort Kearny and the money she'd left for Miranda and Harold, she still had a thousand dollars for Lansing sewn inside the lining. If all went well, she'd make her payment in a few days—ahead of schedule. Unless they had another delay. She wasn't going to think about that possibility.

They'd have to sell some cows at the mining camps to purchase winter supplies, but that was nothing new. Maybe now would be a good time to sell some of the Hereford bulls. They'd proven their value for breeding. She rolled her spare blanket into a pillow and set her Colt under it. Time enough to plan for the future after she was home safe.

She couldn't wait to see the expression on Lansing's face. An icy cold pain—as though she'd been shot with hail—hit her stomach. No, she wasn't looking forward to seeing Lansing. She shuddered. The image of slate-gray skies came to her and she felt the chill in the pit of her stomach spread through her body until she was shivering.

Nate's funeral. It had started that day. Not one to waste time on sentiment, Lansing had remained behind to speak to her as the rest of the mourners filed away.

She still remembered bracing herself when she saw him lingering. She'd never let him see her cry. It would be hard enough to convince him that she'd be able to repay his loan without the help of any men. She couldn't allow him to think her weak.

"Now, Mercy, I don't want you to worry about the loan payments," he said, surprising her with his words, then further surprising her by reaching out and placing an arm on her shoulder.

"That's kind of you, Mr. Lansing," Mercy replied. "With my father laid up and Nate . . ." She swallowed to prevent the tremor in her voice from betraying her emotions. "And with Nate gone, it will take a bit longer. But rest assured, you will have your money and the interest we promised."

"I've no doubt of it, my dear. And please, call me Arthur." The corners of his mouth bent in an approximation of a grin. "Mercy, I am a businessman and not given to emotions. I understand you'll need some time.

When you are ready, I believe a merger of our two enterprises would be most profitable for both of us. And I have my son to consider. He needs a mother."

His words had puzzled her then. She couldn't imagine how joining their ranches would provide a mother for Lansing's son. It was months later, after Lansing deemed that a "proper time had passed" that he made his intentions clear. He wanted her ranch, true, but he also wanted her.

"Don't be too hasty, my dear. I believe that marriage will have as many benefits for you as it would have for me. I know you're fond of my son and perhaps I could succeed where Nathaniel failed in providing you with a child of your own as well." His leer had made her sick to her stomach.

Mercy had worked to control her anger. Lansing's loan was secured by her ranch and she wouldn't risk forfeiting the ranch by losing her temper. She understood why he wanted her land—it was a matter of water. Jake's Creek had proven a reliable water source, while the creek that ran through Lansing's ranch dried up most summers.

She had forced herself to remain calm, begged him for more time. His patience had been wearing thin. Each time they met in public, he greeted her with a warm handshake, which he invariably held longer than necessary. His gaze always settled on her chest, giving her the feeling that she was a horse being considered for purchase. In spite of layers of clothing, Lansing's stare always left her feeling exposed.

She crossed her arms over her bosom. Apparently, she was nothing but a body to Lansing. To Thad and Nate she wasn't even that. Thad and Nate. The only two men who had ever shared her bed and they'd both found her wanting.

Perhaps there was something wrong with her after

all. Her mother-in-law had said that a real woman wouldn't want to wear men's clothes and do men's work. Nate's mother hadn't been surprised that Mercy couldn't conceive. She'd always felt it was jealousy that made her mother-in-law write such mean-spirited things. After all, she'd taken the woman's son so far away from home. All the healers, midwives and doctors Mercy had consulted had told her the same thing—women who had the kind of trouble she did with her monthly visitor often had trouble conceiving. Still, something had made Nate stop desiring her. And Thad clearly didn't want her either.

It was hard for Thad to get used to the abrupt way the sun rose on the plains. Or maybe it was the way Mercy sprang up, ready to move. Thad needed a little time and some hot coffee before he was ready to face the trail.

"Don't let my wife see you cookin'," Sanders said when he saw Thad brewing the coffee. "She'd likely get ideas."

"Self-defense," Thad explained. "You wouldn't want to taste the mud Mercy calls coffee."

"My specialty is the washing up." Mercy's laugh seemed forced.

Sanders chuckled, then walked off shaking his head.

Thad handed Mercy her coffee, watching her wrap her long, lean fingers around the tin cup. He smiled at the familiar ritual as she held the cup under her nose and sighed, appreciating the aroma for a moment before she took her first sip. She was hatless and the morning sun found the gold and copper in her hair.

She turned away without speaking to him. No doubt she was still chafing over his words from last night. Well, he deserved it. That wasn't the way he had wanted to remedy the situation. He had planned simply to keep his distance. Lord help him.

He'd seen plenty of lovely women in his life, but there was something different about Mercy. Even now, he ached for her. Fortunately, after his cold words last night he was certain Mercy would stay far away from him.

He'd miss her when their journey was over. He loved the musical sound of her laugh. He wanted to remember it, along with her smile and her sonorous voice crooning a lullaby to the children. Except that image of Mercy with the children was too domestic. He mustn't make the mistake of imagining her in a role she couldn't accept.

She was right when she said his feelings for her were merely physical. She was beautiful—her body as full of contradictions as the lady herself. Her cheeks were soft, but not the cottony softness of a lady who spent her days protected from the sun, more like kid leather. Her hands were slender and sleek, but callused from years of ranch work; her legs and arms sinewy, in contrast to the delicious curves of her body. Closing his eyes, he could almost feel her breast pillowed against his hand. He snapped his eyes open, drained his coffee cup and smoothed his mustache before his gaze was drawn back to Mercy. He lifted his cup to his lips again, then remembered it was empty. Letting out a long, slow breath, he shook his head. Lust was a powerful force, but he wouldn't allow it to overcome him. For Mercy's sake as well as his own.

Turning away, he watched Mrs. Sanders brushing Dotty's long golden hair while the two little ones sat nearby playing at brushing their dolls. He smiled. Then Dotty kicked at the dirt until she sent a cloud of dust over little Liza.

The toddler started fussing and grabbed a handful of

dirt to retaliate. Her father scooped her up and persuaded her to release the dirt safely on the ground.
Sanders set her upon his shoulders so that she could
"help" him with his chores. He was a good father—the
sort who did things with the children rather than leaving them to their mother. Thad scratched his head,
wondering if he was ready to be a parent.

"You're done now." Mrs. Sanders patted Dotty on the
shoulder. "Come along, Mary."

When Dotty didn't move off her mother's lap, her
younger sister tried to push her off.

"Dotty," Mercy called. "I could sure use your help
over here." Dotty grinned and scampered off to join
her.

Mrs. Sanders mouthed, "Thank you," and Mercy
shrugged before bending to explain her task to Dotty.

At one time, after the bitter losses of the war, Thad
had stopped hoping for a family of his own. But Clarisse's
letters finally brought him to his senses. He had to carry
on. He couldn't waste his life bemoaning his failures.
He'd failed as a soldier, let his mother die and lost the
family farm. So long as he had life and breath, he had a
chance to make up for all of that. If he were very lucky,
he might not only redeem himself, but find joy as well.

His eyes drifted back to Mercy. He couldn't be happy
with someone like her. She was so caught up in her
ranch she didn't want children around to pester her.
He needed sons to carry on his father's name and land
to build a future for his sons.

He watched her packing Clover with help from Dotty.
She pointed to a pack she wanted Dotty to hand her. The
child quickly complied, as if it were a game. She was rewarded with one of Mercy's rare grins. Thad sighed,
knowing she would not have any more smiles for him.

* * *

Thad rode next to Mercy, though she seemed miles away. She had hardly spoken to him since they left the Sanders's camp day before yesterday, except to give him instructions. They'd been riding for over an hour this morning in silence.

"Beautiful day." Thad had to try.

"Hmm?" Mercy turned to him with the same dull look she'd worn all day yesterday. Had his rejection hurt her so badly? He was only trying to do what was best for both of them.

"Let's head down to the river." Mercy's voice was all business. "We need to water the horses more frequently with all the climbing we're doing."

Thad nodded, dismounted and led Zeus to the river. Mercy followed with Annabelle and Clover. While the horses meandered into the shallow water, Mercy walked a few yards downstream, then picked up a stone and threw it into the water. Thad watched her hunt another stone and throw it so that it skipped across the water. The river was too shallow and rocky for skipping stones where he stood, but Mercy had found a place where the water pooled.

She removed her hat and skipped a few more stones, hunting carefully to choose each one before she launched it. His father had taught him to look for a smooth flat stone, preferably round or oval in shape. He remembered more than one fishing expedition turning into a stone skipping contest when Thad had lost patience with waiting for fish. Someday he'd teach his own sons the game.

He walked over to Mercy, picked up a stone and threw.

"Three skips," Mercy said. "Not bad."

She threw four skips and grinned. Her smile broke through like sunshine on a cloudy day and he felt his pulse increase. The reaction was so unexpected he couldn't move.

"Go on," she said. "Try and beat that."

He hesitated, then searched for a suitable rock.

"Here's one," she said and handed him a stone.

He turned it in his hand, feeling the smooth surface. It was round and nearly flat. Perfect. His left side facing the river, he cocked his right arm and let the stone fly. One, two, three. The stone sank.

She was still smiling.

"Guess I'm out of practice," he said.

Mercy bent to retrieve her hat, giving him a view of her round, supple bottom. He turned away.

It wouldn't be fair to indulge his lust with her when he intended to find another woman. A woman who could give him sons. He imagined a stone skipping contest with a laughing child. They'd spend the day together, eating the lunch his wife would pack, and then they'd come home to tell of their adventures.

He watched Mercy checking the horses and knew things would be very different with her. She wasn't the type of woman to sit at home while her husband enjoyed an adventure. She'd go with him. He remembered her, so alive and happy playing with the Sanders children. She would be a wonderful mother. It was a shame she didn't want little ones.

"Coming?" Mercy's mellow voice penetrated his thoughts. He'd missed her voice, her smile, these past two days. Lord, how he would miss her when they parted at the end of the journey.

"On my way." Thad reached for one more stone, took a step toward the water, bent low and hurled it. One, two, three, four, five skips. He punched into the air in triumph. Mercy laughed and he added a bass to her melody.

"I didn't think five was even possible in that small pool," Mercy said.

"Just lucky, I reckon."

She mounted Annabelle. "Not skill?"

He climbed onto Zeus and turned to look into her eyes—sparks of green lightning to match her teasing words. Not the sad muddy-creek green of these past few days. A lifetime of laughing with Mercy, skipping stones and worrying over the cattle would be worth ten lifetimes of quiet domesticity, if he could find a way.

Chapter 18

The next evening, Mercy watched Thad organize the pots over the hot coals while she combed Annabelle's thick mane. If she tried to cook more than one thing at a time, supper would be burned, raw or some of each. Any fool who thought bringing a meal together was a feminine skill had never watched Thad Buchanan set a Dutch oven atop a pile of hot coals, or measure coffee into the pot. It wasn't just a task—it was a ritual. Thad made sure the supper was done right. He moved the coffee pot to the side because boiling too long would make it bitter.

She remembered how he'd insisted on doing things right that night in the soddy with mud all around them. Hell, he'd made her half crazy the way he took his time. As he crouched low near the fire, the locks of gold hair hanging over his collar emphasized the width of his shoulders. He'd removed his jacket and vest and she could see the muscles of his back, arms and legs working. No doubt about it, it was a pleasure to watch the man move.

She shook her head and turned back to Annabelle.

Maybe if she could keep her eyes away, her mind wouldn't dwell on him.

He hadn't tried to start a conversation all day. After days of trying to avoid him, she should be grateful. As much as his rejection stung—it was for the best. For his sake and her own. Definitely.

They'd arrive in Fort Victory tomorrow and everything would change. They'd be neighbors. He'd find the right woman and Clarisse would ask Mercy to sing at his wedding. Her chest felt like someone had cinched a saddle around her a few notches too tight. She leaned against Annabelle's shoulder, rubbing her cheek against the smooth coat. Somehow, she had to find a way to be friends with Thad because that was all she was ever going to be to him.

Mercy walked over to the fire, where Thad used the ladle's curved handle to lift the lid off the Dutch oven. The aroma of cornbread reminded her how empty her stomach was. She poured herself some of his fine coffee, wrapping her fingers around the tin cup slowly as she grew accustomed to the heat. She took a sip for courage.

"It's not like you to brood," Mercy said, coming over to sit beside Thad.

"I'm not brooding, just concentrating on the dinner."

"Hmm." Mercy took another sip of the hot brew. "All day?"

He glared at her, then turned back to his pots. He cut a thick slice of cornbread and set it on her plate, then ladled some beans next to it.

"Thanks," she said when he handed it to her.

She waited until he'd served himself.

"Are you worried about what you'll find in Fort Victory?" she asked.

He took a bite, to give himself more time to answer, she suspected.

"I can't predict the future—no point in tryin'."

"Mmm." Mercy swallowed a spoonful of beans. "But that doesn't keep us from speculating and worrying."

He stared at her, his eyes dark in the fading sunlight. "You, ma'am, are a fraud."

"What?" She dropped her plate, beans spilling over her boots and onto the dirt. She ignored that. "How can you accuse me—?"

"You wear your mask so well, I was completely fooled." He set his plate down. "Not like other women? No. Perhaps you are stronger, more willing to . . . take a risk."

"I don't. I hate gambling."

"Do you? Is that why you sent to England for those Hereford bulls?"

"I—"

"Confronted O'Reilly on the street in Abilene? Took a herd of cattle from Fort Victory to Abilene?"

"Those were calculated risks. I had no choice."

"Didn't you?"

"I have a business to run, Mr.—"

"Don't retreat into formalities with me. I won't be fooled again." He crawled over to her. "Do you know what else I've noticed about you?"

She raised her chin. "I feel certain you're going to tell me."

"You aren't the cold-blooded creature you pretend to be." He grabbed her hand and held tight as she tried to slip away. "You're warm." He brushed a thumb across her palm. "Nurturing." He brought her hand to his lips. "You love children."

"That doesn't mean I want the rascals around—" He kissed her palm and she felt it down to her knees.

"There's more'n one way to have a child."

"I . . . don't . . ." She stared, trying to decipher his words. "What do you mean?"

"Sadly, there's no shortage of orphans in this world. A few of them would be lucky to have a mother like you."

"What?" She swallowed.

He leaned into her and she lifted her arms to push him away. Kissing him would be completely wrong. She cursed her weakness as her palms rested against his firm chest. He deserved much more than she could give him. She shouldn't . . .

His lips brushed hers. Like a beggar grabbing at scraps of food, she threw herself into the kiss. She wanted a feast, a lifetime of his kisses.

He released her lips and nibbled her ear. "I'd be very lucky to have you for a wife," he murmured.

He took her lips again, pressing her back to the ground. She wondered vaguely where her plate was. His hand crept over her ribs until he found her breast. A thrill ran deep into her core, pulsing to the sensual rhythm of his caress. *Wife?*

She shoved both hands against his chest, sitting up and forcing him away from her.

"No." She gasped, took another breath and glared at him. "No. You can't . . . you haven't thought this through— or maybe you've been thinking with your . . ." Her eyes dropped to his crotch.

"It isn't lust." His smile contradicted his words. "Well, yes, it is—partly."

"Of course it is. Lust pure and simple." She choked on a laugh.

"No."

He took her hand, but she pulled it away from him and scooted back until she found herself sitting in her dinner.

"Damn!" she muttered as she swept the beans off her bottom.

Thad cleared his throat. "As I was saying—not simple. I've felt desire before. It came good and strong the first time I saw you. And Lord, seeing you in the bath . . ." He blew out a sharp breath.

He inched closer and she scooted further back. He raised his hands palm forward. "Stop. Another six inches, you'll be sittin' in the fire."

She glanced over her shoulder and realized he was correct. *From the frying pan, into . . .*

"I still feel it—an ache to hold you, taste you and . . ." He turned to stare across the plains. "I'm sure it was only that at first. But somewhere on this journey it grew into something more." He turned and gazed at her then, that searching look that shot straight to her soul. "I love you, Mercy."

She opened her mouth, but had no words.

He studied her face. "I've never felt so complete," he said, "as when we were together. Never felt as empty as I did these past few days of trying to keep away from you. And I don't mean not touching—though, Lord, I do want you. I mean talkin', and laughin', and bein' a part of your life."

"You said there was nothing special between us."

"A lie. Maybe as big a lie as when you said you didn't want a bunch of squalling brats."

"I did want children," Mercy admitted. "But I am glad not to have them. To raise children without a father . . ." She sighed. "It was for the best."

"We can have a family together. Or, if you prefer, we'll concentrate on the ranch and spoil my sister's children."

She saw no hint of teasing in his expression. "I know how much you want to have a family. I can't ask you to give up your dream for me."

"I didn't know what my dream was before." He brushed at the knee of his trousers where the fabric had nearly worn through. "This suit and the pipe I carry are all that's left of my father's possessions. He spent a lifetime building the farm and I managed to lose it all—"

"That wasn't your fault unless you're to blame for the whole damn war."

"I know there's some truth to what you say, but I . . . I can't help believing that one of my brothers or my father would have managed better. I know I can't go back. I thought having a family—making a success of a new farm—might somehow make up for my past failures. I just wanted to find a way to make my father proud of me." He sighed. "It took me this past day to figure it out. Brooding, you called it. I was thinkin' about my father—about what he really expected of me. And what I want for myself. I thought I needed to give him grandsons to honor his name. Now I believe that all he ever really hoped was for me to be a man." His gaze locked with Mercy's. "I swear to you, I'll keep working at that."

"Thad," Mercy inched closer, "you are a good man— brave and honest and kind. Do you have any idea how rare that is?"

He shook his head. "You're a good judge of horse-flesh and . . . cattle, but—"

"Don't you talk that way, Thad Buchanan," Mercy snapped. "You are the most vexing . . . man." She kissed him, hard, weaving her fingers into his hair.

Mercy straddled him and pushed him over, landing on his broad chest. She thrust her tongue deep into his mouth, tasting him. Her chest against his sparked a fire through her belly and between her thighs. She groaned and he responded with a deep growl. Somehow he'd found his way under her shirt and her chemise. His thumb worked her nipple until she was throbbing with pleasure and a growing need.

She raised her head and looked around the empty plain. She smiled and sat up, pinning his legs under hers. She touched the bulge at the crotch of his pants and laughed. Not lust? She opened his pants, releasing each button slowly.

"What . . ." Thad cleared his throat. "What are you doing?"

She grinned when the object she sought sprang to life as she stroked it. "I want to taste you."

She bent and kissed him, then licked the smooth tip of his hard shaft before capturing him. Slowly she drew her lips lower until he filled her mouth. She flicked her tongue against him and toyed with him, enjoying the power of making him helpless with need.

"Ahh," he groaned. "I want to be inside you."

It was exactly what she wanted too. She held him in her mouth as she fumbled with her own buttons until her own frustration overcame her desire to tease him. She released him and sat up as he helped her take off her boots and pants. She straddled him again and opened to him.

He gripped her hips—feeling the weight of her Colt riding on one side as she rocked, taking him deep inside her. For a moment, he felt the exhilaration of joining with her—but he wanted more. Together they moved—slowly at first, then faster until they found the primitive beat that carried them skyward. They peaked together, riding a thunderbolt of hot fire and speed. She shouted his name with a joy that thrilled through him.

She grew still and her eyes locked with his. He pulled her to his chest and held her, both of them panting, their hearts pounding.

She fought for breath, for reason. This man had stolen her sanity. She pushed up and scanned the plain. All was quiet. She turned to see him looking around as he pulled his pants up.

"Sorry," he said, still breathless. "No. Not quite right. I'll never regret that. Still, I know it was dangerous."

She pulled on her pants until she hit her holster. Hell, she hadn't even taken off her gun, she'd been so damn anxious to have the man one last time. She glanced at him, then reached for her boot. She must be the weakest woman in all of Colorado Territory.

He knelt next to her and took her hand. "Mercy, love." He kissed her cheek. "Will you marry me?"

"Thad." The man thought he was in love with her and what was worse, she knew she was in love with him. "I want you—without a doubt."

"It's yes, then?"

"One of us has to have some sense."

The last of the sun shone on his face as his smile faded. She touched his cheek and traced her finger along his strong jaw.

"You think you'll be happy with me, but a year from now, or ten years from now . . . you'll look back and wonder how you agreed to marry a woman who can't bear you the children you want and need. I can't take that chance."

"You're more'n enough woman for me." His smile seemed forced and she knew she must give him an honorable way out.

"You think I'm protecting you, but it's me I'm looking out for." She turned away from him. "I've got to get the dishes cleaned up before we run out of daylight."

"I love you, Mercy."

"Lust is not love!" She picked her upturned plate out of the dirt. "We made a mistake, that's all. I won't let it happen again."

* * *

The next day, Mercy led the way, setting a slow pace. They'd make better time if they could keep a steady pace rather than risk exhausting the horses. They might even make it home today if they could keep going. She watched Zeus and Clover for signs of fatigue that might be brought on by the higher elevation. The mountains loomed close now and the trail was quite high. Annabelle was accustomed to the altitude, the other horses were not.

Mercy itched to be back in Fort Victory, to get away from this man who had worked his way into her heart. She needed time to heal—time to forget him. To stop thinking of what they might have had together.

Tomorrow she'd pay Lansing and get back to work. She'd be too busy for Thad Buchanan to dwell in her mind. She'd forget his searching eyes, the solid feel of his arms around her . . . *Damn.* She threw a glance at Thad. He was still hurt. But it was better to hurt him now than put him through what Nate had experienced.

She turned away, surveying the broad plain and bit her lip. It was natural to be nervous. They were both alert for any sign of danger. Surely that was what was causing her stomach to churn. It wasn't that she was having second thoughts about rejecting Thad's proposal.

"We'd best stop for water soon," she said, being careful to keep her gaze fixed ahead.

"There's a likely spot." He'd come up beside her, his muscular arm pointing toward a shaded spot near the river.

She nodded. It would be good to escape the heat of the sun for a while. They turned toward the river, Thad in front with Clover tethered to Zeus. They slowed, both of them aware that the trees along the river provided not only shelter from the sun, but a place for thieves to hide.

The river was below the trail. They followed a worn path along a ridge that gradually sloped down to the river. To the right of the path was a steep drop of about ten feet to a sparsely wooded area. To the left, the ground sloped up to a thick stand of trees with a cluster of boulders near the river. A movement to the right caught her attention.

"Deer." The sound of Thad's voice was reassuring. He was alert as well.

It took a split second for her to register the sound of a horse in the woods to the left. That wasted second was costly. The roar of gunfire drowned out her warning cry. Leaning low over Annabelle's head, she urged the frightened horse down the slope into the trees where she dismounted and tied her.

She stuck her second revolver in her belt, pulled her rifle and a handful of extra ammunition from the saddle, then plastered herself against a broad spruce tree, peeking out to survey the situation. Thad was down in the dirt, sheltered by a fallen log barely wide enough to cover him. Zeus and Clover had disappeared.

Her heart squeezed into her throat as she watched Thad pinned to the ground, gunfire raining down on him from the pile of rocks on the ridge about fifteen yards ahead of them. She shoved the fear that he was injured out of her mind and focused on distracting the shooters so that Thad could reach the safety of the trees on her side of the path.

She fired her rifle, hoping to draw some fire in her direction. She ducked behind the spruce in time to hear the pop of a bullet penetrating the trunk. More gunshots followed and she saw Thad flatten himself against the log as lead peppered the earth around him. There were at least two shooters above and they appeared to have repeaters. She'd never keep up with them with her Sharps. Without taking the time to reload the rifle she darted from tree to tree, moving until she was close enough to do real damage with her Colt.

A bullet splintered the tree in front of her. She drew a quick breath, then fired around the left side of the tree before darting to the right. Firing as she ran, she emptied her Colt, holstered it and pulled her old Remington out of her belt.

Glancing toward the log, she saw Thad was gone. A bullet whizzed by her head. She dropped low and moved to a tree with low hanging branches. Where was Thad?

The complete silence was eerie. She took a moment to reload her Colt, grateful that it had been converted to accept cartridges. She held her breath—listening. She could hear the whisper of the river, then nothing. This far from the water the rise up to the path was about two feet, but closer it was just a long step. Across the path, the slope up to where their assailants hid was quite steep and perhaps four feet high. She gasped when she saw Thad creeping along the shadow of that ridge.

Mercy stole closer to the river, keeping well into the trees until she was in position to see the men. Holding a rifle at the ready, a big-bellied man with thick, curly black hair, his face covered with a bandanna, stood behind the boulders scanning the path where Thad had been.

O'Reilly. Although she couldn't see his face, she was certain it was him. She was also sure that O'Reilly hadn't been one of the two men who had assaulted them near Fort Kearny—they were both slim.

"I've got it!" A wiry little fellow emerged from the trees behind O'Reilly. "I've got the moneybag!" She'd bet money that nasal voice belonged to Jed. If it was her former hired hand, Luther had to be nearby.

"Hold it right there!" Thad's voice boomed as he revealed himself from under the ridge in front of the gunmen. "Drop your guns, both of you."

O'Reilly and the little man obeyed, their weapons making a dull thud as they hit the ground. Mercy scanned the trees behind Thad. She observed movement—a third man.

"Thad, look out!" she shouted, making the jump to the path where she could get a clean shot at the lanky man who was aiming at Thad's back.

Thad dropped. Mercy squeezed off two shots. The guns up the hill roared, catching Mercy in a shower of lead before she could dive for cover. She staggered back from the force like a kick to her belly. An instant later hot lead burned into her side. She lost her footing and tumbled backward.

Chapter 19

At the sound of Mercy's voice, Thad dropped behind the ridge. He worked his way around to the side nearest the river where he could return fire to the men above him who had now retrieved their dropped weapons.

"Hell, we got the money. Let's move!" *O'Reilly!* Thad recognized that cocky voice.

"No. She shot Luther—she's gonna pay!"

"Don't get yerself riled, boy." O'Reilly always seemed to fall into a brogue when he got excited. "She's as good as dead, I promise you. I got her meself."

Thad glanced over his shoulder to the place where Mercy had been. Where was she? His stomach twisted into a tight knot. *O'Reilly seemed so certain . . .* A bullet whizzed past Thad's head; he dropped back to the ground, crawling forward. The rock above him exploded. He crept backwards looking for another opening.

Thad could hear talking, but couldn't make out the words. He sprang up and fired, dropping in time to avoid the spray of return fire. The three men were moving toward their horses. If they rode away, there would be no catching them. He fired again. O'Reilly went down. The smaller man returned fire. Thad dropped and rolled.

Peering around the rock that sheltered him he saw Jed helping Luther onto a horse. O'Reilly was limping. He turned and fired, bouncing lead off Thad's rock. Keeping low, Thad ran after them as the men mounted their horses.

They fired in his direction, but they weren't really aiming as they pulled away. He stood up to run faster. It was no use—he wouldn't catch them without a horse. They disappeared in a cloud of dust. Thad stopped and caught his breath, then turned back toward the trees where Mercy had disappeared.

"Mercy?"

The knot in his gut wrenched tighter. He moistened his lips. No doubt she was fine, he just needed to find her. He stepped to the edge of the ridge.

"Mercy?"

With the blood pounding in his ears it was difficult to hear anything. He froze, controlling his breathing, listening to the whisper of the trees, a crow's caw, then silence.

"Mercy?" he shouted again.

"Thad?" The voice sounded too high, too small.

He scrambled toward the sound, loose rocks spitting out from under his boots. Then he saw her walking toward him, bent slightly forward, a hand clutched to her side.

"I was afraid you were . . ." Mercy looked as though a slight breeze would knock her over.

Thad took the two long strides to her side just as she collapsed. Her jacket fell open as he lifted her into his arms. A crimson stain spread across her white shirt.

"God, please. No," he whispered as he set her on the ground.

Mercy was unconscious, but breathing. He prayed the bullet hadn't pierced her lung. Thad lifted her shirt to expose a bloody gash at the bottom of her rib cage. He used his kerchief to wipe the blood away and get a better look. He exhaled. Thank the Lord, her rib had deflected the bullet. It hadn't hit anything vital. Unless a stray bit of lead, or bone had . . .

She stirred.

"Rest easy while I—"

She pushed up on an elbow. "Did they get away?"

"They're gone. You need to rest now." He made a pillow with his jacket.

She squeezed her eyes shut, then opened them again and smiled. "It's not so bad. Hit my rib, I think."

He forced a smile. He was supposed to be comforting her, not the other way around. "You'll be fine, but we need to stop the bleedin'." He pressed his kerchief into the wound. "Hold this tight now."

She nodded and leaned back against the makeshift pillow as he examined the rest of her for signs of injuries. Aside from scratches and dirt, he didn't find anything until his eyes stuck on the smashed pocket watch hanging from her belt. He lifted it, pushed his finger into the puncture in the gold cover and pried the cover open, revealing the lead ball that had smashed through the crystal and stuck in the works.

"Best gift my husband ever gave me."

He tried to smile, but his eyes returned to the mangled watch. He swallowed. If the bullet had been an inch away in any direction, it would have ripped her open. She would be dead, or dying. He turned the watch over and stared at the bulge in the metal where the bullet had nearly escaped. Not an inch then, but the thickness of the watch casing had made the difference between life and death.

"Just plain luck, I reckon." Mercy attempted a grin.

"It's not funny," he snapped. "Do you have any idea—?" He sucked in a calming breath. "I've got to find Zeus. He needed the things in his pack.

"Annabelle!" Mercy sat up again. "They had my bag—"

Thad pushed Mercy back down. "We'll find her. But first, I've got to get something to wrap your wound." He touched her cheek and gave her what he hoped was a reassuring smile. "You're going to have to let someone take care of you for a change, whether you like it or not."

She worried her lower lip, but settled back down.

Clover and Zeus hadn't wandered far. He returned within a few minutes, found his jackknife and stood ready to cut the only clean fabric available.

"That's the new shirt you bought to greet Clarissa in."

The woman was impossible. "It's a small sacrifice under the circumstances. You did save my life."

"You'd have done the same for me."

He wished he had. He wished . . . The fabric ripped with a satisfying whoosh. Thad imagined tearing O'Reilly limb from limb. He forced his mind back to the task at hand.

Bay rum would serve to clean the wound. Mercy gasped as he poured. Her whole body went taut as a piano string.

"Relax."

Mercy glared.

"Sorry, I . . ." He shut his mouth and rolled a strip of cloth. "I know all this is painful, but—"

"Just get on with it," she snapped.

"Sorry, I—"

"I know." She bit her lip again.

He pressed the balled cloth into the wound. "Hold this here—we're almost done."

"Good." She winced. "I've got to find Annabelle."

"Annabelle can wait," he muttered through clenched teeth as he wound strips of fabric tightly around her ribs. "I'm sorry I let them get away with your money."

"Thad." She looked up at him. "There was no money in that bag."

She opened her bloodstained jacket. Through the bullet hole, she showed him the corner of a bill. "Afraid it'll all be rather a mess." She laughed, then grunted with pain. "Remind me not to laugh."

"Mercy. Oh, Lord. What were you thinking jumping out into the open? You were safer behind the trees."

Instead of snapping, she gazed at him. "I could see Luther aiming at your back."

"A warning—"

She shook her head. "He'd have killed you for certain." She swallowed. "I had to get into the open to have a shot at him. I had to take a chance."

"You? Gamble?"

"It was a . . . calculated risk."

"Even knowing you might be killed?"

"I wasn't."

His eyes searched hers. "You took a chance for me because you love me."

"I promised to get you—" she sucked in a breath, "to Fort Victory safely. I owe you—"

"Damnation, woman!" He wiped his hands in the dirt, trying to calm himself, but seeing her blood on his hands only made him more angry. "Do you take me for a fool? You may as well try and persuade a river to run uphill as convince me that you don't love me."

"What if I do?"

"Say it. You love me."

"It doesn't . . . We're not going to be together. We can't be."

"Why not?"

"Because you deserve a life that you can't have wit
me."

"You're better'n I deserve. But I love you enough t
think that maybe—"

"You mean you want me. But marriage . . . take
more than wanting." A tear slid down her cheek.

"It takes love."

"Yes," she gasped.

"The kind that would make a person risk a bull
rather than watch her love die?"

Mercy stared at him, then let her eyes drift shut. "
do love you, Thad. But I'm afraid that isn't enough."

"Afraid to take a chance?"

Her eyes returned to his, revealing the pain she wa
trying to hide. *Damn.* This was all his fault. He had le
her into an ambush. If only he'd been more alert.

"I'm sorry," he said. "This isn't the time." Mercy wa
the most mule-headed woman he'd ever met, but sh
was about to learn that he could be stubborn too. "We'
finish this discussion later."

Later. Mercy remembered telling Nate they'd tal
later, but they'd never had the chance. This was differ
ent, she wasn't going to die. She wasn't going to chang
her mind either. Thad dug through his bags and re
turned with the whiskey he'd purchased at Fort Kearn
When they'd discussed the purchase she hadn't imag
ined she'd be the one who needed the painkiller.

He pulled the cork from the bottle and offered it t
her. She curled one hand around the bottle and took
timid sip.

She swallowed and cleared her throat. "It burns . . .
little."

Thad nodded. "Take another sip. It'll help, some."

She took a swallow that would make a sailor prou
and nearly choked. He took it from her and replace
the cork.

"We want it to dull the pain, not make you sick."

Mercy leaned back again. She held her lower lip between her teeth and forced herself to sit up. Every breath hurt. The pain hadn't been this bad when she'd been up and moving. Then she'd embarrassed herself, collapsing like a weak female.

Thad sat next to her and put his arm around her. She rested against his broad chest. She sensed he wanted to give her some of his strength and she tried to take it, breathing him in—bay rum, sweat, gunpowder and horse. Thad.

She would always love him. She loved him enough to risk her life for him. Surely, she could make a small sacrifice for his happiness. It wouldn't be so hard, watching him make a life with another woman. She pushed away from him.

"I can ride." She blinked to hold back her tears.

He nodded, his blue eyes dark with concern. She forced a smile. "No more'n a few hours and we'll be there." She tried to keep her tone light.

Four or five hours. They had enough daylight to make it. She'd be home, back on the ranch where she'd be too busy to be lonely. Soon Thad Buchanan would be only a dim memory. All she had to do was find the strength to stay on Annabelle's back.

Chapter 20

He'd never been more grateful for Mercy's orneriness. She rode for over an hour before she started swaying and shifting in her saddle. He knew from the way she slumped forward, with her left arm pinned to her side, that she was in pain. But, she pressed on, insisting that they keep moving each time he suggested a stop. Their progress was slow, but steady. Until the sky opened up and dumped buckets of rain on them.

He brought Zeus close to her and shouted over the driving rain. "Any shelter nearby?"

She shook her head, but kept looking forward. "It's not so bad. We should keep moving." Her voice sounded miles away.

Thad could see the great peaks ahead, but it was hard to judge distances across the broad expanse of plain. He'd guess it would take them another hour to reach the mountains. Until then, there was nothing but open space for miles around in every direction. Not a tree or substantial rock. Nothing to shelter them from the rain. The temperature was dropping fast and they were both shivering.

Then came the thunder. Lightning flashed ahead. They had to stop.

Mercy dismounted and stood for a moment, unsteady as a newborn colt. He helped her sit, then hobbled the horses. Just as the rain turned into hail, he managed to get one of the oilcloths over her. He quickly piled their supplies and covered them with the remaining oilcloth, hoping to keep their blankets and extra clothing dry. Then he ducked under the first cloth with Mercy. The covering would keep them fairly dry, but it would do nothing to protect them from the lightning.

He rubbed his hands over her arms to warm her. *Damn.* A chill was the last thing she needed. He forced her to drink more whiskey and draped an arm around her shoulders, hoping both to help warm her and to protect her from the stinging hail that was pounding them.

"Thad?"

"I'm here, honey lamb," he said into her ear. "You just rest."

"You'll make sure Pa gets the money I'm carrying, won't you?"

A lightning flash filtered through the oilcloth.

"We'll give it to him as soon as we get you home."

"I mean, if I don't . . . if something happens to me. You'll get it to him."

"Nothing is going to—"

Thunder shook the ground around them. The horses neighed and Thad wished he'd settled them further away.

"Just promise. Please?"

"I swear I will get your jacket to your father. But, you listen to me, sweetheart. I'm taking *you* home to your papa, not an empty jacket. 'Course, he's goin' to have to understand I aim to keep you for myself."

"You can't take 'no' for an answer, can you?" She peered up at him. "Did you just call me lamb?"

"It's a term of endearment."

"Not to a cattle rancher. Do you have any idea what a herd of sheep can do to good grazing land?"

"Sorry," he said. "What should I call you—mule? That's descriptive."

"Very funny."

"You marry me and I'll call you whatever you want."

"I won't—"

"You won't take a chance. I understand. Has it occurred to you—mule—that I just might be right and you're wrong?"

Another flash of light shone through the canvas and Thad pulled Mercy closer. *One. Two.* He waited for the sound of thunder. *Crash!*

They both released a breath at the same time.

"Lightning's moving away, I reckon," Mercy said.

"Don't change the subject." Thad drew back to look at her face. "What if we can be happy together our whole lives just the two of us?"

"Marriage isn't like that. This . . . desire that's drawing us together will fade."

"I suppose when I'm seventy, I might look at you without feeling a desperate need to hold you in my arms and . . . kiss you. Perhaps my need for you will diminish by then. But, I assure you my love won't."

She turned her face toward the canvas.

"I can see you aren't willing to take a chance for yourself, but think about me. You owe me."

"Owe you?" She turned back to him.

"You saved my life. Now it's only fair you make it a life worth living. Marry me. Start a family with me—the two of us. Perhaps a child or two who needs us. Take a chance on me."

Mercy took a deep swig from the whiskey bottle, feeling the heat slide down her throat. "I understand you want a wife and a family. You need someone like Mrs. Hansen who can give you children."

"I don't even know her. But I suppose if I loved her, I'd be willing to raise her children as my own."

"It's not the same. She can give you your own children too, I can't."

"How can you be so certain?"

"I told you. Nate and I tried for years."

"I mean, about Mrs. Hansen. What if I married her and she didn't have another child? I've never fathered a child—how do I know I can?"

Mercy shook her head. "That's different—"

"My point is that nothing's certain. I'd be taking a risk marrying Mrs. Hansen, or any other woman. I'd rather bet on you."

She pulled away from him and hugged her arms tight against her chest. "This is truly what you want?" she asked.

"More than anything." He captured her hand.

She wove her fingers into his. He'd given her a second chance and she might not have another. "I'm sorely tempted . . ."

"Then say yes."

"I'm afraid."

"You're the bravest woman I've ever met. And if you'd met my mama, you'd know that means a lot."

In the shadow of their shelter, it was difficult to make out his features, but that didn't matter—all the moods of his eyes were etched into her heart like a tintype. He might think her brave, but the truth was she wasn't sure she had the courage to face the loneliness of life without Thad Buchanan.

"Thad." She kissed his jaw, cherishing the rough surface. "I do love you . . ." He turned and even in the shadows, she could see his grin. "Let me finish. With the whiskey and all, I can't think right now. If we make it back to Fort Victory—ask me again. I want to be in my right mind and able to stand up on my own, when I agree to marry you."

"But you will. You will agree?"

"You are one persistent man, Thad Buchanan."

He kissed her until she couldn't breathe.

"Got to get some control." He squeezed her fingers. "We'll be home soon. The moment you've recovered, we'll have a proper weddin'. And a soft bed." He caressed her cheek. "Not necessarily in that order."

He kissed her forehead. She was warm, a bit too warm. Even though the wound hadn't caused too much damage, infection and fever were still a danger. Thad pulled her against his chest and held her tight. Mercy was tough, a real fighter. She would recover.

"I thank God you are a mule," he whispered as she slept in his arms.

The lonely howl of a coyote rose with the sparks that jumped from the fire. Thad looked up at the black sky—clouds hid the stars that Mercy loved. At least the rain and hail had stopped. But they would make no more progress tonight. It would be too easy to get lost crossing the plain in all this blackness.

Stepping over to Mercy, he reached out a hand to touch her forehead, then bent his face to hers instead, the way his mother used to check for fever. She was hot.

He brushed a kiss to her forehead. They'd be home tomorrow where she could sleep in a proper bed. She'd be fine.

Thad had done his best to make a nest around her with saddles and packs, but they didn't do much to protect her from the biting wind racing across the high plain. Nor would their piled belongings shield them from another attack. He peered into the darkness around them. The fire made them targets, but Mercy needed hot food and warmth.

He pulled her bag nearer the light of the fire, opened it and pushed garments around until he came to the chemise she'd washed while they were with the Sanders. He'd seen her hang it in the sun to dry. Strange he should feel guilty touching the fabric that she wore so intimately against her skin. He had touched her, had explored thoroughly under her chemise. Well, not as completely as he'd like. That would take years. His gaze drifted back to her sleeping form.

He wanted to watch her sleep in a warm featherbed, nestled against his chest. To walk with her up into the mountains she loved and look down on her ranch. To bring her flowers in the spring and hot coffee in the winter. He wanted a lifetime, but he'd settle for getting her home safe tomorrow.

He brought her chemise to his face. The garment smelled clean, not Mercy's honeysuckle sweet smell, just pure soap. A tiny strip of lace decorated one edge of the garment. He smiled thinking of her hiding that feminine touch under layers of men's clothes. Hating the need to destroy it, he pulled the jackknife out of his pocket and cut the chemise into strips.

"Thad?"

"I didn't mean to wake you." He pulled the blanket back up to her chin. "I need to check your bandages."

Kneeling so he didn't block the light from the fire, he lifted the blanket enough to examine her wound. As he'd feared, blood had soaked through the bandages. Mercy sat up while he bandaged the wound and wrapped several clean strips around her ribs. Except for a suppressed groan when he pulled the bandages tight, she didn't make a sound.

"Go back to sleep," he whispered, covering her.

She looked around, then dropped back against Annabelle's saddle, sucking in a deep breath. Whether it was pain or exhaustion he couldn't be sure, but she took a moment to recover.

"Where are we?"

Hell if I know. "We had to stop. The rain."

Mercy nodded. In the flickering light, he thought he detected fear in her eyes, which scared him.

The coyote howled again, this time there was a response, then another and a whole chorus took up the call. Seeing Mercy shivering, Thad cut a hole in the center of his only dry blanket and pulled it over her head, resting it on her shoulders and drawing it tight around her.

"I'm going to have to take that jackknife away—you keep cutting up your nice things."

Thad didn't feel it necessary to point out that she wasn't strong enough to take anything from him. Besides, he suspected she'd find a way if she really wanted to grab his knife.

"Since you're awake, let's see if you can hold down some food." He turned to the fire. "Nothing left but beans, I'm afraid."

He ladled the bean soup he'd made. When he held a spoon in front of her mouth, she gave an exasperated gasp.

"My hands are fine." She took the cup from him and pushed herself up to a sitting position.

Stubborn woman! Her hands shook so badly he doubted she got much food into her mouth.

He poured himself some coffee and sat beside her. "You're still cold. I could move you closer to the fire."

She shook her head and swallowed another spoonful, letting the cup rest back on her lap as her eyes drifted shut.

"You need to keep your strength up."

She shook her head. "I can't eat any more."

"Try." He could be stubborn too. He shoved the spoon into her mouth. "Can't stand to have anyone taking care of you, can you?"

"I hate feeling useless, is all." She opened her mouth for another bite, chewed it slowly, then swallowed.

He knew she was struggling with pain. The firelight revealed the whiskey bottle was less than half-full. How long did that have to last them? He had no idea how much progress they'd made, or how much farther they had to go.

She'd said four or five hours. They'd gone about two when the rains stopped them, but it had been slow going. They had to make it to Fort Victory tomorrow.

"Take a drink, it'll help you sleep." He handed her the bottle.

She held it a moment. "My pa warned me about fellows like you who ply a woman with drink, then have their way with her."

"You read my mind," he whispered, nuzzling her cheek. As fragile as she seemed right now, ravishing her was the last thing on his mind. All he wanted to do was protect her, make her safe.

She took a long drink and returned the bottle.

"Try to sleep now. We've got a long ride tomorrow."

"How much further do you think?"

He inhaled, releasing his breath slowly. "Two, three hours?"

The fire popped and sparked. As if in response, one of the horses neighed.

"It's hard to . . . think." Her arm came across his ribs as he pulled her close. "I'm tired."

"You rest then."

"Do you know I can hear you breathing, deep down in your chest. And your heartbeat." She rubbed her ear against his chest. "I never sleep—did you know that? I

haven't had a good night's sleep since . . . in a long
time. Except for the night I fell asleep against you. You
breathing's like a lullaby to me." Her hand crept up hi
side. "It's confusing." She sighed, squeezing him. "
can't look at you without butterflies dancing in m
belly."

He felt a bit guilty for letting her say things unde
the influence of the whiskey that she would never admi
sober.

"Looking at you sometimes—like when you were
helping Reverend Sanders with the wagon. You had
your shirt off and the sun was reflecting off that patch
of gold fur on your chest—I could see how solid you
are. I was wide awake then."

She sighed again. He slipped his hand under layer
of blanket and her jacket, feeling her warmth through
her shirt. It wasn't right to let her go on like this. Bu
Lordy, he did love hearing it.

"Curled up against you, listening to you breathe, it'
so peaceful . . . Almost like . . . home." She squeezed
against his ribs.

He was afraid to speak, not wanting to break the
magical spell that had brought forth these revelations.

"You know what else?"

"Hmm?" His conscience told him he shouldn't le
her continue, but he was only human.

"You almost make me feel petite. I never thought I'
know what that was like." She wrinkled her brow. "
think perhaps I've had too much of that whiskey." She
breathed regularly for a moment and he thought she'
fallen asleep. "Do you know what's funny?"

"What?"

"My lips are numb, but my side still hurts like hell."
She pulled away from him. "Sorry. I don't usually curse
You make me forget myself."

He caressed her cheek. "You shouldn't have to be on your guard around me, honey. I love you."

"You really do?"

"Definitely."

"Mmmm. I think I'll sleep now."

"Good."

"Thad?"

"Shh, try to sleep."

"If I go to sleep . . . I'm going to wake up again, aren't I?"

He felt the knot in his stomach tighten. "Of course you are."

"I just worry about my pa." She shuddered. "Now Miranda's with Harold, he'll be all alone. Of course, Buck will take care of him. Buck's a good man."

"Don't worry about your pa, you'll see him tomorrow." He had to ask. "Who's Buck?"

"He's one of the hired hands." She suppressed a yawn. "He's like an uncle to me—almost like family."

An uncle? He relaxed a little. He needn't fear an uncle.

"If I don't . . . make it home . . . you'll tell Pa about everything, won't you?" She pushed herself up to a sitting position and peered at Thad in the darkness. "Tell him we got eighteen dollars a head for the cattle. He should get a good price for the Hereford bulls now—we could sell two or three of 'em." She put her head in her hands.

She would be worried about her damn cattle and her father. Thad let out an exasperated sigh. "You're going home, I'm going to get you there myself and you can tell your father all about the cattle sale. Now, no more worrying—go to sleep." He heard her choke back a sob. "Mercy, I'm sorry. I didn't mean to be sharp with you."

"No, I'm being stupid," she sobbed. "I never cry . . . can't seem to think straight. I'm not going to die . . . I know it." She sniffed, rubbing her damp face against his jacket. "It's just I'm so tired and cold and nothing's ever hurt this bad . . . I just wish I were home."

"Shh, shh." He rubbed her back.

"I can barely sit on the ground. By tomorrow . . . you're having to do everything for me. I feel so useless."

"I'm going to get you home. Zeus is strong enough to carry us both if need be. It's all right to need help sometimes."

"Is that what you think?" She rubbed her sleeve over her eyes. "That I can't accept help?"

"I think it's hard for you."

She sniffed. "I'm sorry. You've done so much and I've been ungrateful."

"You're tired and you're hurtin'." Thad brushed a lock of hair back from her face. "Just sleep now."

She rested her head against him. "Arthur," she whispered.

Thad froze on hearing the man's name.

"I wish I'd never taken help from him." She pulled away, resting her head on the saddle. "No stars tonight— or is my head so foggy I'm just not seeing 'em?"

Thad didn't know what to say, except he felt an inexplicable urge to punch Arthur, whoever he was. What kind of help did she get from him? Thad moved away from her to tend the fire.

"Sometimes I think I've treated Arthur unfairly. I owe him so much. His little boy has been desperate to have a mama . . ."

Thad spun around.

"Tell me about Arthur. He asked you to marry him?"

"Constantly." She massaged her temples.

"You never mentioned Arthur to me." *Not when we were making love. Not when I was proposing.*

"Why would I mention him?" She pushed up on her elbow.

"He must love you." Thad turned and poked the fire.

"You sound like Miranda," Mercy said, settling back and closing her eyes. "What makes you think it has anything to do with love?"

Thad put a pile of buffalo chips on the fire, unable to look at her. He'd been foolish to think she had no other suitors.

"Thad? You're not jealous, are you?"

He turned. She was grinning at him.

"Arthur Lansing is a snake. I wouldn't marry him—not even to save my ranch."

A snake? He could compete with a snake. Thad came to sit next to her. "Arthur Lansing? The neighbor who loaned you the money?"

She nodded. "Ever since Nate died, Arthur has been trying to convince me that we should join our ranches."

"Join?"

"Yes. Marriage is a business arrangement as far as he's concerned. I suspect he married his first wife for her money. That's not fair—I reckon he might have loved her once."

"She died?"

Mercy nodded. "We couldn't stop the bleeding after she gave birth. Clarisse and I were there. No midwife or doctor around."

Thad pulled Mercy close. "I'm sorry."

"I've been watching out for Jonathan ever since—five years now." She sighed. "I love that boy, but I won't marry a snake just to be close to Jonathan." She smiled at Thad. "Rather have a real man."

Thad kissed her forehead. Mercy closed her eyes and leaned against Thad's chest.

"We'll get back tomorrow," she said. "Need to get the payment to Lansing."

"You're goin' straight to bed."

"Don't know if I have the strength for that." She didn't quite manage a full smile. "Besides, my father will shoot you if he finds you in my bed before we're married."

"I mean you're feverish. You'll need to rest in bed for a time—build your strength up for our weddin'."

"I haven't agreed to a wedding."

"But you will—when we get home."

"Home," Mercy whispered. "You'll get the money to Lansing, won't you?"

"You can count on me."

He held her close while she slept. He'd failed his father and his brothers. He'd failed his mother, but he would not fail Mercy this time.

Chapter 21

Mercy woke to the smell of coffee brewing. The diamond-bright, high plains sunrise pierced her brain and she slammed her eyes shut. A moment later, she peeked through half-opened lids. Thad squatted near the fire, pouring coffee. Mercy tried to swallow without much success. Her mouth felt as though a herd of sheep had been sheared inside it. She sat up and groaned as pain pounded through her head, nearly making her forget the stabbing in her side.

"Coffee?" Thad handed her a hot cup.

"Thanks." She stared into the cup, trying to decide whether the hot liquid had any chance of remaining in her stomach. Not yet.

Thad knelt and peered into her face.

She forced a smile. "I'm much better this morning."

"Really?" Thad furrowed his brow. "You don't look at all well."

"You do know how to flatter a woman."

He arched an eyebrow.

"The sleep helped, honestly. I'm strong enough to

ride. I think." She pressed her palm to her pounding head.

"It's the whiskey." Thad seemed to read her mind. "Here." He poured some whiskey into her coffee. "Drink."

"If the whiskey is making me feel—"

"I know it doesn't make sense. But it'll help." He combed his fingers through his hair. "I'm not a drinking man now, but I did overindulge once or twice in my past. You'll just have to trust me on this."

She sipped the contaminated brew and grimaced. Thad glared at her and she decided not to waste energy arguing. She took another sip. He smiled and brushed a kiss to her cheek.

"You're still a bit feverish."

"I wish you wouldn't fret over me." She kissed his cheek in return. "Did you get any sleep at all last night?"

Thad shrugged and she knew he'd spent the whole night watching for trouble. Taking care of her. She felt a sudden warmth deep inside that had nothing to do with hot coffee or whiskey.

"I have something I want to show you."

He took her cup, set it down and gripped her left hand. For a moment or a lifetime, they studied each other, his broad hand supporting her slender one. Those familiar eyes—the color of a glacier fed lake— plumbed deep within her. Instinct made her drop her gaze, but something stronger made her look up again. Back to those tender eyes. Her heart skipped a beat. *I'm not afraid.* She opened her mouth to tell him, but then realized he knew.

His mustache twitched before his lips curved into a smile that caused her heart to race. Mercy sucked in a breath, but had no voice. Thad pulled a ring out of his pocket. The jewels sparkled in the early morning sun as he held it out to her.

"It was my mother's. She—" Thad's voice caught and he cleared his throat. "She wanted my bride to wear it."

"I thought we'd agreed not to talk about marriage until we're safe at home." She studied the ring again. "But even if we do marry . . ." It was the most beautiful piece of jewelry that Mercy had ever seen—a gold band set with six stones, three blue alternating with three green. She shook her head. "It's beautiful." So brilliant and perfect and real. "But I'm a rancher. I could never wear something as pretty as—"

"Of course you can," Thad said. "You wear gloves outdoors most of the time. The stones are small and set into the gold. They won't interfere with your work. And your graceful fingers will show it off perfectly." He bent low and looked up into her face. "Try it on, please?"

She had a lump in her throat the size of an egg. Her hand still rested in his, belonging there. She was beginning to think this was real. Whatever this was between them, it wasn't going to vanish like smoke in the wind.

She nodded and he slipped the ring onto her finger, next to her wedding band.

"Fits like it was made for you." He favored her with another dimpled grin and her heart started galloping again. She'd wear a ring on every finger for that smile.

"But this isn't quite right." She took the two rings off and replaced just Thad's ring, shoving Nate's ring deep into her pocket. "That's better."

Thad swallowed the lump in his throat as he watched Mercy put away the final bit of her armor. The last thing separating them—he hoped. Then he brushed a kiss to her lips and pulled her to his chest, careful not to hurt her injured side.

He ran his thumb under her jaw and she bit her lip.

"What are you frettin' about, love?"

"I have until the fifteenth to pay Lansing. That's only a few days from now."

"We'll get home today." He rubbed his chin over the top of her head. "I'll get you to your pa, and take the money to Lansing. Then we'll start plannin' our weddin'."

"Pa." Mercy looked down at her jacket—torn and bloodstained. "I don't want him to see me like this and worry." She shrugged out of her jacket. "It's warm enough to go without my jacket."

Thad brushed a strand of hair back from her face. "Always lookin' out for everyone, aren't you?" His hand lingered at her cheek and she leaned into his palm. He wanted to sit like this forever, sheltering her and protecting her. As soon as she was stronger, trying to keep Mercy protected and sheltered would be like trying to make a pet out of a cougar.

She pulled his mother's ring off her finger and handed it to him. "You'd best keep this safe until our wedding day. I mean your wedding day."

Thad took the ring and shoved it into his pocket. "I'm not going to find anyone who fits it as well as you do."

She was sorely tempted. "I said we'd talk about it when we get home and I meant it."

"Fair enough. But I heard you say 'our weddin' day'."

He helped her into a clean shirt and bent to kiss her, tasting whiskey and coffee. "Have I mentioned this morning that I love you?"

She shook her head. "As a matter of fact, you haven't."

"Well, let me correct that." He kissed her again. "I love you."

She traced a finger over his cheek. "I love you."

Thad looked away and cleared his throat. "I believe meetin' you must have been the luckiest day of my life. Like gettin' aces on every hand in a poker game." He lifted her hand to his lips, nibbling at her palm. "No. You're better'n aces."

I'm the lucky one. It took all her might to hold back the tears that were pooling in her eyes. All she could do was turn her face toward his, inviting him to kiss her again. Her kiss would have to speak all the words she wasn't able to voice.

After an hour on the trail, they decided to aim for town instead of her ranch. Mercy was anxious to see her Pa, but not certain she could ride the extra two hours it would take to get to the ranch. The truth was she'd be glad to stop. They'd get a message to Pa from Clarisse's place.

Mercy had finished the remaining whiskey and felt light-headed, barely able to stay upright in the saddle. Even with her left elbow pressed against her side, she felt each of Annabelle's steps like a knife in her ribs. Fortunately, the town of Fort Victory was over the next hill, or she'd have been forced to relent and ride on Zeus with Thad.

As they climbed the last grade, Mercy relaxed. She'd followed the curves in this rutted path a thousand times—knew each boulder. She looked around—reminding herself that these familiar rocks could hide trouble.

"After traveling across the broad plains, it almost seems closed in here," Thad said.

The road was barely wide enough for a wagon to pass. "It wasn't easy to build a road here with all the rocks. They used dynamite in places." *Keep talking; stay upright.* "We'll see Fort Victory in a minute. There's not much left of the fort itself—only a small garrison. But the town is growing with all the miners and ranchers coming to the area."

She'd run out of words and all that was left was dizzy nausea. *Only a little further now.*

It seemed like hours later when she reined Annabelle to a stop at the top of the hill. "There." Mercy pointed below them. "Clarisse's store is on the left side of the street. A few doors down is Rita's saloon."

"Where's the doctor's office? That'll be our first—"

Gunfire exploded around them. Annabelle reared back. Mercy couldn't hang on. More gunshots detonated around her as she flew through the air. She landed hard, chest over a boulder. Shooting stars flashed past her eyes as she struggled to breathe. A voice inside her head screamed, "Move! Get to cover." But her legs wouldn't work. She dragged herself forward, six inches, a foot, until she managed to roll over the side of the boulder.

Out of the corner of his eye, Thad saw Mercy go flying. He pulled his Remington, but his horse was crazy with fear and Thad couldn't take a shot.

He managed to turn Zeus and fired at their attackers. The horse bucked again and Thad's shots went wild. He was a hundred yards away before he had control of the animal. He dismounted and ran back toward Mercy. A shower of lead stopped him ten yards from her. He hit the ground and rolled behind a boulder.

Thad peered around the rock. Mercy was huddled behind a large chunk of weathered granite, bent low. She wasn't moving—wasn't even holding her Colt. He shoved one empty revolver back into his holster and drew his second pistol. He scrambled toward Mercy, firing as he went, until he knelt beside her.

"You hurt?" He asked between breaths. She was white as a ghost, her face and hands were scraped, but there were no bullet wounds that he could see.

"Fine," she croaked.

He scowled.

"I don't know." She swallowed. "Hurts everywhere." She blinked.

The shooting had stopped. Thad peered over the rock. How many men were there? Where had they gone?

"Do you think it's O'Reilly again?" Mercy asked.

"No idea." His hands shook as he reloaded, wondering where the assailants would reappear. "Didn't see anyone."

The thunder of hoofbeats pulled his attention away. Annabelle galloped by riderless, the reins flapping against her chest and Mercy's buckskin jacket hanging over her tail. Two horsemen followed close behind. Thad would wager the second man was O'Reilly.

"Annabelle," Mercy said.

Thad couldn't look at her. "It's only money."

Her money. The cash she'd fought to bring here.

"Not only money." Mercy drew her Colt. "It's my ranch." She grunted in pain as she tried to push to her feet. "If I can't pay Lansing—"

Thad pressed down on her shoulder. "You're not going after that horse."

"I . . ." Tears pooled in her eyes. "I don't think I can." She looked up at him.

"No." He growled through gritted teeth. "I'm not leaving you."

"Please, Thad. I'll be fine here. They must have heard the shooting in town. The sheriff is bound to come." She lifted her Colt. "I'm not defenseless."

"No!" Thad looked around now that the gunfire had stopped, Zeus stood calmly a few yards away. He grabbed the gelding's reins and led him over to Mercy. "No sign of Clover. I'm getting you to town. I'll find Annabelle and Clover after you're safe in a doctor's care. We'll worry about the damn money later."

"Damnation, Thad Buchanan!" Mercy fumed. "Why do you have to be so all-fired stubborn?"

"I've been with you for over a month—I was bound to learn a thing or two."

His chest tightened as he watched a tear track through the dust on her cheek. Thad remembered losing his family farm. He couldn't watch Mercy suffer that kind of loss. He squatted next to her. "You promise to wait for me, right here?"

"You have my word."

She smiled that half-smile that could melt lead.

He turned and mounted Zeus. "When I find Annabelle, I'm gonna have that bullwhip of yours and I swear I'll use it on you if you've moved one inch."

Chapter 22

Fort Victory, Colorado Territory
October 1867

Arthur Lansing sipped the foul liquor Rita passed off as whiskey. He didn't know how the Spanish bitch stayed in business. The afternoon crowd of itinerant miners and ill-bred cowboys answered his question with their mere presence. Soon the soldiers from the nearby fort would fill the establishment as they did every night. No one of taste came to Fort Victory. Arthur Lansing was truly alone here. But that suited him.

Before long, he'd be running the town. By the time Colorado became a state, he could well be the first governor. He grinned. His father and brothers had never expected Arthur to amount to anything. They hadn't even invited him to join their banking business. No doubt, they would regret that slight when Arthur returned home to Boston, richer and more powerful than his father had ever been.

He tossed back the rest of the whiskey in his glass. Before he could order another, he spotted his hired man Jed coming through the swinging doors. When did that fool get back to town and why the hell was he showing his face here? Lansing had given the men clear instructions they were not to be seen in Fort Victory, but were to come to him privately.

He strode across the room, nearly knocking Rita over.

"Excuse me, Señor Lansing," the dark haired proprietor said as he rushed past her.

He ignored the woman and grabbed Jed by the shoulder, shoving him back out the door. "What the hell are you doing here?" he demanded.

"I . . . uh—"

"Come with me." Lansing led the way into the alley next to Rita's place. He scanned the area. No one in sight and no windows on this side of the building.

After taking a breath to calm himself, Lansing asked, "Have you lost your mind?" He knocked the thin cowboy against the wall. "Pardon me, I'd forgotten you have no mind. Luther supplies all of the intelligence for the both of you—and where is that son of a bitch, anyway?"

"Shot." Jed licked his lips. "That's why I come into town—to find the doc."

"No." Lansing said. "Not here. Take him to Denver or anywhere else."

"He's in a bad way, Mr. Lansing." The cowboy stood up straight and looked Arthur in the eye.

Arthur ignored the challenge. "Did you at least manage to obtain the money I sent you after?"

"Yes sir, but—"

"And Mercy?"

"She's shot too—O'Reilly got her."

"O'Reilly? Who the hell is he?"

"We found him in Abilene. He—"

"Never mind that." Lansing had no patience for

dealing with trivialities. "Where did you leave her? Is she alive?"

"Don't know. Looked like a chest wound, but she managed to ride on to town—"

"She's here? Did she see you?"

"She's hurt, like I said. We left her on the road, just outside of town. I reckon she got a pretty good look at us before she went down though."

"Damn! Why I hire incompetents . . ." He squeezed the bridge of his nose, hoping to relieve the pain that was growing in his head. "Tell me everything. I'll determine what I must do to set things right."

Lansing fought to catch his breath as he struggled up the hill beyond Fort Victory. He sat upon a rock and stared down at the streets of the dirty little village below. All quiet—no one coming up the hill, no movement around the sheriff's office. He could finish the job his hired men had bungled undisturbed. Of course, if anyone should happen by, he'd tell them he was out walking and stumbled upon Mercy—too late to save her. So sad. He rubbed his aching side. He'd forgotten how bloody steep this hill was.

"Why didn't the idiot tell me how far up this damned hill he'd left the bitch?" Lansing muttered.

He squinted up the hill, no sign of Mercy Clarke. Yet. Lansing grinned. He was going to have Mercy's ranch and her money without having to marry the bitch. He'd certainly need some fine whiskey to celebrate this occasion. And he'd purchase it with Mercy's money. He made a mental note to dispose of the cowboys before they spent their share of the cash. No need to share the thousand dollars with those pathetic fools.

Once he had the money, he would send east for a suitable wife. His son liked Mercy, but Lansing was glad to be rid of the unnatural creature who thought she could compete in business against a man. Jonathan would learn to respect any mother Lansing found for him. Affection was of secondary importance. He supposed old maids willing to arrange a marriage through the mail would not have Mercy's appealing body, but he certainly didn't need a wife to satisfy those needs. More important for her to be a proper mother to his son. And she must know her place. Mercy Clarke never learned how to defer to a man's judgment. That was only one of her many failings. Her greatest fault was her pride. She truly thought she could outwit Lansing.

He shoved back onto his feet and continued up the hill until he recognized a familiar head of brown hair sticking above a large rock. He took a moment to steady his breath before heading toward Mercy, gripping the derringer in his pocket. According to Jed, she was already injured. Lansing congratulated himself on saving her the misery of a slow death from infection.

Not that his intentions were charitable. He simply wanted to make certain she died. Her father would never be a threat to Lansing. The old man's mind had been addled since the accident with the bulls. Mercy, on the other hand, was too damn smart. He wasn't going to risk her discovering his part in the theft of her money. Having her here alone and vulnerable merely saved him the trouble of planning her death.

When he had the chance, he'd take care of Jed, Luther and that Irishman they'd picked up in Abilene. Lansing did not intend to risk any of those stupid bastards giving him away to the sheriff. He had far too much at stake for that.

He stopped to put a neighborly smile in place before he approached her. "Mercy Clarke." Lansing feigned surprise and concern. "What's wrong?"

"Arthur." Mercy grimaced, then made an effort to smile. "I took a fall from my horse. Can't seem to put any weight on my leg."

He took another step closer. The derringer was a powerful little gun, but he wanted to be sure. "Well, that's a shame. How can I help?"

Her Colt was safely in its holster, her arms crossed over her chest. Excellent. Damned if he would let the bitch shoot him. He gripped his pistol, but the clomping of hoofbeats stopped him pulling it from his pocket.

"Thad!" Mercy favored the new arrival with a real smile.

Lansing turned to see a blond man in a dark suit riding a huge black horse and leading another smaller horse behind him. This must be the cheating gambler Jed had told him about. His timing was terrible.

"Mr. Lansing," Mercy said. "I'd like you to meet Thad Buchanan."

The big man held out his hand. "Pleased to meet you, sir."

Arthur glanced at Mercy then took the offered hand. Thad barely looked at Lansing as he shook his hand briefly. He turned immediately and knelt next to Mercy.

"Sorry, I wasn't able to catch Annabelle."

Mercy nodded and reached for the big man's hand with a tenderness Lansing had seldom noticed in the woman. "I'm just glad you're safe. I was beginning to worry."

Unbelievable! The woman who had avoided his marriage proposals for nearly two years had fallen in love with this shabby hulk?

Buchanan beamed at her. Truly, a most hideous expression, as though the man were looking at a mountain of diamonds instead of a dust-streaked woman in dingy men's clothing. Lansing added Thad Buchanan to his list of enemies. He wouldn't be going after either of these two with a pocket revolver again. Next time, he would find a more powerful weapon.

Something was very wrong. Mercy focused on flowered wallpaper, bright in the morning sun. Dark log walls and the angled ceiling of her cabin should surround her. Pushing up, she tried to throw her legs over the side of the unfamiliar bed, then froze, pain screaming through her body. Her head pounded. She squeezed her eyes shut, remembering the gun battle. She'd been shot in the side, but she hurt everywhere.

What had happened?

Gentle hands braced her shoulders, helping her recline again.

"Thad?" Her voice cracked; her mouth was dry as tumbleweed.

"He's not here." The genteel southern voice belonged to Thad's sister.

Mercy opened her eyes and looked into familiar azure-blue eyes speckled with green. Funny she'd never noticed Clarisse's eyes before. Her small, heart-shaped face was nothing like her brother's but there was no mistaking the similarity of the eyes, even down to the same look of concern Thad had tried unsuccessfully to hide from her. Clarisse took hold of her hand and gave it a squeeze. Mercy's eyes fluttered closed, then open again. She had a misty memory of Thad bringing her here. Yes, he'd carried her up the stairs in Clarisse's house.

"He's okay, then? Thad wasn't injured?"

"He was falling asleep on his feet. I forced him to find a bed and rest."

"Good, I . . . worry about him."

"Do you feel up to taking some water?" It wasn't really a question. Clarisse gently lifted Mercy so that she could take a sip of water. The cool liquid soothed her parched throat.

"You rest now," Clarisse said.

Mercy nodded, which sent a shock of pain from her head to her neck. "Before we got to town . . . there was shooting . . ." It was so hard to think. There was something she was supposed to be doing. Mercy looked up. "The money."

"Thad gave me strict orders not to let you fret over that." Clarisse squeezed her hand. "My brother managed to fall in love with you, didn't he?"

Mercy focused on Clarisse's smile. "You're not disappointed? Thought you might want to introduce him to Ingrid Hansen."

"Ingrid?" Clarisse laughed. She brushed the hair back from Mercy's forehead. "Ingrid's a fine woman, but I had higher hopes for my baby brother."

Mercy stared at Clarisse. Her friend knew her and all of her flaws. Was it because Mercy couldn't have children that Clarisse wanted someone else for Thad? Perhaps Clarisse knew another woman who would be better for her brother. She wanted to tell Clarisse not to worry, that she wouldn't stand in Thad's way, but the darkness drew her in.

The next time Mercy woke, it took her only a minute to remember she was in Clarisse's home. The pretty wallpaper seemed comforting now. Clarisse helped Mercy drink some beef broth and some medicine before she drifted back to sleep. Time became meaningless for Mercy as she alternated between sleeping and waking. In her waking moments, she thought about Thad. She'd promised to give him her answer when they reached town—if he asked her again. She wasn't certain what her answer should be, but that didn't matter, since he still hadn't come to see her.

A cool hand grasped Mercy's. She squinted up into a loving face. "Pa," she breathed.

"I'm here, Mercy gal, you're gonna be fine." He sniffed twice.

Mercy's eyes pooled with tears as she watched her father wipe his sleeve over his eyes.

"I'm sorry, Pa." She tried to sit up, but sank back into the pillow exhausted. "Sorry to worry you."

"It ain't your fault." He brushed spindly fingers across her forehead. "You need to rest. There's a bit of a fever is all." He cleared his throat.

There was something she needed to tell her pa. "Miranda." Mercy ran her tongue across her lips, but still felt parched. "Left her in Fort Kearny."

Pa nodded. "I know. Thad told me all about it. You've been sleepin' a good while."

He helped Mercy take some water. Her throat felt like she'd been drinking sand. "Sleeping how long?"

"A full day and a night."

Still time then, but not much. She blinked until she had a clear view of her father's face. "The money is gone."

"I know. Thad explained about that too. Told me how it was stolen from you."

"Annabelle too."

"Your horse is here," Pa smiled at her. "Wendell Wyatt found her near town—no saddle though." He looked away from her, as though he couldn't meet her eyes.

"I have a few days, Pa. I'll think of some way to get the payment—"

"We'll take care of everything—don't you worry yourself. Just rest and get your strength back."

"Lansing won't accept a late payment."

"No, he won't." Pa squeezed her hand. "I already asked him."

"I'm so sorry Pa. I—"

"Don't you be apologizin' now. I don't care about the damn money or the ranch for that matter. I'm just grateful to have my daughter."

She smiled at him. Her eyes drifted shut. She was too tired to think about the ranch. There had to be something she could do. She just needed to sleep. She'd find a solution tomorrow.

"Pa?" Mercy forced her eyes open. She just had to ask. "Did Thad say anything about . . . me?"

"Told me you were very brave. You saved his life."

"Is that . . . all?" *He didn't by chance mention loving me?*

"He told me you got eighteen dollars a head for the cattle. Said if he didn't tell me you'd likely use that whip of yours on his hide. Now, why would he say that?"

She closed her eyes and let sleep take her away.

Chapter 23

Thad kicked at some straw on the floor of Clarisse's barn. He had managed to foul things up again. He'd lost Annabelle and the money. The one thing Mercy had asked him to do for her and he hadn't been able to accomplish it. She'd never be able to forgive him—not that he deserved her forgiveness. He glanced over at the stall where Annabelle was placidly chewing oats. At least Mercy's horse had wandered into town on her own. Mercy loved the mare, but the ranch was her life.

He paced across the open area where his brother-in-law stored his wagon, kicked at some loose straw, then paced back again. He counted six stalls along one wall. Zeus, Annabelle and Clover each occupied one. Two more stalls for the horses that were now out pulling the wagon, leaving one empty. Fine, now he'd accounted for all the stalls and horses. Hell, he was a bloody genius.

He had to do something. What he really wanted to do was drive his fist into O'Reilly's gut and keep punching until he'd knocked the man back to Kansas. But that wouldn't help Mercy. The fact was there was nothing he could do for her. Not without money. The more he thought about it, the more certain he became that Mercy would be better off without him.

He heard footfalls and ducked into an empty stall. He'd come out to the barn to be alone, the last thing he wanted was conversation. Late afternoon sunlight shone on the petite woman's golden hair for an instant before she shut the big barn door. Thad bent low so his sister wouldn't see him. He wanted to avoid her questions most of all.

"Thad Buchanan, you can't go on hiding," Clarisse scolded. She stood, hands on hips, shouting into the dim barn. "I know you're in here."

She clucked her tongue and shook her head in a way that brought their mother to Thad's mind. He couldn't help but smile at how Clarisse favored Mama in appearance and demeanor. She marched across the barn and started peering into each stall. Before she came to the one that hid Thad, he stepped into the open.

"I want an explanation." Clarisse glared up at him. "You may frighten others with your size, but I still remember my skinny twelve-year-old brother and I am not afraid to demand some answers from you."

"I know we haven't had a real chance to talk. I'm sorry."

"You've been worried about Mercy." Clarisse squeezed her brother's arm. "I understand that. But I want to know why you're out here instead of sitting with her?"

He looked into Clarisse's eyes and turned away, not knowing what he should tell her. Mercy was not obligated to him. She'd been careful not to agree to marriage as much as Thad had pressed her. Thad could honorably leave her—give her a chance to find someone more suitable. A better man.

"I can't help feeling responsible for what's happened to her. After all, she asked me along for some protection—"

"Mercy?" Clarisse laughed. "She asked for help from you? I never thought I'd see the day. Lordy, she is in love."

"No!" Thad cleared his throat. "I mean . . . What makes you say that?"

"My dear little brother. It's one thing to hide in the barn—that's childish, but at least it did make it more difficult for me to find you. Trying to conceal something in plain sight is another thing—just silly. Can't be done. I know you too well." She reached up and placed her palm against his cheek. "Mercy's a fine woman. You've chosen well."

"Did she . . . say something to you?"

"Thad Buchanan, you aren't listening to me." Clarisse chuckled. "I'm your sister and Mercy's my closest friend. Do you think either one of you has to tell me? I saw it when you carried her in. Didn't I nearly have to lock you in another room to get you to rest?"

"It's natural for me to worry about her. We became friends in the past few weeks."

Thad walked over to Zeus and made a show of checking his legs. Perhaps if he looked busy . . .

"I asked you before to explain yourself. What are you doin' out here when Mercy needs you inside?"

Thad left Zeus's stall and paced around the barn. One wall had pegs holding everything from torn bridles to garden tools. He ran his fingers over the wooden handle of a shovel, thinking how good it would be to dig into earth again.

"I'm waiting," Clarisse said.

"She doesn't need me. She has her father with her and you—"

"But you're the one she keeps asking for."

"Likely she wants to tell me what she thinks of my carelessness, losing her horse—"

"The horse has been found."

"But not her money."

"And I suppose there's something you could have done differently that would have prevented that theft?"

"There must have been something."

"Name one thing?"

"I . . . I don't know. She got herself shot trying to protect me. Did she tell you that? I should have been the one to keep her safe."

"Protect Mercy Clarke? Thad—you can ride alongside Mercy. You can help her, work beside her. You might even be able to make suggestions. But you are never going to be able to protect her if that means keeping her from doing what she is bound and determined to do."

"I'm the man."

"Maybe I was wrong in thinkin' you'd understand her. From readin' your letters—the way you talked about working beside Mama and learning from her—I thought here is a fellow who knows how to be a man without feeling he has to be lord and master over his woman. A man like my Wendell, only not so short and skinny." She chuckled. "You're supposed to laugh at that. I've seen more smiles at a funeral."

"I'm not feeling jolly at the moment."

"No, I see that. Well, it occurred to me from readin' your letters and Mama and Papa's too—"

"Papa mentioned me?"

"He surely did," Clarisse said. "I saved every letter, if you don't believe me."

"I didn't think he . . . What did he have to say?"

"He said I'd never recognize you. That you'd grown

to be such a man—not just in size, but in the way you carried yourself, the way you talked. Well, he went on and on. And I see he was right. I'd know your face anywhere, but you have grown up, little brother." Clarisse used the hem of her apron to wipe at a tear. "Now you've distracted me. I was sayin' that you'd be just about the perfect man for Mercy. One who would take care of her without ever stealing her pride."

"But I didn't take care of her, that's what I'm trying to tell you."

"Didn't you?" She squeezed his hand between both of hers. "You did everything you could for her before you brought her here." He met her gaze. "I imagine you wish you could have stopped the bullet in midair or performed some other magical feat to keep Mercy from being injured. We all want to be able to shield our loved ones that way. You can't blame yourself because you're only able to do what is possible." She stepped back and put her hands on her hips. "Now, you get on up to the house and finish what you started. Mercy needs you."

"Clarisse, it hurts. Seeing her in pain."

"Of course it does, baby brother." She patted the back of his hand. "As sure as roses will have thorns, love will bring you pain."

Thad stood just inside the door for a moment before he approached the bed. Sunlight filtering through the lace curtains showed Mercy's face—gaunt and flushed. He found himself breathing in time to the rising and falling of Mercy's chest. Each breath was reassuring on the one hand, and on the other hand reminded him of just how fragile she was. He sat on the bed next to her and pulled her into his arms.

"Mercy," he whispered in her ear. He kissed her hot cheek. "Mercy, love."

He held her for a moment, then set her gently on the pillows, wet a towel and washed her burning face and neck.

"Come on, honey. Time to stop sleepin' now. You've got to fight. Come back to me."

She coughed and drew another ragged breath. Her eyes fluttered open.

"Thad?"

"I'm here."

"I thought maybe you'd left me . . ." A coughing spell shook her fragile body. He pulled her into his arms and held her until she was breathing steadily again.

"Take a drink, sweetheart." He held the glass to her lips and she gagged on the water. "Small sips now." He tilted the glass. "There, that's better."

She collapsed against his chest, exhausted from the effort to swallow.

"Rest now, Mercy." He stroked her cheek. "I'm not leaving you again."

Mercy looked up at Thad. She tried to smile—to tell him she was glad to see him. No. She had to tell him she'd let him go if that was what he wanted.

"Thad?"

"More water?" He lifted her and she swallowed as much as she could.

"I want you to know." She stopped for a breath. "Now we're home, everything's different." She closed her eyes again to concentrate. "Clarisse will help you find the right woman to marry."

That wasn't quite what she had wanted to say. She felt him stand and move away from the bed or perhaps she was the one moving. It was so damn hot and she was sweating . . .

Mercy leaned on her shovel. Mucking out the stalls was hot work. She should stop and take a drink to replace all the sweat that was dripping from her head and pouring down her back, but she kept working.

"You've been avoiding me." Nate stood near the window, the sunlight showing streaks of yellow in his tawny hair, his lips curled up in a lopsided grin. "Think you can stay in here forever?"

Mercy looked around. She didn't remember coming out to the barn. She had been with Thad, but he was gone. She glanced back at Nate.

"I just need to finish cleaning." She looked down at her feet, sinking in a pile of mud and manure that seemed to be growing. "I was going to talk to you tonight."

"We need to talk, sweetheart, but tonight will be too late."

"Mercy!" Miranda's panic-edged voice carried through the window.

Mercy tried to run, but her feet were stuck fast. She looked back at Nate. His shirt was covered with hoof prints.

"You're going to die?"

He nodded.

She tried again to move—to run to him. "I need to tell you . . . I love you."

"I love you too, sweetheart."

"I let you down."

"Never."

She tried to use the shovel to free her feet, but the shovel stuck fast too.

She looked back at Nate. "You didn't belong on a ranch."

"I belonged wherever you were," Nate said in his calm voice. "I wouldn't trade our years together for anything."

"Oh, Nate." She managed to pull one foot out, but the other sank deeper. She pulled her sleeve across her face, not knowing whether the salty moisture was sweat, or tears. "I should have let you go back to Chicago. You could have been happy there— had children."

*Nate walked toward her, but didn't seem to be getting closer.
"I was happy. I just wished I'd been able to give you children."*

*"It was you who wanted them." Mercy frowned. "You
talked about children before we were even married."*

*"Because you were always so happy playing with Emily and
Will's boys. I knew you'd be a wonderful mother."*

"That's what I said." Thad walked up behind Nate.

*"I hope you can convince her," Nate said. "She can be
rather stubborn, did you notice?"*

*"It so happens I did notice an ornery streak about a mile
wide."*

*"I once caught her giving stubborn lessons to the mule."
Nate winked at Thad and they both laughed.*

"Mercy!"

*Miranda sounded frightened. Mercy looked to where the
men had been standing, but there was no one there.*

*Miranda called her again and Mercy moved toward the
sound, her feet suddenly free. She ran to the pasture looking for
Nate, but found her father instead, bent over an unconscious
figure.*

"Nate?"

*She looked down and saw herself on the ground in a pool of
blood. Her father sat with his hands over her ribs, trying to
stop the bleeding.*

*From the ground, she looked up and saw Nate was walking
away. "No! Don't leave me. I have something I have to tell
you."*

He studied her patiently. "What is it, sweetheart?"

*"I love you. I'll go to Chicago with you. We'll leave the
ranch."*

*"Too late for that." He backed away from her, climbing up
into the mountains.*

*She pushed herself up to follow him, but didn't have the
strength to stand.*

"No," she whispered. "Nate?"

She knew it was all her fault. If he had stayed in Chicago, he'd have been safe. Except that it had been Nate who insisted on coming with her to Colorado. Why did he have to go near the bulls? He didn't know how to handle them. He was always careless—his mind wandered when paying attention was crucial. Now he was dead and her father would never be the same.

She choked back a sob.

She looked around the tranquil meadow, thick with grass and beautiful wildflowers. She could hear a meadowlark calling in the distance. Nate was gone and she felt completely alone. . . .

She opened her eyes and focused on the wallpaper, its pretty flowers seemed to be waltzing. Her head pounded, chest ached. Thad poured a cool liquid into her mouth. She swallowed it, opening her mouth for more.

He settled her back onto her pillow, placing a cool cloth on her forehead. She stared into his blue eyes and knew she didn't have to be alone any longer.

Clarisse handed Thad a warm cup of broth and he helped Mercy drink.

His sister placed a hand on Thad's shoulder. "She's growing stronger."

Mercy frowned. "I can understand you—no sense talking about me like I'm a horse."

"First sign of recovery—the temper is back." Thad winked at his sister.

"I am recovered." Mercy sat a little straighter. "It's time to settle how I'm going to pay Lansing," she croaked.

Thad set the cup down.

"I've searched everywhere, hoping to find some clue that would lead to your money." He glanced at his sister. "All I found was the bag you carried your clothes in."

He pointed across the room to a leather bag sitting on a chest under the window. "I'm sorry."

Mercy smiled. "Thank you for trying, but I . . . I know the money is lost. I aim to find another way to pay Lansing."

"It's Saturday." Thad said. "The money is due on Tuesday. There's no time."

"There has to be a way." Mercy sighed and her eyes drifted shut.

He had let Mercy down. Now she was better, he should just leave. Except that he couldn't bear to imagine days without her.

She opened her eyes and looked back up at him. "I'll think of something." She had to. "I'm sure I will."

He brushed a lock from her forehead, his fingers lingering at the side of her head. "You sleep now. Maybe you'll dream something that will help."

She nodded, remembering the dream she'd had of Nate and Thad. Clarisse bustled about the room, cleaning and straightening. Mercy would talk to Thad later, when Clarisse wasn't around. His sister had someone else in mind for Thad, but Mercy was certain her friend would accept her if it was still what Thad wanted. She glanced up at Thad. He'd been acting strangely—tender and loving one moment and distant the next. She'd make sure he knew what he wanted, before she told him of her decision. It was important he not feel his proposal on the trail obligated him. She wanted to be with him, but not if that meant he would be unhappy.

A tremendous crash that sounded as though the ceiling had collapsed in the next room, startled all of them.

"Oh, Lord," Clarisse said. "I wonder what those boys are doing now." She hurried out the door.

"I'd better help," Thad said before following his sister.

Mercy sighed as she watched Thad run out the door. Her eyes dropped to those muscular legs. She was most definitely better.

"How are you feelin' this morning, Mercy?" Clarisse brought a tray in and set it down.

"I hope you brought me some coffee," Mercy said.

Clarisse laughed. "I have some buttermilk for you— that'll give you some strength."

Mercy pulled a face, but she sat up and took the cup. "Mmm." She glanced over at the tray. "I didn't realize how hungry I was."

"Glad to hear it," Clarisse said. "I thought you might try a real breakfast—do you think you can eat some eggs?"

Mercy's stomach growled as she smelled the food. "I'm willing to try."

Clarisse arranged the tray on Mercy's lap and sat near the bed while she ate. "I brought somethin' to show you."

Mercy glanced over, her mouth full of eggs. Clarisse laid a long string of pearls out beside Mercy. "Thad was able to save some of Mama's favorite jewelry for me. She always promised to give me these pearls when I married." She looked up at Mercy. "Papa didn't approve of Wendell. His family was poor—he had no education. When we couldn't get Papa's permission, we eloped and came West lookin' for gold. I always thought Mama would send me the pearls, but . . . Well, perhaps she didn't trust the mail to carry anything so valuable."

Clarisse opened a blue silk bag. "There are earrings too—with pearls. And some rings."

Mercy glanced over the collection. The ring Thad had showed her wasn't among the jewels. "Your mama must have liked white."

Clarisse smiled at Mercy. "She always said simple things are more elegant. She did have a ring with colored stones—her weddin' ring. Papa had it made specially, with her favorite colors—blue and green. She had a pendant and earrings to match that ring too, but she had to sell them." Clarisse ran her fingers over the pearl necklace. "They were her most valuable jewels. She couldn't bear to give up the ring, though."

"I imagine she wore it until she died."

Clarisse shook her head. "No. All of these things," Clarisse waved a hand over the jewels spread out on the bed, "and the ring too, Mama had Thad bury them until the war was over. It wasn't safe to keep valuables in the house."

Clarisse opened the bag and put the earrings into it. "Mama gave Thad clear instructions to save the ring for his bride and he's doing that." She lifted her eyes to Mercy's. "You've seen the ring, haven't you?"

Mercy felt her face warm. "He might have shown it to me—"

"I knew it. He proposed marriage to you, didn't he?"

"Clarisse . . . I. What did Thad tell you?"

"He won't say. You didn't turn him down, did you?"

"I haven't said he asked me." Mercy crossed her arms over her chest.

"Well, somethin's causing my brother to act like a rooster who's had his feathers plucked."

"What do you mean?"

"When I mention your name around him, he clamps his mouth tight and won't talk." She put the necklace into the bag and began picking up the rings. "And he won't look me in the eye. You love him, don't you?"

"That's a mighty personal question." Mercy studied the flowers on the wall. "I won't have him feeling oblig- ated to me just because—" She looked at Clarisse. "We

did speak of marriage on the trail. But I was wounded
and half-drunk with whiskey and he was worried about
me. Not the best circumstances for making such an important decision."

"Have you told him how you feel—now that your
head is clear and you're mending?"

Mercy looked back to the wall. If Thad gave her the
slightest encouragement, she'd be in his arms, kissing
him. Damn, she missed his kisses. She missed *him*.

Two quick raps on the door drew Mercy's attention.

Rita Diaz entered the room and strode over to the
bed. The dark-haired beauty greeted Clarisse, then bent
to kiss Mercy on the cheek. She straightened, holding
her head high, seeming as independent in her way as
Clarisse was in hers. Yet they couldn't be more different. Clarisse was bosomy and fair, quiet and dedicated
to her family. Rita was slender and dark, tempestuous
and passionate. She kept the men in her saloon in control with a sharp sense of humor and the derringer she
carried in her skirt pocket. The saloonkeeper had a
reputation for changing lovers more frequently than
most women changed their undergarments. Mercy knew
that image of Rita was completely wrong.

"No more fever, eh?" Rita smiled. "*Muy bien.* You will
be strong again soon."

Rita always bubbled over with energy and enthusiasm.

"I am quite well, thanks to you and Clarisse and all
my friends."

"Clarisse—she has done all the work. I only visit and
bring you stories."

"Don't underestimate the value of a good yarn,"
Mercy said. "I'd have died of boredom in this bed without them."

Rita pulled a chair up next to Clarisse. "I have not a
good story today. It is bad news."

Mercy wrinkled her brow. "What is it?"

"I tried to speak with Señor Lansing."

Mercy's stomach twisted at the mention of the foul man's name.

"I hoped he would consider . . . *Como se dice?* Extending the loan, until you are better."

"Oh, Rita." Mercy sucked in a deep breath. "I appreciate your efforts, but—"

"It is only right." Rita moved to the edge of her chair. "The whole town knows what happened—that you had the money so close before it was stolen. *Cabron!* Idiot! He has more money than one man can spend. He could not wait for you to pay him, one more year?"

"Lansing is probably glad the money was stolen. He wants my land."

"It isn't fair," Clarisse said.

"You and Rita are good friends. I appreciate your loyalty. But . . ." Mercy sighed. "I do owe the money. Lansing is within his rights to demand cash payment—on time." She looked from Rita to Clarisse. "If anyone is to blame for this, it's me. I took a tremendous risk importing the Herefords." The whole adventure had cost her dearly.

"And your idea has proven itself," Clarisse said. "Just look at the fine price—"

"Which means nothing since I didn't get the money home." Mercy blinked back a tear. She hated to appear weak in front of her two closest friends.

"You are upset now, I should not have mentioned Lansing." Rita reached out and took Mercy's hand—her coffee brown eyes filled with concern.

"It isn't anything you've said, Rita. I was worried about the money before you walked in the door."

"I wish there was something we could do," Clarisse said.

"It isn't your problem," Mercy said. "I know that both

of you are anxious for me—and I do appreciate it. haven't given up yet." And she hadn't. Except that, fo the first time, it did occur to her to wonder what sh would do if she lost the ranch.

Chapter 24

Mercy blinked twice—she'd been dozing. Her father leaned close. He hadn't shaved. Damn! He looked terrible. "You need your rest, Pa. Have you been sleeping?"

He grinned at her. "I believe you're back, praise God!" He kissed her forehead. "I never thought I'd hear you nag me again."

"She walked all the way out to the privy this morning, while you were restin'," Clarisse said.

"I'd prefer to keep some things private, Clarisse," Mercy said.

"Well, I thought it was worth tellin' your pa. I'll bet it sets his mind at ease some, doesn't it, Fenton?"

"Yes, indeed," Pa said. "I'm right proud of you, daughter."

"Make fun," Mercy said. "It's bad enough I've been saddled to this bed with folks constantly hovering over me. You have to tease me too?" Mercy sat up higher. "My greatest accomplishments—nagging and using the necessary." She pulled her braid over her shoulder and brushed the end against her palm. "But since you brought it up, I did walk out back on my own—"

"With a little help," Clarisse corrected.

"With a little help," Mercy admitted. "Now, I need to go see Arthur Lansing. I'd appreciate a little help getting to his ranch."

"Where do you get these mad ideas?" Clarisse asked.

Pa pressed her gently back into bed. "You'll go nowhere. You ain't strong enough to be chasing out to Lansing's place."

"I can't put this off. I want to talk with him about trading the Herefords and some of our herd. It isn't cash—but it could benefit him far more than cash."

The bell from the front door of the store rang and Clarisse turned her head. "I've got to go. Wendell is out making some deliveries. Will you talk some sense into her, Fenton?"

"Damned right I will," Pa said, then added. "Beg pardon, ma'am."

"Hellfire, Fenton. Don't you think after eight years of livin' in Fort Victory, I can tolerate strong language?" Clarisse went out the door.

"You ain't goin' nowhere." Pa crossed his arms over his chest. "You know danged good and well the man wants cash. It's a waste of time tryin' to talk to him. And you aren't so far recovered you can be runnin' across the countryside. I won't allow it."

"I have to try."

"No."

Mercy settled back down on the pillow. No point in wasting energy fighting. She closed her eyes to wait until Pa fell asleep.

As Mercy had guessed, it wasn't long before her father was dozing. She threw back the blankets and sat up, then took a moment to catch her breath. Slowly. No need to rush. She glanced at her father. His head was bobbing in rhythm with his snoring. He wasn't going to awaken for a long while. Mercy stood and crossed the room to the bag with her clothes. She ached everywhere, especially her right knee. She must have injured it when she fell. The pain didn't matter—she had no choice. Time was running out.

She was a hell of a lot stronger than Clarisse and Pa thought she was. It was less than two hours to Lansing's place. A short ride really. She took a deep breath and lifted off her nightshirt, feeling as though a blade cut into her ribs when she raised her arms. She eyed the laudanum on the table and took another deep breath. The medicine might lessen the pain, but she needed a clear head when she talked to Lansing.

Thad jabbed the shovel deep into the earth, turned the soil over, then drove the shovel in again. Nearby, his brother-in-law supervised his nephews as they harvested the last of the potatoes and carrots. Thad turned over more dark soil. It felt good to be accomplishing something, but he wished he were helping Mercy.

He stabbed the shovel into the earth again, pausing to wipe a handkerchief over his brow. He looked up at her window. She was better, much stronger now. It was time to talk to her. To make some decisions. If only he weren't such a coward. He replaced his hat and stalked into the kitchen, the smell of tart apples and sweet cinnamon tickling his nose.

"You're not avoiding Mercy again, are you?" Clarisse pulled an apple pie from the oven.

Thad poured water into the basin, then splashed some on his face before washing his hands. Clarisse handed him a clean towel.

"She doesn't need constant care now. I thought perhaps I could make myself more useful." He looked out the window, pretending to be interested in Wendell and the boys working in the kitchen garden. His eyes drifted to the blue gingham curtains that matched the cloth on the table behind him.

"I think Mama would be surprised to see the civilized home you've made here," Thad said.

"I hope she'd be proud of me. I could never tell from her letters . . . Do you think she understood that it wasn't her I wanted to leave, or Papa either?"

"I don't know how they felt when you left. I do know she was always proud when she talked to her friends about your growing family and your successful business."

"I'm glad." Clarisse placed a hand on his arm. "Now as for you—why don't you go up and talk with Mercy? I'm sure her pa is sleepin' by now."

He handed his sister the towel. "Just came in to see if you need any help with dinner."

Clarisse grinned at her brother. "Miss cooking, do you?" She handed him a bowl and a knife. "How 'bout peelin' some potatoes for supper?"

Thad nodded and sat at the table to commence the chore.

Clarisse sat across from him, peeling carrots. "If you intend to end the relationship, the least you can do is tell the lady yourself."

He looked at his sister. "I'm not sure what I intend."

"Humph." Clarisse nodded. "I suppose you think because we've been separated all these years I've forgotten that look."

"What look?" Thad kept his eye on the potato he was peeling.

"The same look you had when you told Mama that Tom and Cal had nothing to do with the fire out back of the barn."

Thad looked up.

"Mama knew very well you were lying for them, but

she hoped the boys would feel guilty when they saw you taking their punishment."

"Little did she know they were pleased to see baby brother get punished for once."

She smiled and came around behind him. Clarisse stretched her arms around his shoulders. "I'm so glad to have you here, little brother." She gave him a peck on the cheek.

"Well, then." Wendell let the door slam behind him. "A fellow comes in for a cool drink only to find his wife kissing another man."

"Now, now." Clarisse hastened to kiss Wendell's cheek, but he wrapped his arms around her and gave her a deeper kiss that had Clarisse blushing like a bride.

Thad smiled, seeing his sister so happy. He dropped his eyes to the potato in his hand and resumed peeling. Clarisse fetched a drink for her husband and they continued to chatter. Thad was ashamed for the spark of jealousy he felt, seeing the love between them. His parents had been the same way, so close they could communicate without speaking. Now he knew that was a rare gift that few would ever enjoy, but he and Mercy had a chance at that kind of love, he was certain of it. Except that the loss of her ranch would always stand between them.

He looked up when he heard Wendell's boots stomping out the door.

Clarisse came back to the table. "I know you and Mercy love each other. Seein' Mercy so ill—is that what's troublin' you?"

Thad shook his head. "I keep thinkin' there's something I should be doin'... I can't just stand by and watch her lose her ranch."

Clarisse pursed her lips, then bent her head over the carrot in her hand. "Unless you have a thousand dollars..."

Thad pulled a small cloth bag out of his pocket. "I

have eighty-five dollars in gold coin here and another hundred in greenbacks."

Clarisse stared at him. "That's nearly two hundred dollars. Wendell and I probably have another two hundred on hand." She shook her head. "That's still less than half . . . what about Rita? She takes in quite a lot of cash at the saloon and I know she'd want to help Mercy." Clarisse stood. "And Thad." She grinned at him. "Mama's jewels—they must be worth another couple hundred, don't you think? What am I going to do with pearls?"

"Are you sure, Clarisse? I know Mama's necklace means a lot to you."

"Knowin' Mama thought of me, that means a lot. I have no occasion to wear pearls in Fort Victory."

Thad reached into his pocket and pulled out the one piece of jewelry he'd kept. The blue and green stones sparkled.

"No, you can't, Thad. Mama would want that ring to go to your wife."

"It's the most valuable piece." Thad looked at his sister. "Maybe he'd take it as a pledge—I wouldn't have to give it to him outright."

She nodded. "I'm going to see whether Rita can help us. You get your horse ready—you've just enough daylight left to get to Lansing's place and back."

Thad nodded, but he was still looking at the ring, remembering how right it had looked on Mercy's finger. Mama had cried when she took it off and asked him to bury it. She'd made him promise to keep it—to be sure he had found the right woman before he gave it away. He'd kept his promise—he'd found the right woman. If the ring could save Mercy's ranch, it was a small price to pay.

*   *   *

Zeus was so anxious for a ride he could hardly stand still for Thad to saddle him. How many days had he let the poor horse stand in the barn? Thad pulled the last cinch tight, then led the animal past three empty stalls and into the yard. He stopped. Something wasn't right.

Thad wrapped his gelding's reins around a post and marched back into the barn. The two horses that Wendell used to pull the wagon were in their stalls next to Clover. Where the hell was Annabelle?

"Rita gave me every dollar she could spare." Clarisse bustled into the barn. "Nearly three hundred. That brings our total to—" She stopped short and looked up at Thad. "What's wrong?"

"Annabelle is missing." Thad looked back into the stall, then walked around to where Wendell kept the tack. He turned back to Clarisse. "Isn't there a saddle missing?"

"Yes, my old saddle is usually next to Wendell's."

Thad felt his stomach knot. "Would Fenton have taken Annabelle?"

"Fenton wouldn't leave. He's upstairs with—" Clarisse spun around. "Lordy, that woman will be the death of us all." She lifted her skirts and sprinted toward the house with Thad close behind her.

Chapter 25

Lansing was grateful for the cool day. A pleasant fire in the parlor would be most welcome and he intended to make a lovely, hot blaze. He carried the bucket full of kerosene closer to the fireplace—the magnificent stone wall was the one masculine touch in this room. He held the pail steadily in front of him. Damned if he'd spill kerosene on the fine imported rug—his late wife had paid a fortune for the ugly thing.

"Papa—"

Lansing sloshed kerosene on his trousers and the rug.

"Dammit, boy—what did I tell you?"

"But—"

"You're to stay in your room. No arguments!"

"Yes, sir." Jonathan turned toward the door.

"Wait a moment, young man." Lansing was pleased to see his son stop instantly. He was an obedient boy—though he did tend to be forgetful. "Bring the strap."

Jonathan walked slowly across the oriental rug to the secretary that stood next to the window. He opened the bottom drawer and pulled out the leather strap.

The lad brought it to his father and without being asked, lowered his britches and turned his bare bottom toward Lansing.

He smiled. A good boy, indeed. "You should have twelve strikes for direct disobedience of my order. But I'm in a good mood today and I know you didn't mean to disobey, did you?"

"No, sir."

"Fine." Lansing pulled his arm back to begin. "It will be just ten hits then." Jonathan counted each hit aloud as Lansing had taught him.

The boy turned and looked up at his father, a single tear rolling down his cheek. He swallowed. "Thank you, Papa."

"You're welcome, son. I only did my duty. The strap is a necessary part of your discipline. You understand?"

The boy nodded and Lansing scowled at him. Perhaps he'd been wrong to be lenient.

"Yes, sir," Jonathan corrected his mistake. "I understand."

Lansing smiled and patted the boy's head. "Very well then—off to your room with you now. And no more tears. Crying is for babies."

Jonathan slipped out the door and pulled it closed behind him. Lansing stared at the door. The one thing he'd learned from his father was proper discipline. A firm hand turned a weak boy into a powerful man. The old man had grown soft by the time his younger brother was born. Father had spoiled Benjamin. Lansing would not allow his son to suffer that fate.

"Now." He grinned. "Back to the task at hand." He took the iron poker and shoved it into the bucket, pressing the leather jacket under the kerosene. It had been thoroughly soaked. After an hour sitting in the oil, Mercy's jacket should burn nicely.

Lansing set about starting the fire. No kindling, blast

it all. He shouldn't have to worry about such things, but it had been weeks since the last servant had left. No loyalty. A man should be able to wait a few weeks for his wages. Well, it was their loss—all the men who had left his employment in the past few months would regret their decision. Lansing had plenty of money to hire new servants now and he wouldn't consider rehiring any of those who'd betrayed him by leaving.

With his expanded ranch, he stood to earn even more money. If Mercy had obtained eighteen dollars a head for her cattle, he imagined he could negotiate twenty dollars or more for the animals. Perhaps he could drive the other cattle ranchers out of business. So many plans to make. First, he had to get rid of everything that might connect him to the theft. Not that it was really stealing; after all, the money was rightfully his.

He looked around. He'd have to go outside and collect some kindling. No—there was a pile near the stove in the kitchen.

He hurried out of the parlor and down the back hall to the kitchen. There he filled his arms with kindling and carried it back to the fireplace, dumping it on the stone hearth. He arranged half of the small pieces of wood in the fireplace, then chuckled. With all the kerosene he had, kindling was almost unnecessary. He dipped a few sticks into the bucket and set them under the pile he'd made. Then he added three small logs. Finally, he set the soaked jacket over the top and allowed kerosene to drip on the wood. Son of a bitch, he'd dripped kerosene on his shirt. No matter, he'd change clothes and burn his shirt and trousers later.

He lit a match and dropped it on the pile of wood. The first match went out, but the second burned in a puddle of kerosene. In a moment, some of the sticks caught the flame. It wasn't long before the jacket started to smolder. Lovely. He watched the blaze grow.

He debated whether to leave the pile of kindling in the parlor, or take it back to the kitchen. A banging at the front door interrupted his thoughts. A most inopportune time for a caller.

Mercy had managed to saddle Annabelle and ride out of town unnoticed. The five-mile ride to Lansing's house had brought her near exhaustion. She filled her lungs with cool autumn air. Tomorrow would be soon enough to rest. After she'd talked to Lansing. At least then, she'd know for certain whether she was going to keep her ranch.

At the sight of Arthur's sprawling house, she slowed Annabelle. Mercy drew herself taller and rolled her shoulders, trying to shake off the aches and pains that throbbed through her body. *Almost there.*

She had to convince the man to take his payment in cattle. She'd give him more than a thousand dollars worth of animals. She felt certain that the Hereford bulls were worth over a hundred dollars each now they'd proven their breeding value. Her eyes still on the house, she stroked Annabelle's neck, feeling the horse's warmth through her leather glove.

"Annabelle, can you imagine living in a fancy house like that?"

Annabelle nickered.

"You're right, the house Thad grew up in was grander."

She'd nearly forgotten Clarisse's description of her childhood home. Thad's home, too. How could Thad be willing to share her simple life? Because he was a practical man who cared about the land, the beasts— *and me.* She felt a warmth deep in her chest in spite of the chill air.

Seven chimneys rose from Lansing's house. With cow chips plentiful, Lansing preferred to burn logs, although there was no forest within a mile. He paid to have firewood cut and brought to him from the mountains. Perhaps Lansing should just burn money to keep warm. All of these trappings were important to him, but his ranch was dying for lack of water.

She sighed. Mercy's ranch could provide Lansing with a steady flow of water, enough for him to double or triple his herd and make his ranch profitable. She couldn't blame him for wanting her land, but she hated to give it to him. He'd never care for it properly. Raising cattle was only a business to him. For her, it was a way of life.

If she lost the ranch, she and Thad could take Pa and move to Denver. She disliked the thought of living in a city, but knew she'd be happy with Thad anywhere. He still hadn't mentioned marriage to her, but she was certain he would. If he didn't, she would swallow her damn pride and ask him herself. No more wasting opportunities.

Thad loved the land as much as she did and she'd be happy to work with him to build another ranch if she had to. But she certainly wasn't going to give up on her own place without a fight. She drew a breath, pulled her hat down and clicked her tongue, signaling Annabelle to trot.

It had been a while since Mercy had visited Lansing's place. The empty yard felt strange with no cowboys working. *They must all be out with the herd.* Not even any horses in the corral. Very strange.

Mercy dismounted, hitched Annabelle to a post near the stable, then walked to the house. She moved slowly to work out the stiffness from the long ride.

She had to knock several times before Lansing answered the door. When he did, he hardly glanced at her. She hadn't expected an enthusiastic greeting, but Lansing was usually at least civil.

Where were the butler and the other servants? He

didn't step aside to let her in, but stood blocking the partly opened door. He glanced over his shoulder.

"I'm, uh, glad to see you've recovered so speedily," he said in his emotionless voice.

She peered over his shoulder into the cavernous entrance hall, but didn't see anything unusual. Arthur's wife, Vivian, had decorated the space with family daguerrotypes hanging on one wall and a large oil painting of an English hunt on the other. Mercy knew the house well from the weeks she'd spent here caring for Arthur's son, Jonathan, after Vivian died giving birth to the lad. Everything appeared in order.

"May I come in?" she asked.

Lansing glanced at the closed parlor door. "Of course." He took a step back from the door. "What can I do for you, my dear?" He smiled, with an effort that betrayed his lack of experience with the expression.

Mercy took one step inside the door, which was all Lansing allowed her. It seemed odd that he didn't invite her to sit. The parlor was a showpiece as grand as any mansion she'd seen when Nate took her to Chicago. Lansing loved to display it to visitors. The room reflected Vivian's taste, decorated with lace curtains, brocaded furniture and carpets from the Orient. When visiting, Mercy had always felt out of place among the fine furnishings, but today she would have been glad for the opportunity to rest in one of the comfortable upholstered chairs.

"I'm very busy." Lansing glanced over his shoulder at the door to the parlor. "Did you come to pay me?"

"No." Mercy took a step toward him. He reeked of, what? Kerosene? "I had hoped to come to another arrangement."

"Arrangement?" Lansing sneered.

Mercy stood taller. "I know you heard that my cattle fetched eighteen dollars a head in Abilene."

"Ha!" Lansing sneered. "Meaningless, since you have no money to show for it."

"It does mean one thing. The Hereford bulls are more valuable now. I'd say they are each worth one hundred and twenty-five dollars." Mercy raised her chin. " can give you four of them—worth five hundred."

"Even if I were willing to accept, that's only half what you owe me."

"I understand that. But, I can give you the rest in cattle—figuring a low price of twelve dollars each, I'll give you forty-two head. You could sell them for even more in the mining camps, I'll even sell them for you—"

"Enough!" Lansing raised a hand palm forward. " am not interested in these negotiations. I want a thousand in cash, or your land. Nothing else will do."

"Think it over, Arthur. I'm offering you an opportunity. You can be among the first to raise the new breed—"

"Why don't you take your rebel lover and do your own breeding?"

"There's no reason for insults."

"Why do you find my words offensive? You're the one who chose to take a lover rather than accept an honorable—"

"My relationship with Thad Buchanan is not your business." Lansing was fishing, he couldn't possibly know that she and Thad were lovers. "I came here to discuss—"

"You play the role of the business woman—making decisions without emotion as a man would. Ha! You are truly naïve. You wouldn't even consider my proposal—a match that would have benefited both of us. You'd have had a fine home, beautiful clothing and a son. Instead you jump into bed with a no-account gambler."

"You don't know Thad." Mercy fought to keep the anger from her voice, to keep from giving Lansing the long list of reasons she had never seriously considered becoming his wife.

"Humph," Lansing snorted. "Love. It has a way of blinding people. I've never cared to feel so uncontrolled."

Mercy drew a breath. "Sometimes love can make a person see more clearly." She reached a hand back to the wall to steady herself. She wasn't going to be able to stand much longer.

"Our business is concluded . . ." He took her arm and moved her toward the door. Yes, the odor was kerosene, no doubt about it. Lansing was burning something.

She pushed past him and through the parlor door.

"Stop!" he shouted, but she was already striding toward the vast stone fireplace that dominated one wall.

The odor of burning kerosene permeated the room. On the hearth sat a pile of kindling and a bucket half full of the fuel. In the blazing fire, Mercy spotted the remains of her buckskin jacket. If Lansing had the jacket, he had stolen her money.

She grabbed the poker and tried to snag a bit of the burning jacket. Lansing clutched her arm and she dropped the iron tool as she shrugged out of his grip. A bit of burning leather stuck to the poker as it crashed to the hearth.

"You!" She turned to Lansing. "You had my money all along." He moved toward her and she pulled her Colt. "You hired Jed and Luther to take it."

"That's right. I should have offered them a bonus for killing you. I nearly got my wish without paying for it. Damn O'Reilly for being such a poor shot. He should have killed you. Hell, I'd have killed you myself if that rebel oaf hadn't happened by."

"You missed your chance then." She gripped the gun with both hands, but still had a difficult time keeping it steady. "We're going to see the sheriff now."

Behind Lansing, the kindling pile on the hearth started to burn.

"Do you honestly think he'll take your word ove mine? I'm too important in this town. Everyone be lieves I have plenty of money—they'll never accept tha I would resort to theft." Lansing took a step toward he "You can't defeat me. You had every chance to becom an ally—my wife. The arrangement would have ben fited both of us, but you were too damn stubborn. waited as long as I could. I'm out of money and no on left to borrow from. I will not return to Boston a fai ure," he growled. "Now you're going to regret interfe ing with my plans."

"And you're going to find out what happens to thos who break the—"

Lansing lurched at the gun, knocking it out of he hands. He shoved her against the stone wall. The pai shot from her shoulder into her ribs. She kicked he knee into his groin. He doubled over and she butte her shoulder into his chest, shoving him away. He stum bled, knocking over the bucket of kerosene. She dov for her gun. Behind her, Lansing screamed.

He sat for a moment in a puddle of flaming kerosene then jumped up, running across the room, his trouser blazing.

"Stop!" she shouted. "You're making it worse." Sh pulled a linen cloth from a table, overturning a sma wooden box. She chased after Lansing, intending t smother the flames with the cloth, but he, half-crazy wit pain, wouldn't let her near him. The flames climbed u his back and he set the curtains ablaze as he passe them.

Mercy felt helpless. A trail of fires soon marke Lansing's path. She caught up with him in the corne but he still wouldn't let her close enough to smother th flames. She threw the cloth over him. Within second that cloth was also burning.

The room filled with smoke from the many blazes

Mercy's heart pounded as she made her way toward the door, stumbling over an upturned table. The air was cleaner near the floor and she crawled forward. Near the door, she bumped the overturned wooden box. The spilled contents included a pile of bloody greenbacks. She scooped up a handful of money and shoved it into her pocket. At the door, she turned to see Lansing rolling on the carpet. Even if he smothered the flames he would be badly burned. He'd need help, but she needed to get outside and breathe some pure air or she'd be no use to either of them.

She pulled herself to her feet and staggered into the entrance hall, aiming for the large front door.

"Jonathan," she whispered.

Mercy turned away from the door. Smoke poured out of the parlor and drifted up the stairs. Soon flames would follow. She dragged herself to the second floor and into the nursery.

"Mercy?" Jonathan's small voice greeted her from his bed. "It smells funny." She could see the lad had been crying.

"There's a fire. We need to go outside."

"Papa said I must stay in my room today."

"He wants you to go outside now, Jonathan." Mercy drew a breath and choked on the fouled air. "It isn't safe in here."

He shook his head.

"You must, Jonathan." She took his hand and pulled him toward the hall.

As the smoke and heat hit them, Jonathan pulled back into the nursery. She lifted the boy in her arms and staggered back toward the stairs. Flames had escaped the parlor and several small blazes showed through the smoke below. Every breath hurt. She took a step. Collapsed to her knees.

"Ow!" Jonathan cried.

"Sorry," Mercy panted, and then choked. "You nee to be brave . . . a little longer."

She crawled forward, dragging Jonathan. The hea from below felt like an oven. They wouldn't make down the stairs. There had to be another way. She kep moving, towing the boy behind her. The smoke seeme to cloud her brain. She couldn't think. Couldn't see. Th floor lurched up to her head. She clutched Jonathan t her breast and tried to catch her breath, to make plan. She turned away from the stairs and felt along th wall for the hallway. If she could find the back stair they might make it.

Mercy took a breath to clear her head, but it burne her throat. A black curtain threatened to close over he She stopped to rest, then crept forward, pulling Jonatha a few more inches. He felt like a dead weight in he arms. She looked at his face—he was unconscious. Dea God, she hoped he was breathing, but she didn't dar stop to check. She had to keep moving. They must b near the back stairs by now. She couldn't see anythin through the smoke, but the heat wasn't so bad here She crawled forward, keeping a shoulder against th wall and dragging Jonathan.

"Not much further now, son." She choked on th words.

She wrapped her arm more tightly around the bo and pulled him along. Inches were all she could man age, but she wasn't going to stop. Her lungs screame for air. She reached the top of the stairs, and tried t stand. Her legs wouldn't carry her. Jonathan slippe out of her arms and she pulled him close enough t feel his heartbeat. The back stairs were steep and nar row; she had to find the strength to crawl down wit him in her arms. She was not going to let him die.

"Wake up, Jonathan," she said. "Please, you mus help me!"

The fire roared behind them. In a moment, it would be on top of them, if the floor didn't collapse first. Through the gray smoke—the haze that was around her and inside her head—she thought she heard Thad calling her name.

Chapter 26

The rock at the bottom of Thad's stomach sank deeper yet again as he rode Zeus away from town. Mercy was riding to Lansing's place. He'd bet all the money he was carrying on that. Nearly seven hundred dollars. Together with his mother's jewels, it was a good deal more than Mercy owed Lansing.

Thad still hoped to persuade the bastard to take the money and hold the jewels until Thad could raise the rest of the cash. But right now, his first task was to find Mercy. He would make sure she was safe and then he would wring that long, graceful neck of hers.

Lord only knows why that woman feels she has to take everything on herself. She could have asked for his help. If she trusted him, she would have.

Clarisse said Mercy was still weak and should be in bed. His sister claimed to know Mercy. Well, she couldn't know Mercy very well if she was surprised that mule-headed woman would be trying to do everything herself.

Thad fought the urge to push Zeus to gallop. If he went too fast, he just might ride past Mercy lying help-

less in a ditch. He scanned the road for any sign of
Annabelle. His stomach twisted into a tighter knot. It
was possible that Mercy hadn't made it as far as Lansing's
place before collapsing. Sheer stubbornness could only
carry a person so far. If the doctor had been in town,
Thad would have dragged him along, but the man had
been called out to a ranch five miles the other side of
town. Thad swallowed. Mercy would be fine—she just
needed rest and he was going to make damn sure she
got it, even if he had to tie her down.

Thad peered ahead. There was smoke rising out of
buildings in the distance. And, if he wasn't mistaken—
flames. Hell, that had to be Lansing's place. He urged
Zeus to a gallop. As he raced into the yard, Thad brought
his horse to a rest near where Annabelle stood tethered.
He looped the reins over a post and nearly tripped over
the water trough before he raced to the front door of
the burning house. He flung the door open.

"Damn!" Flames danced up the wall. He ran back to
the trough, soaked his hat and jacket, then charged back
to the house.

He peered into the thick black smoke, then plunged
inside. Thad lifted his wet sleeve to his face to block the
heat pouring into the entrance hall from the room to
the right. Fire crawled across the floor—on top of a person.

"Mercy?" Thad threw a rug over the body, fear clutching his gut.

He bent closer and saw it was Lansing. "Where's
Mercy?"

The man peered at him, half his face charred. Thad
could only imagine how badly his body was burned. "My
son . . . upstairs . . ."

Lansing had crawled out of the burning room, but
there was no entering that room now. God, Thad hoped
Mercy wasn't in there. How to find her?

"Mercy?" he shouted.

Dear God, if the boy was upstairs . . . "Mercy?" he shouted up the stairs. Flames covered the stairs. He raced into the hall looking for another way up. "Mercy?"

"Thad?" The voice seemed so distant, for a moment he thought he'd imagined it.

There was another staircase. He sprinted up the stairs, praying she was alive up there. His lungs burned from the smoke as he reached the second floor. Mercy sat curled up at the top of the stairs with a child in her arms. Flames crept across the floor behind her.

"Thad?" she choked out his name.

He took the boy from her arms and pulled her up. She clung to him as they made their way down the stairs. The hall he'd come through was engulfed.

"Kitchen," Mercy said. He turned and found the kitchen and the rear exit. They stumbled out the door. He scrambled for a hundred yards, clutching the boy with one arm and dragging Mercy with the other. He didn't dare stop until they were clear of all the smoke.

He set the boy on the ground and Mercy collapsed next to him, gasping for breath. Thad's jacket and hat were steaming and he ripped them off.

"Mercy?" He traced a finger over her soot-covered cheek.

She coughed, tried to sit up and collapsed again. Tears streaked her cheeks.

"It's all right." Thad would scold her later for scaring him half to death. Now he'd just be grateful she was alive.

He touched the boy's chest and bent low over him to listen for breathing. The lad coughed in his ear.

"Jonathan?" Mercy muttered, reaching for the boy's hand.

Jonathan sat up and looked at Mercy. "Papa?"

"I don't know if . . ." Mercy panted.

Thad raced around to the front door where he'd left Lansing—and saw the front entrance collapse as he came around the corner. Thad drew in a deep breath and coughed until he thought his lungs would burst. If he'd been a few moments later Mercy would have been trapped inside too.

He stood bent, with his hands on his knees for a moment, catching his breath. He couldn't get Lansing's charred face out of his mind. That could have been Mercy. He stood tall and walked around to where Mercy sat with her arms around the boy.

"Are you injured?" he asked as he collapsed next to them.

She shook her head and coughed again.

"The whole house is on fire now," Jonathan said softly.

Flames shot out the windows on both floors now. Thad wondered for a moment whether he should look for water.

"There's nothing we can do, son." The house was lost. "We'd better move farther away," Thad said. He helped Mercy and the boy walk around to the front of the house.

"Papa?" Jonathan asked again as he looked up at the house engulfed in flames.

Thad knelt beside the boy. "I saw him inside. He was trying to save you, but the fire burned him."

"Where is he?"

"I'm afraid—" Thad glanced at Mercy, then back to the boy—"I'm afraid he didn't get out of the house in time."

Jonathan swallowed and stared at the house.

"I'm sorry, sweetheart," Mercy said. "Your father died."

Jonathan buried his face in Mercy's chest. She held him close while Thad put his arms around both of them.

"Mercy, don't you ever scare me like that again," Thad whispered. "What were you thinking, coming here alone?"

"I . . . I didn't know," Mercy croaked.

Jonathan wept. "Papa? I want my father."

"Shh, shh." Mercy patted Jonathan's back.

Thad looked back at the house and relaxed his fists. It appeared the man he wanted to punch was in God's hands now—or more likely in hell.

Thad had commandeered a buggy from Lansing's stable. Mercy sat next to him with her arms wrapped around Jonathan. He didn't think he was ever going to be able to pry the boy out of her arms. It was just as well—she had to ride in the buggy to hold him, which meant she hadn't insisted on riding Annabelle home. Any fool could see she didn't have the strength to stay upright on a horse's back, but Thad knew that wouldn't have stopped her from trying.

Thad's chest ached, and not just because he'd swallowed so much smoke. Something was squeezing his heart until he feared it would stop altogether. He had plenty of time to think about his future as he drove the buggy into town, and he didn't like his choices.

"Thad, there's something I need to tell you."

He braced himself for rejection. She needed her independence, he understood that now. Hell, if she hadn't been willing to ask him to help her deal with Lansing, she was never going to be able to trust him with anything.

"I want you to know I love you," Mercy said.

"You . . . you do?" Thad glanced at her face—she was looking down the road.

"I do."

She leaned against him and he wrapped an arm around her, wondering how many baths it would take before they stopped smelling like smoke.

"I'm too tired to talk now, but I wanted to tell you. Mustn't postpone saying important things," she mumbled.

"We'll talk later. You rest, darlin'." He watched Mercy slowly fall asleep in the dusky light. His greatest desire was to have a lifetime with her. A chance to watch her sleep every night. To help her with that ranch she loved so well and perhaps to raise children together.

Her confession of love might mean she had finally decided she wanted the same thing. Unless it was exhaustion talking or hidden fear from nearly dying in that fire. As the rutted road rolled past them, Thad imagined life with Mercy and life without her. She'd told him several times that she wanted her independence. He wasn't sure a person could be independent and married at the same time. More importantly, he wasn't sure that was what he wanted in a marriage.

It was nearly dark when they rolled into town. The wagon rumbled to a stop in front of the store. Mercy sat up and looked around as Clarisse and Wendell came rushing out.

Wendell carried the sleeping child inside. Thad swept Mercy into his arms. She opened her mouth and he thought she would protest. Instead, she closed her eyes and leaned against his shoulder as he cradled her in his arms.

"Mercy?" Thad whispered.

She lifted one lid and made a feeble attempt to smile. "Tired . . . I'm just tired."

He pulled her close and followed Clarisse up the stairs.

He loved the woman in his arms—that was a fact. Mercy was asleep by the time he set her on the bed and bent to pull her boots off.

"Thank you, young man," Fenton said. "Clarisse and I—"

"I'm not leaving her." Thad pulled one boot off and threw the old man a look that dared him to argue. Then he reached for the other boot, but Clarisse beat him to it.

"You two men had better settle your differences now." Clarisse pulled Mercy's second boot off. "Mercy's been through enough without having to watch you two men fighting like a couple of angry roosters."

"It isn't decent for this young fella—"

"Can't see how it's indecent," Thad said. He stared her father in the eye. The man was as tall as he was, but scarecrow thin. Thad stuck his chest out.

"Enough!" Clarisse stood between them. "You boys take the argument down to the kitchen."

"I'm not leaving!" the two men shouted at once.

"Thad?" Mercy's voice seemed small.

"What is it, sweetheart?" Thad pulled her slender hand into his.

"Pa's so fragile these days. You'll be gentle with him, won't you?"

"Mercy," Fenton leaned over her. "I'm fine, don't you be worryin' about me."

"You should rest, Pa." Mercy looked at Thad. "See he rests, will you?"

"I'll . . ." Thad swallowed. "I'll make certain he does."

Thad poured Mercy some water and helped her drink. He brushed a stray lock back from her face. "Rest now, sweetheart."

"Hold me," she whispered. "So I can hear your heart-beat while I sleep."

He sat next to her and pulled her head against his chest. "Go to sleep now, love." He glared at her father.

She drew a breath and released it.

"Mercy?" Fenton leaned close to her.

She slanted a weak smile at her father. "There was so much smoke. I'm fine now . . . just tired, Pa." She reached for him and he took her hand in his.

Thad watched the old man shed his tears over her hand. *Her father loved her before I ever met her.*

"I'm sorry, Mr. Chase."

She peered at her father. "Don't let Thad . . . take the blame. He saved my life, you know. Mine and Jonathan's."

"You love this poker playin' rascal?" Fenton asked.

"I do."

Fenton looked at Thad. "I think you'd better start calling me Pa, young man."

"His name's Thad." She took in another raspy breath. "He wants to marry me. Reckon he can fit in that cabin of ours?"

"I think we'll have to build another room on the house you bring home a man this size."

"We'll talk about all this tomorrow," Thad whispered.

Mercy closed her eyes and settled against his chest. His heartbeat lulled her to sleep.

Thad held Mercy until soft, steady breathing signaled she was asleep. He could stand and walk away now without waking her, but he was a selfish bastard and he wanted to extend his last moments with her. He brushed a kiss against her cheek and she smiled in her sleep.

He would miss her smile. Her laugh. Her touch. Lord, he'd probably even miss her wild temper. He kissed her again and gently set her on the pillows. She didn't stir. He stood, put out the lamp and walked out the door, feeling as if he'd just left a piece of himself behind.

His boots grew heavier with each step down the stairs. He couldn't leave without telling his sister, but he didn't have any idea what he was going to say. Clarisse was scrubbing a huge pot when he walked into the kitchen. He stood near the door watching her work. Her petite frame and golden hair were so like their mother's, for a moment he almost thought he was seeing his mama.

He swallowed and stepped up to the sink. "Let me work on that," he said.

She looked up at him and grinned. "Mercy will love you even more when she finds out you scrub pots too." Clarisse handed the rag to her brother and wiped her hands on her apron. "Did she tell you she can't cook?"

"Yes." Thad tried to smile, but couldn't. He reached into the pot and scrubbed at the bottom where some of tonight's supper appeared to be stuck.

"I have a warm plate for you in the oven," she said.

"Not hungry."

"I'd have thought you would be half starving after what you've been through today." She leaned over the sink to look at his face. "I know you haven't eaten much the past few days."

Thad shrugged and bent to work harder.

"I don't believe you came down here to help me scrub this pot."

Thad cast his sister a look. "Just came in to bid you good-bye."

"Good—?" Clarisse put her hands on her hips. "What are you talking about?"

"I'm leaving. I can probably get to California—"

"You mean to say you're leaving—now? Alone?"

Thad nodded. "You'll explain to Mercy, won't you?"

"You haven't even told her?" Clarisse drew a breath. 'I'm not relievin' you of that task. After what she's been through? Thad Buchanan, you are . . . Hmph! A lady does not use the kind of language I have in mind to describe you!"

Thad dropped the rag into the dirty puddle at the bottom of the pot. "Call me what you will. Maybe I'm selfish." He wiped his hands on a dry towel. "Any woman I marry is damn well going to trust me enough to ask for my help occasionally."

"You're angry."

"You're damned right I'm angry. She nearly got herself killed today." Thad threw the towel down on the table. "Next time maybe she won't be so lucky. I am not going to stay around and watch."

"Thad." Clarisse squeezed her hands together. "You're upset about what's happened. That's only natural, but think about Mercy. She loves you."

"I know that. Don't you think I know that?" He stomped across the room and sat in one of the ladder-back chairs. "Walking away from her love—walking away from Mercy is the hardest thing I've ever had to do."

"You'll break her heart."

"Her heart will heal. When she decides she needs a man—really needs him—she'll find someone who's right for her."

Clarisse placed her hands on his shoulders and peered into his eyes. "You can't believe this is best—"

"I know it is." He stood and wrapped his arms around his sister. "Zeus is still saddled. I'm going to be on my way. Tell Mercy—"

"You can't go now. Wait until morning at least. Give me a chance to pack you some food for the journey."

Thad sighed. He wasn't sure he could muster the courage again if he didn't leave now. He looked out the window at the black night. He wouldn't get far in the dark.

"I'll leave at first light."

Maybe he was a coward, but he knew he had to be gone before Mercy woke up.

Thad checked the straps holding his guitar in place one last time before leading Zeus out of the dim shadows of the barn. Sweet memories of singing with Mercy through a rainstorm floated through his mind. One day the memories would stop hurting.

"You weren't even going to say good-bye?"

Her voice crackled with anger.

"Mercy?" Thad's voice caught as he turned to look at her.

"I thought you loved me." She raised a brow.

He shrugged, not daring to speak. She was so beautiful with the morning sun reflecting on her hair. A bit of color had returned to her cheeks, perhaps because she was angry with him.

"Clarisse shouldn't have awakened you," Thad said.

"It wasn't Clarisse—it was Pa." She placed her hands on her hips. "He heard you talking with Clarisse last night and came to tell me this morning. Lucky he did. Your sister is apparently more loyal to you than she is to me."

"She's loyal to both of us. That's why she understands that I'm doing the right thing." He tugged on Zeus's reins and led the horse away from Mercy. "You deserve better than me."

"Better?" Mercy caught up to him. "There isn't a better man for me."

"If you really believed that, you'd have trusted me yesterday."

"Trusted? What do you mean?"

He shook his head. "You don't have any idea, do you?"

"You're the best man I know, Thad Buchanan. I'd trust you with my life."

"You want to place a wager on that?"

"I already bet my heart."

"Then why the hell did you go to Lansing alone? You didn't even tell me—" Thad pulled his hat down on his head.

"It's my ranch. I had to take care of it myself. At least, I thought I did."

Thad started to walk away.

"Please, Thad. Hear me out."

Thad shook his head. "As I understand it there's more'n twice as many men as women in Colorado Territory. You won't need to look far when you decide you want a man."

"Sure, there are plenty of men—but how many of them will make me feel the way you do?"

"That's lust, honey lamb." He spit out the term he knew would make her angry. "As you have pointed out, it doesn't last."

Chapter 27

Mercy was confused as hell, but she was certain of one thing—she was not about to let Thad Buchanan walk out of her life.

"All right, I admit it. It's lust!" She focused on his azure eyes. "And maybe Colorado Territory is filled with men who could satisfy my desires—though I wouldn't place a wager on that." She brushed back a loose lock of hair, trying not to think how she must look in Wendell's night-shirt with her pa's jacket thrown over it. "I suppose I could try them out—maybe work my way from one min-ing camp to another, shall I?"

"That's not what I meant and you know it."

"So you admit that maybe you have some other tal-ents. Perhaps something besides your great physique might have caught my attention?" She leaned toward him. "Do you want a list? You make me laugh for one thing. And hope. Hell! I can't remember the last time I felt hope before you happened along. You make me feel loved and protected—"

"Protected?" Thad snapped. "I nearly got you killed."

"You're going to take the blame for that? I put myself in danger."

"I should have known—"

"You couldn't have known. Hell, I didn't know that Lansing was so far in debt he was desperate enough to commit murder. Since you're running away, I haven't had a chance to tell you about all I learned yesterday."

"You had no business going—"

"I probably shouldn't have . . ." Ice shot through her remembering the way Lansing had looked at her, the way he'd talked about wanting her dead. "I had no idea just how desperate Arthur Lansing was, or I'd never have risked going to him alone." She sucked in a deep breath. "Looking back on it, I should have talked to you. I was wrong."

"If I'd have been there—"

"You were there when it mattered. You saved my life and Jonathan's."

"I managed to do one thing."

"More than that, Thad." Mercy wrapped her hand around his. "Much more. Do you have any idea how many things you are really good at? Not just poker either. Music, and coffee, and loving. You are tender, and sweet, and a damn fine shot. You're brave—patient and understanding. I could go on—you're one hell of a man."

"I can't stay."

"You have to stay."

"You'll find anoth—"

"You owe me."

"Owe you?"

"Damn right, you do." She put her hands on her hips and arched one brow. "You saved my life. Now you are obligated to make it a life worth living. I am not letting you walk away until you've paid your debt."

"Debt?"

"Did I misunderstand? You told me when I saved your life I was obliged to make it a life worth living. Now you've saved mine—you owe me."

"You really want me?"

She wrapped her hands around his neck and pulled him down to her. "Thad, I need you." She kissed him with all the strength she could muster, kissed him until he surrendered to the kiss. His arms pulled tight around her waist and she felt her exhausted body reviving. Maybe they could make their way into the barn and . . .

"Now, son," Pa's voice sounded a thousand miles away. "If you're gonna carry on like that, you're gonna have to marry my daughter."

"Mercy?" Jonathan asked. "How come we couldn't stay for the whole party?"

"We wanted to get home before dark," Mercy said and she gave Jonathan a squeeze. He snuggled up against her on the high wagon seat and his eyes closed. The little boy was tired and excited at the same time and she couldn't blame him. It had been quite a day for all of them. The wagon rumbled along and she thought he had fallen asleep, but he shook his head and sat up. The excitement of the wedding had apparently won out over his exhaustion.

"I get to sleep above the kitchen." Jonathan was excited about his new room. He had been sleeping in Miranda's bed with Mercy sleeping up above. But now Mercy was moving into the new room with Thad.

Mercy pulled the blanket back over Jonathan's legs.

"Starting tomorrow," she said and she planted a kiss on top of Jonathan's head. "Tonight—"

"Tonight me, Grandpa Fenton, and Buck will stay in

the bunkhouse and celebrate. We're going to play cards and checkers, and sing songs all night."

"That sounds like fun," Mercy said.

"You and Thad can come too, if you want."

Thad chuckled. "You bachelors are having a special celebration. We married folks aren't allowed."

"Oh." Jonathan sounded disappointed.

"Just as the preacher said, we're a family starting today. You and Thad and me." Mercy hugged Jonathan close to her.

"And Grandpa Fenton."

"And Grandpa too." She pulled him close to her. "Cold?"

"No." He shivered.

"Here," Thad said and he handed the reins to Mercy while he took off his coat.

A minute later Mercy returned the reins and draped Thad's great big coat over Jonathan's shoulders. He looked up at Mercy.

"We're going to be taking care of you, from now on. You understand?"

He nodded and she could see him trying to hold back tears again. Of all the things that Lansing had done in his life, Mercy thought the cruelest was trying to convince his son that crying was for babies.

"Shh, shh." Mercy bent low and whispered in his ear. "You just cry as much as you like, Jonathan. Sometimes it helps you feel better."

Jonathan rubbed his wet face against the new wedding dress Mercy was wearing. "I know Papa's gone to be with my mother. I should be happy for them."

"Who told you that?" Thad asked.

"Lots of folks said they are in heaven and—" Jonathan wiped his sleeve over his nose to catch the drip.

"It's never easy to say good-bye, son." Thad pulled a

handkerchief out of his pocket and passed it to Jonathan "Don't let anyone tell you different."

The lad blew his nose. "You never did cry." Jonathan peeked around Mercy and up at Thad. "You're a full-grown man."

"I've cried lots. When my mama and papa died. When I thought I was goin' to lose Mercy."

She squeezed Thad's leg and hugged Jonathan close. "There's no shame in a boy crying," Mercy said. "Don't you forget that."

"Papa said." The boy sighed. "Maybe I didn't understand what he meant. Do you think that could be?"

"Yes, Jonathan," Mercy said. "I expect that even your father cried sometimes. I know you're a very brave boy. But sometimes even brave people cry."

"Is it right to be sad and happy at the same time?"

"Sometimes feelings don't make sense. It's very possible to be happy about one thing and sad about something else at the same time," Mercy said. "I'm happy that you're coming to live with us, but very sad . . . that you have lost your father."

Jonathan snuggled back against her. In the distance, a coyote howled and Mercy pulled Jonathan harder against her side. She watched him struggle to keep his heavy lids open for a moment. Mercy hummed "Amazing Grace" as Jonathan drifted off to sleep.

Thad closed the door behind him and threw his coat over a peg before he wrapped his arms around Mercy. His skin was cold from the long wagon ride, yet Mercy felt a rush of heat when they touched.

"He never even woke up when I carried him into the bunkhouse," Thad said.

"It was a big day for him," Mercy said.

"Not just for him." Thad bent his face to hers. "My bride."

While her lips melted into his, she fretted over the layers of clothing separating them. It had taken Clarisse over an hour to help her into all this satin and lace. She hoped Thad would take less time getting it all off. They'd waited nearly a month for this wedding. Sometimes it was downright frustrating to be in love with a man who had that much self-control.

He stepped back, examining every inch of her. "Have I mentioned how very beautiful you are, Miz Buchanan?"

"A few times." She felt giddy, like a schoolgirl who had pleased her beau. "Maybe several."

The wedding had been nearly perfect. Mercy had planned to wear her good Sunday dress, but Clarisse insisted on making her a new gown of emerald green that brought out the color in her eyes. Mercy was glad she'd made the effort when she saw Thad looking magnificent, closely shaved, trimmed and wearing a new black suit.

After the wedding, Pa had helped them escape the wild celebration at Rita's and make their way home. They were finally alone. Glory hallelujah!

The main room of the cabin she'd lived in for nearly six years hadn't changed much—a stove, a table and chairs, shelves filled with books and her piano. Hanging blankets provided small private areas for Pa and Miranda.

Miranda. Her sister had been the one thing missing from her perfect wedding. Surely, Miranda would write soon. Mercy wasn't going to let her worry over her sister spoil this night.

Mercy bit her lip and glanced at the new door next to the spinet—a door that led to the private bedroom Thad had built for them. He'd stretched a blue ribbon across it and tied a bow.

"A wedding gift wasn't necessary," she said, squeezing his hand. "You gave me the best possible gift when you invited Jonathan to live with us," Mercy said. "It will be hard on you, Thad. As wretched as his father was, Jonathan loves him."

"I'll do my best to be a friend to the boy. He'll accept you as a mother and maybe one day—" Thad sounded excited.

"He might never want to think of himself as a Buchanan."

"No. I won't force him to take my name."

"I mean, it won't be the same as having your own son."

"Mercy." Thad caressed her cheek. "I thought that was settled. Marrying you is not a sacrifice for me. We'll have our family. You and me and Jonathan to start— nothing's certain, ever. It's a great risk, opening our hearts to a boy grieving as Jonathan is."

"Not so much of a risk." Mercy leaned into his chest. "Knowing what I know about the power of love to heal a heart."

She reveled in the feeling of him all around her. His solid chest against her breasts, his arms around her shoulders, his lips hot against hers. He nibbled her hand, then kissed the bejeweled wedding ring.

"I still say it's too ostentatious for a rancher," she said.

He smirked. "That's the idea. One look at this ring and people'll know you're spoken for."

"You make me sound like a cow you're branding."

He pressed searing hot lips against hers. Not branding iron hot—forge hot. He wasn't merely branding her as his, but making her a part of him. They released each other, gasping for air.

"Penny for your thoughts," she whispered into his neck.

"My thoughts are worth a great deal more than that," he echoed the words she'd used in another lifetime.

She stepped to the corner and reached up to a high shelf.

"What are you doing?" he asked.

"Fetching your price."

He knitted his brows. "I was only funnin'."

She grinned, pulled a can down and picked a coin out before handing it to him. He stared at the half eagle.

"For your thoughts," she said.

"I was thinkin' I'll never deserve you."

"You deserve more, but I won't question my luck."

"You've become quite a gambler."

She swallowed. "Sometimes you have to take a chance to get what you really want."

Hot blue flames shone in his eyes. "And what is it you want, so badly?" His voice was even deeper than usual.

She looked into his eyes, wanting to tell him everything.

"You're not afraid to say, are you?"

She'd promised Thad she wouldn't hide her feelings from him. Even more important, she'd promised herself.

Mercy lifted her chin. "I want a man who'll respect my business sense and still think of me as a woman."

For a moment she was certain he would laugh.

"I hope you're not expectin' me to treat you like a man," Thad said.

She placed her hands on her hips. "I hope you're not expecting to run this ranch, now we're married?"

He raised an eyebrow, and flashed that roguish dimple. "Now why would I do that? You've done a fine job so far. But I reckon I can make a contribution or two."

"Of course, I didn't mean . . ." She'd forgotten how much it meant to him to be working the land again.

"You'll have your say. I was just afraid you meant to take over. I'd like us to be partners. Equal partners."

"Equal. I like that. I was afraid I'd have to start as assistant and work my way up." He set his hands on her waist and pressed her back against a rough log wall. "I confess I can't quite imagine you as my boss, givin' me orders all the day long." He bent to her neck and nibbled. "On the other hand, I don't think there's a man livin' who could boss a wildcat like you. I sure don't intend to try." He looked into her eyes. "Agreed?"

She nodded. "If you'll agree to treat me as a partner all day and a woman at night."

He shook his head. "That won't do."

"Why not?" She shoved both hands against his chest.

"You're my woman night and day." He breathed fire into her ear. "I am not agreeing to keep my hands or various other parts of my anatomy"—he suckled her throat until she arched with pleasure—"away from your tender body," he muttered, "just because the sun happens to be shining. Do I make myself clear?"

Was he asking her something? "Uh . . ." She swallowed. Flames licked deep inside her belly as his palm covered her breast. Any moment she was sure she would melt away.

"Daytime loving is allowed then?" He lifted his head.

"Yes. Yes. Whenever you want only . . . please?"

"Please? Did you want something?"

The man was infuriating. "Please, I need . . . you . . ."

"Do you?" He smiled. "You don't want to chat a bit more about runnin' the ranch? I'm not sure I've given you your money's worth—that's a gold coin—"

"No. No more talking."

He laced his fingers through hers, pulling her to the ribboned door.

"I reckon it's time to open your wedding gift, Miz Buchanan."

She pulled on the bow and managed to create a tighter knot. Thad held his jackknife out to her.

"It's such lovely ribbon," she said.

"Fine," he said. "I'll just wait over there." He inclined his head across the room.

She took the knife and cut the ribbon near one end. "I'll get the knot out tomorrow."

He grinned and pushed the door open. She stepped inside and gasped when she saw the huge four-poster bed.

"Like it?"

"It's beautiful." She ran a hand along the polished cherrywood. "But how did you—"

"Clarisse had it shipped from Denver. Amazing what that woman can do. She insisted a man of my size needed a large bed, though I told her we manage fine in a small space with mud closin' in around us."

"You told your sister about that?" Her cheeks flamed as the image of their night in the cabin danced through her mind.

He looked around the room. "We'll need a few more things, including a stove, when we can afford it. Meanwhile . . ." He brushed a kiss on her forehead. "We'll just have to find another way to keep warm at night."

The room was nearly dark and Thad set about lighting some candles. "We don't need light, do we?" She crossed her arms over her chest, thinking of the revolting scar on her side.

"I want to see you." He set a candle down on the bedside table and turned his gaze on her.

He pulled the combs from her hair and allowed it to drape over her shoulders. He brushed it back and nuzzled behind her ear. His hands meandered down over her ribs. She leaned against him to let him know he needn't worry about hurting her. His thumbs found her nipples—the sensation through layers of clothing was electric.

He brushed kisses on her jaw. Somehow, he opened the buttons down the back of her dress and it dropped over her shoulders, revealing her throat to his kisses. His tongue stroked the hollow at the base of her neck until she groaned. Her hands shaking, she undid the buttons on his vest.

Clothing dropped to the floor around them until he knelt before her, caressing her legs as he pulled her stockings down. He bent to kiss her knees, moving slowly up her thighs.

"Thad!"

"You promised, no bossing." He slid another inch up her inner thigh.

She couldn't stand it any more and pushed against his shoulders, bowling him over. Thad helped her finish the job of stripping him before pulling her down against him. She shivered as her bare breasts rubbed against his furred chest.

"I was beginning to think you'd never . . ." she mumbled through wet kisses.

He rolled over, positioned one knee up between her legs and caught her nipple between his teeth, teasing her with his tongue until she trembled on the brink.

"Thad," was all she could manage to say. The rhythm of the flickering candles matched the cadence within her.

He ached to plunge inside her, but this was their wedding night. He was determined to take his time and do things right. With his last ounce of control, he led her to their bed and crawled in beside her, running his hand along her waist until it rested on her bare hip. He bent to kiss the scar under her ribs.

"Don't," she said.

"Does it still hurt?"

"I don't want you to pretend it's not ugly."

He bent to kiss the scar again. "I'm gonna say this

once, love, so you listen carefully." He touched her face. "You've never mentioned my scars." He touched the worst one, a broken spider web that went from his collarbone to his right shoulder.

"I don't see those things, I . . . but you're a man."

"You think it's different for me? All right, I admit I notice your scars. I see them and remember—your courage, your strength." He grinned. "Your mule-headedness."

"My what?"

"Let's face it, you were too dang stubborn to die. This scar reminds me to cherish each moment we have together." He smiled, revealing his dimple in the candlelight. "You've got the heart of a cougar—ferocious when you're protectin' your own, but I can make you purr like a kitten."

"Kitten, am I?"

She bit his ear and he growled, rolling her onto her back.

"I love you," she whispered as she opened to him.

He thrust inside her, marveling again at how perfectly they fit together. His body covered her like a canopy, but it was her body that held them linked together. She wrapped her legs around him, pulling him deeper. He lowered his head to her breast, inhaling the scent of honeysuckle and Mercy. He'd been given the precious gift of time with this woman and he didn't intend to waste a moment. He flicked his tongue against her erect nipple until he felt her throbbing around him.

He drove further inside Mercy and she arched her back to meet him. Her pulse became his. The song had no words. Needed no words. Only rhythm. Beat. He watched her eyes flame and the sound of her voice calling his name rang in his heart.

His breath came in short bursts until he soared with her.

"Mercy!" he gasped.

He collapsed beside her, their arms and legs tangled together. Hearts pounding as one. Soft echoes of her pleasure tickled him as he lingered inside her. Still holding her, he settled his head on the pillow a few inches away so that he could observe her lovely face glowing in the candlelight. Neither of them spoke. Her smile said more than mere words could. He watched her eyes drift shut and pulled her closer, feeling her heartbeat grow quiet.

She rested against him. He spread her hair over his chest and combed his fingers through it. She opened her eyes and allowed him to look deep into her heart.

He pressed a kiss to her forehead. "I'll love you every moment, 'til I take my last breath."

Mercy smiled. "I'm betting on it."

ABOUT THE AUTHOR

Teresa Bodwell grew up in the West, writing stories in spiral notebooks, journals and on the odd scrap of paper. After serving in the U.S. Army, where she helped make the world safe for John Phillip Sousa music, she read her first romance novel and knew she had found her niche. Teresa lives in western Montana and practices law, marriage, raising children and leading Girl Scout Troops. She hopes to get all of these things right one day. Visit her website at *www.tbodwell.com*

If you liked this book,
try these other titles from Zebra!

Jude's Law **by Lori Foster**

When It Comes To Love, He Plays To Win

There's only so much frustration a guy can handle before he gets a little nutty. For Jude Jamison, his frustration has a name—May Price. She's everything the former Hollywood bad boy actor came to Stillbrook, Ohio, hoping to find: open, honest, lovable, and full of those luscious curves you don't find on stick-figure starlets—curves May doesn't seem to appreciate in herself. Every time Jude tries to get close to the skittish businesswoman, to take her in his arms, she thinks he's joking. Joking? Joking does not involve lots of cold-shower therapy.

Time for new tactics. If May can't respond to his sly compliments and sexy innuendos, he'll just have to spell it out for her. Jude Jamison is going to lay down the law for May Price. And after that, she'll have no delusions about just how much he wants her . . .

Murphy's Law by **Lori Foster**

Anything That Can Go Wrong . . .

Nothing is going to go wrong. Ashley Miles has worked too hard for her independence to let some Bentley-driving hunk named Quinton Murphy interfere with her plans—or her freedom. Yes, the chemistry is phenomenal. Kind of scary, actually. But that's it. NO emotional commitments.

. . . Will

But he's SO wonderful—a woman could fall in love . . . How did that happen? That wasn't part of the plan! But can she trust him? Really trust him? The man is just so mysterious. There's only one solution: put it all on the line and see what Quinton does when she tells him how she feels. And hope everything that can go wrong . . . won't . . .

Texas Wildflower by Susan Wiggs

Known for her soulful stories brimming with adventure and heartfelt emotion, *USA Today* bestselling author Susan Wiggs has captured the hearts of readers everywhere. In *Texas Wildflower*, she sweeps readers into a tale of the American West, where a bold spy falls in love with the very woman sworn to bring him to justice . . .

Texas Wildflower

All her life, beautiful Shiloh Mulvane has wanted to follow in her father's revered footsteps as one of the Texas frontier's greatest detectives. Now, she finally has her chance—by bringing sexy outlaw Justin McCord to her employer, a powerful judge who wants him to marry the daughter he allegedly compromised. But Justin has other ideas. The secret spy has a mission to complete, one that holds the fate of a free Texas in the balance. He knows what will happen once they reach Houston: he'll be forced into a sham of a marriage that will allow the corrupt judge to destroy the dream of Texas independence he's fought for, unless . . . he's already married. In one bold moment, the tables turn, and Shiloh finds herself the captive of a new husband she cannot trust or completely resist. What begins as a desperate ruse soon leaves them both vulnerable to a passion as wild and unforgiving as the land they both love, even as they are pursued by those who would stop at nothing to destroy everything they hold dear . . .